MW01228953

CONTENTS

TRIGGER WARNINGS

This story contains themes of abduction and captivity, exploring kidnapping and imprisonment with depictions of psychological and physical control. Violence and gore are present, including physical harm, blood, and intense combat. The story also delves into death and loss, portraying grief and mourning. Sexually explicit content, including graphic depictions of sexual acts, is present and may not be suitable for all readers. Additionally, dark themes such as betrayal, helplessness and survival in morally ambiguous situations permeate the plot.

This novel is intended for mature audiences (18+) and explores complex, dark, and sometimes uncomfortable subject matter. Reader discretion is advised.

If you've made it this far and you're still here... well, let's just say you're exactly where you're supposed to be. Now go ahead and dive in, good girl.

This one's for you.

GODS BLESSED

BOOK ONE
IN THE BLESSED SERIES

KAY HUGHES

CHAPTER ONE

I t has been thirty-two days since I have seen another person. That's forty-six thousand and eighty hours. I've never been the best at math but I've been in here so long, I don't really have anything else to do with my time. I tried recalling the tales of old, poems my mother once recalled and even thinking of recipes I would make once I was free. But I had long since grown bored with these thoughts. So, I've been counting the minutes, double checking my math again and again until the numbers themselves seem to blur in my mind. This would make my father quite proud, as I have always hated the subject and refused to practice as I should.

Thoughts of my father make me think about what

is happening outside of this cell. Though I know everything is probably close to the same as it was before I was captured, I have no window to confirm that is the case. Though I have only been in our small section of the lands, Alblasia is a province with nine separate nations, all holding their own nobility and diverse civilizations. It is said that this once was a peaceful land, and the gifted traveled between the lands freely, but that changed after the Dark War three decades ago. Now, most gifted stay within their own territory lines and try to keep the peace. Though not all of them, which is why I wonder what may have happened in my time tucked away.

I am surrounded by four towering stone walls, their rough texture grazing my fingertips as I reach out. The stone floor beneath me feels icy against my bare skin, sending shivers down my spine. Above me, the stone ceiling sits high above, its presence suffocating even with the distance. The coldness of the stone seeps into my very bones, leaving me trembling with no blankets to shield me from the chill. Despite the harshness of my surroundings, I notice a glimmer of beauty as well. The stone walls, a deep black hue, display delicate specks of gold that add a touch of luxury to the space. This is a sure sign that I have ended up in the lands of Promental, as there is no nation who would flaunt their wealth in this way other than them. Promental is known as the Land of the Prominent, and my father said that their Lord Soren is known to flaunt his wealth in any way possible. On good days, it keeps me solace to know I have ended up here, in a land my father had told me of. I like to think that if this is their idea of a prison cell, it would be so incredibly worse in another land, and that would be quite bad, considering.

In this desolate place, devoid of human interaction, I am isolated, left to my own thoughts. Once, in the safety of our cavern, the beautiful songs of birds would drift into my room, filling it with life. But now, all that remains is a suffocating silence that seems to fill my very being. The absence of any sound amplifies the emptiness, a void that echoes within these dark stone walls. Longing for the sweet symphony of life that once surrounded me, I am constantly reminded of my solitude by the deafening stillness. The silence is the worst part.

It is so gods damned silent.

Although I do miss the vibrant autumn colors of the trees that bloomed outside of my room in my homeland of Mygreen, I have come to realize that my current situation could be much worse. If the lands of Arrakis had captured and imprisoned me, I would most likely be dead by now. Nulls are not accepted in any lands within Alblasia, not even Naboo, our version of the mainland that prides itself on being "inclusive of all". But Arrakis is the worst of them all. They consider themselves the Land of the Dreamers, but we refer to them as the Land of the Cult. They execute even the most peaceful-natured gifted within their borders, all in the name of the cruel god they worship. But I am not considered a peacefully natured gifted. No, the gifts I have landed me in a cell, where most Nulls would wish for salvation or a second chance.

I am refraining from wishing to the gods at all, because I know they will listen, and every wish has it's cost.

However, thirty-two days of being in this room is something I would wish on nobody. And based on the scratch marks on my right wall, the last person had been in here for over seven hundred days. The faint metallic scent of blood still hangs in the room from where it has stained some of the jagged marks. I can't help but wonder what they had used - a rock, or possibly a weapon. Some lines etch so deeply that they appear to penetrate the very soul of the stone, while others barely leave a mark. It makes me question my strength, my thoughts on how I would endure counting my days after spending over two years in this room.

As my thoughts drift, a fist interrupts them, crashing against the steel door in the front of my cell. The loud impact sends shockwaves through the air, assaulting my senses. Against the force, the heavy door trembles, its metallic echo lingering in the confined space. The narrow slot at the bottom of the door creaks open, allowing a sliver of white light to enter the dimly lit room. The scent of stale air wafts in, mingling with the smell of the meal they have left on the tray.

With a swift and resounding thud, the slot slams shut again, sealing off the outside world. Even through the thick door, I can sense their fear. The metallic cuff around my wrist renders my physical gifts useless, but still, their caution is palpable, tangible in the air, as they refuse to leave the slot open for more than a fleeting moment. As the sound of the guards' retreating footsteps gradually fades, I cautiously approach the door, my fingertips brushing against the cool, rough surface. I reach out and grasp the tray left behind, feeling the slight warmth of the food against my palm.

Today's lunch appears to consist of a porridge made with some type of fruit I have never seen and a glass of water. It is a slimy, inconsistent texture and I can tell that it was not properly mixed by the clumps of powder throughout. I try to push those to the side and only eat the fruit and mostly cooked through porridge. I learned quickly that the food may keep me mildly sedated, but that is better for me than what they do when I refuse to eat.

I try not to look at the small scars on my hands from

the last time I had left my tray untouched. Though I do not have to look to picture the pale scars that dance along the entirety of my palms.

They do not have to touch you to make the tray burn your hands with the fire magic of some elemental they surely have in their ranks. Hell, they don't even have to see you to laugh at the screams tearing from your lungs while your hands burn of a magic you hoped to never feel in real life. The cool, soothing balm they tossed through the narrow slot at the next meal may have healed the burn wounds, leaving only the faint, pale scars now etched across my palms. Yet, the intense, searing pain lingered for weeks, like a flame scorching my senses.

That was on day six in my cell (eight thousand, six hundred and forty minutes), back when I still believed I may break myself free. I plotted my escape, thinking that eventually someone would enter my cell or take me out for a shower. I have since realized that is not possible, as they do not plan to ever let me out of this small room, nor risk one of their own by sending them in. With that realization came the one I most feared, that what I will have to do to get out of this cell is the only thing I promised myself I would never do.

With my mind burdened by the weight of my thoughts, I take thirteen slow steps towards the dimly lit bathroom in my cell. The sight that greets me is disheartening; a solitary toilet tucked away in the corner, devoid of any semblance of cleanliness or comfort. The absence of a sink or shower is a harsh reminder that I have no way to clean myself. The stench of my own body fills the air, mingling with the dampness of the cell. As I run my fingers through my tangled, unkempt hair, I can almost feel the knots and snarls pulling at my scalp, a constant reminder of the neglect I have grown used to. I almost dread the first bath or shower after I am freed, as I know cleaning my hip length silver hair will be a long and painstaking process.

The heavy knock and quick drop of my dinner comes a few hours later, consisting of the same slimy fruit porridge. I eat while thinking of the decision I know I will have to make tomorrow and if it is really worth my life.

But that's the main question, really. What is my life worth?

It's possible that the world is safer with me here, where I can hurt none and no one can hurt me. It is possible that I was never really a danger at all, otherwise how would I have been captured only four days into fleeing for my life to begin with?

But then I remember I was not fleeing in Promental, where I now sit imprisoned, but in Mygreen, where I know the terrain better than most know the back of their own hands. I have been in the woods throughout Mygreen hundreds of times in my life, without ever being seen by another person. With that reminder, I remember that, remember is the one thing I do not.

I do not remember being captured.

I do not remember being transported to a prison in Promental, or coming to Promental at all.

I remember nothing past falling asleep at my campsite, on the way to the wishing tree, and that is the problem with staying here. I was not the only one traveling to the wishing tree, and I would burn the world down to get back to my brother.

Aparently, even if it means pulling him into danger first.

CHAPTER TWO

I wake up in the morning knowing that I will see my brother again soon, because I am finally ready to do what needs to be done. I have pushed it off in fear of dragging him into the same position, but knowing him, he will end up worse if he does not know where to find me.

With a deep breath, I steadily exhale all the air in my lungs, close my eyes, and make my wish to the gods.

Without fail, every wish I have ever made in my life has been granted. Whether for food, protection or an escape, there has always been an answer that granted my wish. Even if I had wished by accident, the word gracing my mind or lips out of mistake. This has led to me being considered as "God's Blessed" by the few I had around me. Throughout Alblasia, there are many gifted who have been blessed with sway, wealth, or extraordinary gifts, but it is very rare to discover which god you are favored by. I try not to think about which god is blessing me, as that thought only leads to the countless gods I have studied in my time at home by myself.

I know they'll hear me, and I can almost feel the familiar warmth of Arden's presence. He is my only hope, the one person who might risk everything to pull me from this cell. But the thought of his safety sends a fresh wave of dread crashing over me. What if they capture him too? What if my desperate wish brings him nothing but danger? I can't bear the thought of him suffering because of me.

I draw my knees to my chest, wrapping my arms around them as I try to fend off the chill creeping into my bones. Memories flood my mind, vivid and haunting. I recall the day Father told me about the Null found in a nearby village, how the townsfolk turned against him, driven by fear and hatred. I remember my father's voice trembling as he recounted the male's execution, the way his hands shook when he spoke of the injustice. The fear in his eyes was palpable, a reflection of the terror that lay just beneath the surface of our lives.

"Nulls are a danger," he had said, his voice laced with urgency. "You must never let anyone find out what you are."

Now, I sit here, both terrified and ashamed. With Arden and me as Nulls, what chance do we have in any part of Alblasia? The very land that should be our home feels more like a prison, a place that would rather see us dead than living among its gifted. My heart aches with the weight of our shared fate, and the walls of the cell seem to close in around me, a constant reminder of our precarious existence.

What if we can never find a safe place? What if the world outside remains a hostile expanse, forever out of reach? I press my forehead against my knees, feeling the tears welling in my eyes.

Am I even worth saving?

Four days later, when I hear the harsh knock on my cage door that should signal dinner, I notice the sound of wind. It is soft, like the first gust you feel in the morning as the world wakes. After Thirty-Seven days in this room, hearing nothing but absolute silence, I almost convince myself that I have lost the sanity holding me together. But, as the slot in my door opens, the sound only gets louder and louder. The sound of the wind grows to be as harsh as the knocks on my steel door and as strong as the dragons found in our lands. The light gust turning into a draft, and quickly rise as if a tornado was coming through the small slot in my door. I stand up from the corner I have been huddled in, walking towards the sound, ignoring the anxiety stirring within me. I know my wish has been answered when no tray comes through the slot, and it does not slam shut, but instead there is a hand I have seen as many times as my own reaching in. Without hesitation, I reach out and take it, closing my eyes and wishing for a safe escape.

As the air fills with a mystical scent, a tingling sensation tickles my nose, signaling the presence of magic. The world seems to sway beneath my feet, causing a subtle shift in my equilibrium. Slowly, I open my eyes, revealing a breathtaking sight before me. I am standing before the enchanting canopy of the wishing tree. In the tales of old, people believed it to be a terrifying and powerful tree that steals wishes from poor souls too unlucky to cross its path, but I have long since known that this tale was just that.

A tale.

The Wishing Tree stands proudly, towering over seventy feet tall, its branches cascading with shiny silver flowers that glisten in the sunlight. A faint scent of earth and moss wafts through the air, mingling with the sweet fragrance of the silver flowers. The tree's branches, adorned with deep black thorns, create a stark contrast against the sky, their jagged edges casting ominous shadows on the ground. From afar, it can look a tad frightening, as you must wish entry to see the heart of the tree itself, and that is something that was lost in the tales long ago. If you attempt to touch the tree without first wishing permission, the black thorns are sharper than the teeth of a Cayman, capable of tearing through flesh in an instant.

My brother Arden found this tree almost a decade ago, and it has been our place of solace ever since.

"Emory,"

I turn my head to the right, and my eyes widen with delight, causing my face to break into a wide smile. My brother's face mirrors the expression, with his bright eyes shining. Without saying a word, I take two brisk steps towards him, feeling a surge of excitement coursing through my body. I eagerly wrap my arms around his neck, relishing in the love flowing from him.

"Arden, it feels like you've grown five inches in the last month! How am I supposed to tell people I am the elder sister when you keep growing so much taller than I am?" I say jokingly.

Arden laughs, his silver eyes seeming to glow. "How do we know they didn't slip something into your food to make you shorter in there? You seem quite short now that I'm thinking about it."

I gently punch him on the arm, my eyes measuring the space between us, aware of his towering height that now exceeds mine by nearly a foot. The metallic jingle of the cuff, restricting the use of my gifts, resonates in my ears as I note its presence, still firmly fastened to my wrist.

"We'll have to take care of getting this removed pretty quickly, or I will be no help to you in the forests." I say.

Although Alblasia is not a warring nation, that does not mean the lands are safe. Since the end of the Dark War, there have been an increase in sightings of monsters and other creatures in the woods, appearing in areas where they were previously unheard of. Rumors suggest that this surge in activity is a result of the birth of the New Gods, which started twenty-nine years ago. It is said that the Fates are striving to balance out their divine presence. The exact number of new gods remains unknown, with only one officially introduced and four witnessed by the gods themselves. However, judging by the significant number of encounters with these creatures, it is safe to assume that there are quite a few of them.

Arden laughs. "I'd wish for a hot bath and shampoo before that. Your odor is even worse than what lingered on father after his long hunting trips!"

Rolling my eyes at him, I turn to the wishing tree and wish for the tree to grant me safe entry and for it to prepare hot water within the bath. Remembering the state of my hair, I crinkle my nose, thinking that it may be easier to cut it for the first time in my life. Dismissing the thought with a quick shake of my head, I go through the leafy silver flowers and find myself in our camp.

The delicate silver flowers cascade down, their petals shimmering in the sunlight as they create a lush, vibrant wall that envelops the tree's base. Their sweet fragrance fills the air, mingling with the soft sounds of nature that surround the tree. The inside of the tree is just a tree base and empty space we have made into our camp surrounding it. An earthy scent fills my nostrils, mingling with the faint smell of stale air. The sight before me is no different from when I was here last- the neatly arranged furniture, the untouched cots- all giving the illusion that time has stood still, which tells me that Arden has not been staying here while I was in the cell.

"Where have you been camping?" I ask.

He turns to look at me from where he is setting his bags down next to his cot. "I met a traveling party that was helping me search for you. I would like for you to meet them in the morning, so we can decide if we would like to continue with their party or go on our own."

I walk over to my cot on the other side of the tree base. As I sit down, I feel the rough fabric of the cot beneath me, and let my thoughts wander. I imagine the bustling sounds of a vibrant traveling party, the laughter and chatter of companionship. However, my mind is swiftly brought back to reality, as I have never been around anyone other than Arden or my mother and father before they passed this last winter. As a Null, my gift steals the gifts of any other person I touch, leaving them as a Plain. I cannot give the gift back and to be a Plain in these lands without having been born one is a death sentence.

As I sit down on my cot, I let out a sigh. "Do you really think it's a good idea to include me in a party? I wouldn't want to steal the gifts of those you may call friends."

Arden walks to my side of the base and crouches down, bringing himself to my level. The sun shines down on us from gaps in the branches, casting shadows that dance across his face. His eyes, a reflection of my own, lock onto mine, piercing through the silence. "You will not hurt them Emory, we have found a way to guarantee it". I tear my eyes away, scared of the hope blossoming in my chest at his words. My fingers graze the worn fabric of the cot beneath me, the coarse texture a grounding reminder of reality.

When I finally lift my gaze again, I lock eyes with Arden, his eyes mirroring my own. "How could you possibly guarantee that?" I ask, my voice barely a whisper.

He cracks a soft smile, lifting only the left side of his mouth and showing off the dimples that I was not lucky enough to inherit from our father. "They have a Mymic in their group, Emory, and he is God's Blessed as well. His gift can never be stolen and he can steal yours!".

He laughs now, a big laugh, full of joy that we have known little of in our short lives. "You do not have to fear hurting anyone, Emory, and nobody will want to hurt you. We will be safe to be ourselves in this group, make friends and even hunt! I caught a deer last week with a bow and arrow, and I want to teach you to do the same. This is our chance, Emory."

Mymics are rare within our lands, as they can steal the power from another gifted and take it as their own, but only temporarily. The gift returns to the original gifted when the Mymic falls asleep, so they are not hunted like the Nulls. Though they are not widely trusted, either.

I smile at him, with both sides of my mouth, and sadly, no dimples. "I guess I better get this cuff off than",

I joke.

Turning to the base of the Wishing Tree, I gently run my hand along its rough and flakey black bark, feeling the intricate patterns beneath my fingertips. With closed eyes, I take a deep breath, inhaling the earthy scent of damp moss and fresh leaves that fills the air around me. Amidst the soft rustle of the tree's swaying branches, I wish for the cuff to be removed from my arm and when I open my eyes; it is gone.

Walking over to the area we have made into our bathhouse, I find the tub full of steaming hot water. Forcing the muscles in my neck and shoulders to relax, I roll my shoulders and know I must begin. Reaching over to grab the bar of shampoo we keep here and closing the curtains, I walk over and remove the brown dress from my body. It had once been a lovely off white color, now covered in dirt and surely unsavable. Once I am fully unclothed, I gingerly lower myself into the tub. The cool porcelain sends a shiver down my spine as I settle in. My body quakes, trapped between being both freezing and boiling hot. As I dip my head beneath the surface, my ears are filled with the muffled symphony of bubbles and water swirling around me. Holding my breath, I feel the pressure building, my chest tightening until I finally emerge, gasping for air. Tiny water droplets cascade down my face, tickling my skin and collecting in the corners of my eyes and on my lips.. The water feels softer than I remember, like it is mixed with the fabric softeners my mother used to bargain for at local markets. I wipe the water off of my face, smoothing my hair back and leaving it submerged. I sit like this in the tub until the water grows cold, and then I begin washing the months' worth of oil, knots and dirt out of my long silver hair.

CHAPTER THREE

After my bath, we take some time getting settled back into the space and changing the linens on our cots before making a quick dinner. Many years ago, we wished upon the tree that food brought here would not go bad, and I am extra thankful for that wish tonight. We sit at a small wooden table Arden built when he was sixteen and start to eat our dinner of Braised Lamb and Potatoes. It was one of the last dishes our mother made before she passed and we brought it here to save for a day when we wished she were close to us again. Arden had decided that today was that day and I agree. The lamb is perfectly cooked and the potatoes are slightly charred, just how my father liked them.

Though none of us preferred the char, we continued to eat them this way after his passing and I doubt me or Arden would ever stop. There is very little in this world that brought true joy to our cavern, but on the days where father returned from the village hunt and got to stay for more than a few hours, our home was full of it. Our parents loved everything about one another, their affection palpable in the tender way they looked into each other's eyes and held hands. Our mother, once vibrant and full of life, became a shadow of herself after our father's passing. The heaviness of grief weighed on her, visible in the deep lines etched on her face and the sadness that lingered in her once sparkling eyes. When she passed just seven months after we lost him, Arden said it was a surprise to no one in the village.

"Tell me of your time since I last saw you! I want to know everything that happened while I was gone." Looking at Arden, it is like no time and years have passed all at once.

Ardon smiles that boyish half-smile of his, a charming mix of mischief and warmth. At three years younger than my twenty-three, he carries an air of youthful exuberance that's hard to ignore. It's incredible to think back to the small boy I remember sitting at this very table all those years ago. Now, he towers over me at over six feet tall, his frame solid and muscular, a stark contrast to the scrawny kid who once struggled to reach tabletops within our cavern.

His silver hair, longer than I ever remember him keeping it, cascades down to brush against his eyes, giving him an almost ethereal look. As he moves, the locks sway with him, and he absentmindedly pushes them off his forehead, tousling them in a way that feels both deliberate and carefree. It's as if he wants to maintain that sense of boyish charm, despite the man he has become. I find myself momentarily lost in the memories of his childhood—his laughter ringing through the air, the way he would bounce in his seat with excitement, and the innocent dreams he shared with me.

Yet, as I look at him now, I see not just my brother, but a young man who carries the weight of the world on his shoulders, and I can't help but feel a mix of pride and concern. The playful glimmer in his eyes is still there, but under it lies a depth that only experience can bring.

"When I got to the wishing tree and found that you were not here, a sense of dread washed over me. You've never been late for a meeting or lost your path in these woods. It felt wrong, so I immediately turned toward the Northern Woods, searching for you. I hadn't been wandering long when I spotted an orange Wolfer stalking Bundra with another Wolfer I hadn't seen before. I tried to keep my distance, but it heard me pretty quickly."

My body tenses at the thought of him facing a Wolfer alone. Wolfers are massive, aggressive beasts, larger than any wolf found on the mainland—more akin to a bear in size and ferocity. They are merciless hunters, tearing their prey apart without hesitation. Arden is strong and capable now, no longer the scrawny boy I grew up protecting, but I still shudder at the thought of him in such a dangerous situation. "What happened?" I ask, anxiety churning in my gut like a storm.

He looks up from the potato he's eating, his brow furrowing slightly as he sighs. "It shifted into a fucking woman who told me that if I was going to be in the Northern Woods, I should know better than to sneak around a Wolfer."

Shifters are somewhat common in Mygreen, having traveled here from other lands as our woods have easier prey for them to hunt. Like the common Wolfers, they're not known for their kindness. Arden takes another bite of his lamb, chewing thoughtfully before setting his fork down with a clink.

"I asked her if she was out hunting alone, or if she had seen a woman with silver hair like mine and she told me no to both. That's when I felt the presence of the other Wolfer behind me. He was a giant beast, and I knew that if I had to face them both, it was going to take everything I had to escape the battle alive. I had reached for my sword in preparation, but the woman told me to stop. She said they did not want to fight. She asked me if I was looking for my sister, and when I told her yes, she smiled and said that I was welcome to join their party."

He looks down at his plate, picking up his fork and spinning it absently in his fingers. "I asked why they would want me to join them and she told me that everyone in the group was looking for something, and everyone in the group had once been alone as well." Suspicion rose in me, knowing that while I was not allowed out of our home during my twenty-three years and Arden was, he was still known to be a tad naïve when it came to trusting others.

He sets the fork down again, looking me in the eye with a light grin. "I followed them back to their camp and, to my surprise, everything they said was true. I was welcomed in with open arms and they helped me search until I got wind of the new prisoner in the Promentals Null Grounds. They helped me break in and I whisked us out with a plan to meet them back at camp in the morning." Some of my unease was tempered down, though I was still unsure if they were to be trusted, as he claimed.

I laugh, smiling, "and they say it's me who's been God's Blessed." Some of my unease ebbs, though doubt still lingers in the back of my mind.

Arden smiles. "I know when you are faking a smile, Emory, and I can tell you aren't sure that they can be trusted. I was cautious at first as well, but they are all a mess in their own right. None of them wish to be found. The party was started specifically for those looking to find someone or something they had lost. And, as you know, it is not safe to be in these woods without a larger party."

He's right. These woods are filled with both magical and ordinary creatures, both deadly in their own ways. Though Arden has embraced the gifts he was forced to steal over the years, whether during attacks or other circumstances, I have not been able to fully develop my own. We are strong together, but we may not be strong enough to survive the winter between fighting off both the cold and the creatures we encounter. Releasing a harsh breath, I know that this would be the best option for him, and I would do anything for my brother. He has done worse for me.

"Alright", I sigh, shifting in my seat. "We leave at first

light and we will meet with this party." Though I am apprehensive that they will accept me as easily as they have accepted Arden, I must try to fit in.

Arden is smiling his big, goofy smile. "They will love you, Emory. I just know it." He takes the last bite of his lamb, along with the last charred potato in his bowl, and chews it slowly, his eyes closed and head lowered. I follow suit, taking the moment to remember the laughter that filled our cavern during a childhood dinner with Mother and Father. The aroma of the charred potato wafts through the air, evoking a vivid picture of us gathered around the rough-hewn table, the flickering candlelight dancing in their eyes.

I can almost hear Father's hearty laugh, a deep, rumbling sound that always filled me with warmth, as he teased Mother about her insistence on seasoning everything with spice. Her soft chuckle would follow, a melodic counterpoint, while Arden, just a boy then, would giggle and try to mimic their banter, his silver hair catching the light as he leaned in, eager to join the joke. Though I was not allowed into the village, I never, for one moment, questioned how much I was loved.

"I missed you, Emory." Arden says softly. "I am not used to spending time away from you, and I was worried that I would not find you in time. I have never been so scared in my life." I hear the wood creak as he moves in his chair and open my eyes to look at my younger brother. I feel tears form in my eyes at the look on his face and in a quaking voice I respond, "I missed you more than I thought was possible, and I'm so sorry I waited so long to wish on the gods. I did not want to put you in danger to release me, but I knew that was the only way."

With steel in his eyes, Arden sits on the edge of his chair and says, "I would burn the world to ashes to find you Emory, I will always find you."

With teary eyes, I look at my younger brother, knowing the sentiment is shared between us both. Arden closes his eyes and sits back in his chair again as he asks, "what happened in there, Emory? I saw your hands and you've lost weight."

He pauses.

"Did they hurt you?"

His voice trembles, and I can see the pain in his eyes as the thought sinks in. I wish I could tell him I'm completely unscathed, but the memory lingers. I lower my head, trying to push away the chill that threatens to consume me.

"They burned my hands with a Fire Elementals gifts when I refused to eat the food they'd laced with sedatives. After that, I kept eating, and they left me alone. Nobody touched me or even spoke to me—I was alone in that cell the entire time. There's really nothing else to share."

Arden opens his eyes wide, the weight of my words settling heavily between us. I can see he's close to tears, though he hasn't let any fall since he was just a boy. "The solitude must have been unbearable. I'm so sorry, Emory. You'll never have to be alone again, I promise. I swear it."

His sincerity washes over me, and I believe him.

CHAPTER FOUR

I lay in my cot, attempting to be still so I don't bother Arden while he sleeps. My mind is restless and I cannot stop thinking about meeting the party in a few short hours.

Growing up, I spent most of my days reading any books my mother could find within our village or my father brought back from his hunting journeys. I knew, mostly, how to interact with other people. Though my experience in real life was quite limited. Arden would come home and tell me all about the school drama, tossing around slang that felt foreign to me. I'd nod along, trying to absorb it all, but deep down, I worried I wouldn't know how to keep a conversation going. Sure, mother taught me a ton about herbal remedies and historical creatures, and father always said I was well-versed in most topics, but what if that stuff doesn't even matter anymore?

Lying awake on my cot, I think back to those cozy evenings when we'd chat at the dinner table. We'd laugh about silly things, and I'd share wild theories I read about, like the latest rumors of gods starting wars or tales of brave souls standing against dark forces. But what about the world outside? What do normal people even talk about?

Would I bring up the chilling whispers I'd heard about the gods stirring unrest, or the legends surrounding the last great conflict? What if someone asked about my thoughts on the shifting alliances and I fumbled over my words? I think about my gifts, too. When do you even open up about things like that? I fear I might share too much or not enough, leaving people confused or uncomfortable.

And love? The thought sends a wave of anxiety through me. What if I never find someone who understands me—someone who sees beyond my gifts or my past? Will I ever have the chance to share my hopes and fears with someone I love? I almost want to go back to those carefree days, where the hardest thing was finding the next good book to dive into. Instead, I'm left overthinking every possible conversation I might have, worrying about who I am and who I might become.

As I lie here, the weight of tomorrow presses down on me. I can hardly fathom meeting all those new people for the first time. What will they think of me? Will I fit in, or will I feel like an outsider? The uncertainty coils in my stomach, a mix of excitement and dread.

"Emory. I can practically hear your thoughts from all the way over here," Arden says as I hear him shift in his cot, the linens rustling under him.

I sigh. "Arden, what if I don't know how to speak to them? What if I say too much, or gods forbid too little? What if-". He cuts me off. "You will not, because you communicate perfectly fine."

"I've never had to make friends, Arden. What if I reveal something too personal too fast or if I do not know how to open up to another person the right way and they think me suspicious?"

"You just have to be yourself, Emory. That is what will make them trust and like you. It's okay for things to be a tad awkward. Everyone has those moments. There is a man in the party who rarely speaks at all, and they accept him just as he is as well."

That does make me feel a bit better.

Arden sighs, "Though grumpy no sleep you isn't usually the nicest, so you may want to attempt to get some rest if you wish for your first impression to go well."

I know he is right. I tend to be a tad ill tempered when I do not get proper sleep and we have a hike to make in the morning that will require my energy. "You're right", I sigh, "I'm going to get some rest. I'm sorry if I woke you with my rustling." Rolling onto my side, I close my eyes and attempt to sleep.

I awake a few hours later to Arden, ruffling through his bags. Groggily, I open my eyes and take in the dimly lit surroundings. The faint glow of the dawn peeks through the trees, casting long shadows across the floor. I can smell the earthy scent of damp moss and hear the distant chirping of birds welcoming the new day. I glance at the makeshift sun tracker we have, its wooden frame casting a faint shadow on the ground, and see that we should be leaving shortly. Slowly, I rise from my cot, feeling the coolness of the floor beneath my bare feet. I start to pack my bag, carefully folding my belongings and rolling up my blanket. As I do, I can't help but notice the lingering chill in the air, a reminder of the cold that has been with me since my time in the cell.

Arden fills our food bag with non perishables and easy snacking foods. I refill our canteens with water and put them in the bag we use when transporting them all. With nothing left to do, Arden looks over at me. "Ready to go?"

"Ready as I'll ever be", I smile lightly, knowing he can

sense my anxiety.

We wish upon the tree for a safe exit and enter the woods to begin our hike. The air is filled with the crisp scent of pine, mingling with the earthy aroma of moss and damp soil. I can hear the gentle rustle of leaves as a light breeze blows through the trees, accompanied by the symphony of chirping birds and buzzing insects. As I gaze back at the tree, I can't help but wonder to myself when the next time I will return here is, and how much time will have passed since now.

As we walk, I think about the day ahead of us. This is my favorite part of the day, when the sun has just risen and the world is still asleep. I reach out and graze my fingertips against the velvety leaves of the vibrant green fig tree, feeling the cool morning dew trickle against my skin. A delicate fragrance of freshness wafts through the air, as if nature itself is awakening alongside us and I thank the gods for another day of calm weather. Though the weather is most likely being determined by Belene, God of the Elements, you never know what god has their hands involved, so I tend to thank them all.

Our hike is going to take us approximately four hours by Ardens' calculations, and thankfully we are going through the Eastern Woods, which are known to be much more docile than the Northern Woods. We pass Bundra as we walk, and I see a few deer in the distance with their fawns in tow. The sunlight filters through the thick canopy above, casting dappled shadows on the ground beneath my feet. With each step, the twigs snap and crackle under the weight of my boots, breaking the serene silence that envelops our surroundings. I marvel at Arden's ability to move so silently, his footsteps barely making a sound, as if he's become one with the woods themselves. He walks a few feet ahead of me, checking our surroundings every few seconds as though he were worried that something was getting ready to pounce. He's always been like this, overly worried about me when I am out in the woods. Though, I guess I am not one to talk, as he has always been my only priority as well.

"Can you tell me about the people in the party?" I ask. I've been curious about them, almost as much as I've been nervous.

I can hear the smile in his voice when he responds, "Absolutely! There are eleven others. The leader of the group's name is Ryat, he's the Mymic. He's a few inches taller than I am and has black hair. He has a sister, Teirney, who's also in the party. She looks just like him and is just as tall. She's a Boost."

Boosts are also incredibly rare in our lands. Boosts make those around them stronger, boosting their gifts and increasing strength and stamina. It doesn't take any skill or training, it's just a blessing from the gods, and the range is determined at birth but doesn't increase.

"It's crazy that two rare gifts would be born into a sibling group. That's not common."

Arden looks back. "We were both born with rare gifts as well, Emory. It must not be as uncommon as we were made to believe."

I've never really thought about our gifts the same way Arden has. He believes the Gods gave us the gifts we would need to one day fulfill our "destinies", though I'm not so sure I believe in all of that. "You're right", I say.

Arden faces forward again, picking up his pace a bit. "Then there's the two Lorics, Nox and Fenris. Nox's father is the god Teos, The God of Dreams. Fenris' mother is Vivas, The God of Medicine."

Lorics are halflings, born of one god and one gifted. They typically hold a gift derived from the Godly parents' power. "What powers do they have?" I ask.

"Nox has the power to enter your dreams and change them as he wills. Nothing that happens in them is real, but it would be remembered if he wishes it. Fenris has the ability to heal, though he pulls from his own energy source to do so, so he mostly heals minor illnesses and wounds unless the situation is life or death."

My steps falter thinking about Nox's gifts. Dreams are sacred in our lands and the gift of dream walking is one that some Lands rulers count as cause for execution. The more I hear of this group, the more nervous I get. Secondary to the danger of being around such powerful gifted, I wonder what use I will be to the group. I can barely control the gifts I have stolen and the only one I've mastered is the gist of being able to read a person's emotions. Though it can be quite useful, it tends to remind me of the Celtic I stole it from.

Celtics are empaths with emotion reading and are typically very kind, but a few years ago, three men attacked us at our cavern and he was the unfortunate soul who came for me. I begged him to leave and never return, but he tried to kill me and I was successful first. Arden and my father took care of the other two, leaving Arden with a new shifter ability and me with a mountain of guilt.

Arden continues, "there's two Elementals. Hellion controls fire and Eira controls water. I think you'll like Eira. She's quiet, but very kind when you get to know her."

Elementals are common in our lands, gifted with the ability to control one of the elements. Fire Elementals tend to be temperamental and loud, while Water Elementals tend to be calm and peaceful.

"There's the two shifters I met, Azrael and Haven. They're both Wolfers. Both Alphas as well, which is an interesting dynamic considering they're lovers."

All shifters are born into one of three categories; Alpha, Omega or Beta. Alphas tend to be the leaders, Betas are usually even-tempered and Omegas are known to be quite reserved. Having two alphas in one group, as lovers, and neither of them being the leader is an interesting dynamic for sure.

"There's another shifter, Fenor, as well. He's a Beta Foxe shifter."

Foxe are a lot like Wolfers, in the way that they are larger versions of the Fox they have in the mainlands. They are around the size of a normal wolf and typically have a coat matching the terrain in which they were born. They can also be regular animals or shifters.

"Then there's Vor and Vulcan. Vor is a Warrior and Vulcan is a Scribe."

It is rare to come across warriors in Mygreen. They

are born in Ulopia, which is known as the Land of the Unlucky. It is a land of harsh landscapes and harsher inhabitants. The terrain is all desert and the summer weather never relents. Between the frequent sandstorms and the creatures, it is a very rough place to survive, and all people born there are born plain. This started the Warrior race. They are born stronger, smarter, and stealthier than the average person. Though, with their upbringing in Ulopia, they do not tend to be the friendliest.

Scribes have the ability to steal a person's memories by touching them and are known to have photogenic memories. They are usually from Promental, and are typically quite wealthy and a tad uptight.

"That is quite a group of gifted Arden," I sigh. "Have you told them of our different gifts?"

Arden slows down and stops beside me. I stop and turn to face him. He looks me in the eye, "I would never betray your secrets and by revealing that about me, it would in turn lead to suspicion of yours. They know that my touch can steal gifts, but they do not know that

I have actually done so yet. We will tell them together once you have decided if we shall stay."

"Do you believe they will be angry that we kept it from them, or that they will think we are monsters?" Fear surrounds me as I think of the possibility that I find the place I can belong, only to ruin it by holding onto this kind of secret.

"Only time will tell Emory, but no, I do not believe that they will hate us or think that we are monsters." He says as he starts to walk again.

I release a breath, set my shoulders and start walking as well, quickening my steps to catch up. The woods seem to grow louder, animals rustling in the bushes and birds chirping above. The thoughts in my head do the same, swirling around and jumping between thoughts so rapidly I have a hard time catching just one.

CHAPTER FIVE

Arden was correct with his estimate of four hours. Right at the time he said we would, we walk into a small grass clearing, fully surrounded by tall maple trees and blooming lilies. The grass is taller around the edges and the lilies are a bright yellow color, decorating the tall weeds as if they cannot grow in the middle of the circular clearing. My thoughts are stuck on the lilies as Arden walks over to one tree and sets his bag down, along with the food bag and water canteen. He refused to let me carry them at any point during our hike, much to my dismay. Dropping to take a seat on the ground beneath the tree, he leans back against the base and looks up at me. I walk closer to him and squat down, my mind going back to the task at hand. "When will they be here to meet us?" I ask.

"Right behind you, princess," a deep voice says. I jump up and spin around, hand going to the blade at my side. Behind me is who I believe Arden described as Ryat. He is a few inches over six feet tall, just as Arden said. He has pale skin with black freckles, the kind of eyelashes women dream of having, and deep black hair hanging just above his eyes. I sense no ill will from his emotions, and I slowly pull my hand away from the short sword I have strapped to my hip. I begin to feel silly for the reaction. If I had been more focused on my surroundings than the lilies, I may have sensed the new emotions joining us in the clearing. Looking him in the eyes and pulling my shoulders back, I try to smile softly. "I'm sorry. I didn't hear you come into the clearing. You scared me."

The man (who I believe to be Ryat) smiles, showing that he has deep dimples on both sides of his face. "I've gotten quite good at walking quietly in these woods. You wouldn't have heard me if you were trying to, princess. I'm glad your first reaction was to protect yourself. That will help you in these woods."

"I've been in these woods for most of my life. Protecting myself and Arden has become second nature." I shift on my feet and Ryat steps closer to me, our bodies only a couple feet apart now.

"I share that habit princess, my sister and I have been doing the same for a long time. You'll meet her soon, and if you're anything like Arden, you'll quickly become best friends. She's just as quick to reach for her sword and even quicker to steal your heart."

"Why are you calling me princess? My name is Emory." I ask, confusion swirling inside of me..

He smiles again, a bit wider, and a bit of mischief fills the air around him. "I know, but you were locked up in a tower and you look a hell of a lot like what I'd imagine a princess to look like."

What does that mean? I know I am pretty, but princesses have not been in our land for centuries. They were known for being close to the goddesses and were worshiped for their beauty. And a tower? I never left my cell, but I did not know that I had been in a tower. I guess that would explain the chill.

Turning his head, he locks eyes with Arden, giving him a quick nod of the head. The air is filled with a faint scent of pine, as if we were standing in the heart of a dense tree bed instead of the clearing.

"I'm Ryat. I'm the leader of the traveling party, and I'll be the one taking your powers each day to ensure everyone's safety." He turns his gaze back to me, his honey brown eyes twinkling with kindness. The soft smile on his lips brings me a sense of comfort. "I assume your brother told you that this was the plan?" he asks, his voice velvety smooth.

I nod my head, averting my eyes. His eyes are a bright honey brown and when I look in them, I want to get closer to him, which seems like a very weird thing to do when you first meet somebody.

Looking back up, I see him looking down at me. The soft sound of his breath fills the air, mixing with the distant hum of wildlife around us. Once we make eye contact again, he nods. "Alright then, let's get moving. The camp is about an hour hike away and everyone is really excited to meet you."

I shift my gaze towards Arden as he rises from his seat on the ground. The sound of his footsteps echo in the clearing as he lifts the bags, effortlessly balancing two on each shoulder. The weight of the bags creates a faint rustling sound as he begins to make his way towards me. Suddenly, I become aware of how close I am still standing to Ryat, feeling his warmth radiating from beside me. I take a deliberate sidestep, feeling the grass crunch under my boots, and start walking towards my brother. Behind me, I hear the sound of Ryat's footsteps growing fainter as he walks in the opposite direction, presumably towards their camp.

Once I reach Arden, he gives me a smile and punches me softly on the shoulder. "You're blushing, you dork," he says softly, and I feel the heat grow even hotter along my cheeks and move to my ears as well. Being born with the inability to control my blush is a curse all on its own. I put my head down quickly and turn to follow Ryats' path, quickening my steps and hear Arden laugh behind me.

Jerk.

We walk in silence for almost the entire hike. The only sounds are the occasional twig snap from my steps or animals moving in the forest. The scent of earth and moss lingers in the air, intertwining with the crisp freshness of the surrounding woods. After being in the cell for so long, I have not grown to be fond of the silence, but there is something soothing about the light background noises that come from being in the familiar woods. I continue to name the trees we pass in my head, cataloging the different herbs and edible plants that line the trail Ryat forges through the underbrush. The earthy scent of damp soil fills the air, mingling with the sweet, musky aroma of ripe blackberries hidden among the thorny brambles. Oak, with its sturdy trunk and broad leaves, stands tall and proud beside us. I spot clusters of bright red raspberries glistening in the dappled sunlight, their tartness practically beckoning me closer. The unmistakable tang of tomatoes wafts from a wild patch nearby, their juicy promise tantalizing.

"Pine," I think, inhaling deeply as the crisp, resinous scent envelops me. "Oak again," I note, mentally ticking off my list. "Pine again," I chuckle to myself, amused at their abundance. Fig trees sway gently in the breeze, their leaves whispering secrets, while the soft rustle of wild onions peeking through the underbrush adds a hint of familiarity.

This has become a habit for me over the years, a sort of treasure hunt during my solitary excursions. I was always in the woods to gather, not to explore, so I've turned it into a game. "Find five herbs, and you win a bronze; find five edible vegetables, and you win a silver; find five edible fruits, and you win a gold." I grin at the thought, recalling the thrill of discovery each time. I may or may not have snatched a handful of blackberries while we walked, the sweet juice bursting on my tongue as I savor each one.

But they're my favorite, so can you really blame me?

Suddenly, as I spot my fourth edible vegetable—plump and vibrant against the earthy backdrop—Ryat halts ahead of us. The soft crunch of leaves underfoot fades as I slow to meet him, my curiosity piqued.

He turns around, his silhouette framed by the sun filtering through the canopy above. "We're getting ready to enter the camp, so now would be a good time for me to cancel out your gift. It's quickest if I hold your face but can be done with me touching just your hand as well, if that makes you more comfortable."

The Idea of him holding my face makes me nervous. I have never been touched by a male and I'm not sure I'm ready for that kind of connection yet. Before I have the chance to tell him, Arden speaks up. "Her hand would be best. We can spare a few minutes."

I am forever grateful that my brother seems to read my mind as Ryat steps forward and holds his hand out in front of me. His hand is large, his fingers long and dusted with scars. I wonder briefly where all the scars came from. Some seem to have been deeper than others, and some seem to be barely there at all. Putting my hand out, he grabs it as if we are just shaking hands and I close my eyes.

I feel the tingling in my nose as the sensation of magic stirs within me. Ryat is silent while he cancels out my powers and my mind is focused on the fact that this is the first time I've touched anyone on purpose other than my mother, father, or Arden. I have always been so scared of stealing gifts that I would have never dared touch another person. My parents were terrified I would be executed, like so many of the Nulls found before me, that I wasn't even allowed out into the village. Everyone there thought I was a plain, and in our world it made sense for me to be kept safe at home. Arden, being a male, meant that nobody would touch him, so he was safe to go out. Males of low class were not to be touched, nor were they to touch each other, and it was heavily enforced. He told people his power was the original he got from our father on first touch, and it made sense to everyone in the village.

Suddenly, my thoughts are brought back to Ryat

canceling out my gift as it suddenly feels like everything and nothing at all has changed. I had not known that there was a buzzing feeling I felt constantly until my brain wonders where it has gone.

I open my eyes as Ryat releases my hand and I look over at Arden as he takes Ryats' hand next. My body feels strangely empty, like a piece of me is missing. I had not thought that any part of me would miss my gift, but it seems my body is not in agreement. I extend my arms, feeling the weightlessness of emptiness, and twist my ankles with a gentle creak, as though trying to awaken dormant sensations. The sound of rustling fabric accompanies each movement, the soft swish blending with the sounds of the woods around me.

When Arden opens his eyes and releases Ryats' hand, I see him shake out his arms as well.

"Do you feel like something is missing when he does that?" I ask, still popping my joints and wiggling my fingers.

"Every time," he replies. "It's like my body has gone

still and it's used to being in constant movement."

Nodding, I look down at my body. Nothing looks different. My black dress is still flowing around my thighs, my silver hair is still hanging down my back, my skin looks exactly like it always has. Feeling as if I have gone still is a good way to explain it.

"Come on, princess. It's time to get to camp," Ryat says, turning to walk farther down his path.

CHAPTER SIX

We enter the camp and I count fifteen towering brown tents, their sturdy frames reaching towards the sky. The air is filled with the crackling sound of logs burning in the large circular fire pit, nestled firmly into the earth. The distinct scent of wood smoke dances in the breeze, mingling with the earthy aroma of the surrounding woods. There are eight people sitting around the fire, on logs, tree stumps and other structures they have put around the fire to use as chairs. After a few moments of us approaching the camp, a large man with bright red hair looks over and spots us walking in.

He stands up, taking large steps towards us as he

yells, "Arden! Boy, you left your tent a mess! Who do you think they made clean that shit up?"

If he wasn't smiling one of the craziest smiles I had ever seen, I would have been on high alert from the tone of his voice.

Arden laughs. "I left it just for you, old man!"

As they get closer to each other, they grab each other in a weird side hug and smack each other's backs quite hard. I've never really seen guys hug, but I really hope that's just how they do it and I won't be expected to do the same. I think a smack from him may break my shoulder.

I'd really like to keep my bones in their current unbroken state.

Ryat, who is standing next to me (quite close if I might add), lends down to whisper in my ear, "that is Hellion, he and your brother have grown quite close in Ardens time with us."

The others have gathered around us now and

being around this many people has made me feel claustrophobic. The men are all quite large and they are all clapping Arden on the back harshly, in that same weird sideways hug.

I've never been around more than three people at a time in my entire life. I'm not sure how I'm supposed to greet this many people at one time. Do I say hello to everyone at one time or will they all want to give me that angry hug?

I don't want to hug; I think.

As their eyes lock on me, I feel my cheeks grow hot. Chatter and laughter fill the air, blending together and cluttering as they make their way to my ears. My hands tremble, betraying my inner unease, as two men and a woman make their way towards me. Their smiles radiate a contagious energy, enveloping the atmosphere with an electrifying buzz. The emotions pour into me, full of positivity and enthusiasm. Yet, the intensity of it all becomes overwhelming, an avalanche of sensations crashing into my senses.

Lost in this whirlwind, I become panicked, wishing for someone to step in and help me.

Suddenly, I feel a strong arm, radiating warmth, gently pressing against my lower back, pulling me towards the side of a solid body. In those initial moments, the sudden surge of warmth, a sensation I haven't experienced in what feels like forever, overwhelms my senses. The touch of the arm against my back sends a comforting tingle down my spine, instantly making me feel safe and protected.

When is the last time I remember being this warm? Definitely before my cell.

The wonderful way he smells follows that thought, reminding me of a freshly cut tree and cinnamon. I think it is a pine tree, and mixed with the cinnamon, it reminds me of holidays in the cavern.

Then I fully realize I am touching a male.

Trying to pull away, I fail and look up to see that it's Ryat, holding me to his side. I forgot he was standing next to me. I also forgot that wishing is a dangerous thing to do because it always gets granted.

"Let's backup everyone. No need to crowd our newbie. Everyone will have time to meet her, and I have canceled out her powers, but for now, please refrain from overwhelming her." Ryat says loud enough for everyone to hear him.

He looks down at me, but I've been looking up at him this entire time. He's touching me, while telling people not to overwhelm me. Is that normal? Why is he touching me? My body is warm and tingling a bit where we are touching, and I'm not sure if that's normal. I'll have to ask Arden later. He had lots of female friends in the village who could touch others and had told him about it.

Ryat speaks up again, looking back out at the people who had approached us, "I will bring her to lunch and we will do introductions, but for now she needs to rest and regain her bearings."

The crowd backs up and goes back to the fire, but

I hear the muttering of apologies as they go. The onslaught of emotions I had felt eases and I feel the tension release from my shoulders as I release a breath I hadn't realized I was holding. My hands have stopped shaking and for some reason, I feel safe still.

I can sense that Ryat is amused, excited and also some emotion I do not know. It's warm though, and I like it. Ryat smiles, "you okay princess?"

"Um, yeah, yes, I mean, I think so." Being this close to him makes me feel nervous, making me shiver. He rubs his hand in a slow circle over my hip, and I jump a bit. "You just told them not to overwhelm me, but you're touching me a lot."

"Does me touching you bother you?" He asks.

Averting my eyes, I think about it. My thoughts are racing and the circles he is tracing on my hip are not helping that matter. Does it bother me? No. Does it make me nervous? Absolutely. Does it confuse me? 100%.

"Um, no, I wouldn't say it bothers me. Maybe it

confuses me?" Why did I say that like a question? Ugh. He's going to think I'm stupid now.

He laughs, a big dimpled smile taking over his face, "oh princess, I'm sure it confuses you. Arden told me how you were raised. After so many years of isolation from other gifted and touch, I can imagine a lot will confuse you over the next long while. But that's okay, you'll get used to being touched and you'll find when it does and doesn't bother you."

Nodding, I look down at where our bodies are touching, seeing our black clothing pushed together, almost the same shade, but not quite. My clothing was made by the seamstress in our village. Arden would buy them for me as gifts when he went out with his friends. He said her name was Iraya, and that she had a lovely shade of shiny pink hair. I wonder where Ryat and the others get their clothes, where I will get my clothes. He continues to rub circles on my hip for a few moments as I think about the clothing situation and then I hear footsteps approach us.

Looking up from where our bodies are touching, I see

Arden looking at me with a soft smile and holding out his hand for me. I go to remove myself from Ryat and he gives my hip a small squeeze before releasing me.

I take Arden's hand and he leads me toward the tents. I can sense that he is content, though there is a bit of confusion laced in there as well. I guess that makes sense.

Looking back, I see Ryat watching me walk away, his eyes seeming to glow with an intensity that only confuses me more. I will need to ask Arden about a lot of things, it seems, because apparently I understand males a lot less than I thought I did.

Turning back, I follow Arden into the tent sitting closest to the fire, seeing that it has a fur covered cot and small full dressing wardrobe in it. "Who's tent is this?" I ask. The clothes in the wardrobe seem to be made of feminine fabrics and colors, and the linens and furs on the bed look to be freshly cleaned.

"This is your tent. They prepared it for you. I have the tent behind yours." He plops down on my cot, sinking into its soft looking fabric. The sound of it creaking fills the air as he stretches his legs out. He is so long now that the tip of his boots brush the other side of the tent as he stretches.

I take a seat next to him and rub my hand over the soft furs covering the cot. Looking over at me, he smiles again, "The clothes should all fit, though I'm not sure they'll all match your usual style. Ryat bought anything we couldn't get from other people in the group. He decided you were a princess right away, so good luck with whatever he chose." He laughs.

I grimace, thinking of what type of clothing a "princess" may wear in the woods, hoping he had been practically in his decision making. I really hope I will not be fighting in gowns and frills. Fights within these lands typically led to bloodshed and tears, which did not bode well for fancy outfits.

Arden stands up, hunched over slightly, as he is taller than the tent itself is tall. "I'm going to go take a nap in my tent sis, I would recommend that you do the same. The afternoons around here can be pretty lively, and I'm sure you'll want your energy. Make sure you drink some water, too. You didn't drink enough on the hike."

I roll my eyes, "you got it, water and a nap, pronto."

Arden leaves, and I secure the tent flap behind him. It covers the entire entry way and is secured with a velcro material, making it easy to seal. I wish that he had stayed longer, so that I could have asked him some of the questions piling up in my mind.

Walking to the back of the tent, I push the dressing wardrobe open fully, and a wave of color and fabric greets me. It's mostly filled with short, flexible dresses, much like the one I'm currently wearing, but these are adorned with frilly sleeves that cascade delicately and flowing skirts that seem to dance with an unseen breeze. The corsets are intricately laced, their silver accents glinting in the soft light that filters through the tent's fabric, creating a shimmering effect.

I run my fingers along the hem of one dress, the fabric soft and cool against my skin. I can already picture how beautiful they will look, yet I can't help but feel they're far too extravagant for a life spent in the woods. Who needs such finery while walking and fighting in the rustling leaves and earthy trails?

With a sigh, I close the wardrobe again, the wood creaking slightly as it shuts. It's a discussion for another time—one I know will come, but for now, I turn away, the weight of expectations lingering in the air like the scent of wildflowers outside.

Turning, I pull my dress off and walk the few steps forward to climb into my cot, draping the furs over my body and lay still for a moment, appreciating the softness against my skin. Based on the softness and coloring of the furs, I assume it is from a Foxe. It is a light copper color, the color of the sun right before it goes below the horizon at nighttime.

After my time in the cell, I'm not sure how long it will be before I become used to the softness of blankets again.

After being cold for that long, when will I feel warm again? Other than when I was being held against Ryat's body, I have been bone cold ever since Arden got me out.

I wonder for a moment what we will have for dinner, remembering the porridge. I hope I never have to see porridge again.

I refrain from looking at the scars along my palms as I drift into a light sleep.

CHAPTER SEVEN

I wake to the sound of rustling and what sounds like somebody saying my name? As my heavy eyelids reluctantly flutter open, I am immediately greeted by the sight of Ryat standing over me. My eyes go wide and I gasp out, "Oh!" I pull the warm fur up farther, which uncovers my toes and sends a shiver of cold up my body. "I'm sleeping!" I all but yell.

Ryat laughs lightly, still looking down at me with his honey brown eyes, "I can see that, but we're getting ready to eat lunch, so I figured I would come grab you. It's time to meet everyone."

Oh, right. I had forgotten.

I look down at my fur covered body, "okay, but you'll have to leave my tent before I can get up." I may not be uncomfortable touching him, but I am definitely uncomfortable with him seeing me naked.

Ryat looks down at my body, confused. "Why would I need to-", he stops and I see realization in his eyes as looks back up at me and laughs. "Got it, got it. Okay, princess, I'll wait outside. Wear the pink dress."

Once the heavy canvas tent flap closes, I spring to my feet and secure the flap behind him. Walking to the wardrobe, the sound of my heart still pounding in my ears, I open it up and without even thinking about why I'm following his directions; I feel the cool silk of a pink dress brush against my fingertips as I step into it. It's got short butterfly sleeves and a V neckline that accentuates my collarbones. Paired with the corset top, it makes it a bit more revealing than my usual outfits. The skirt cascades down in a flowy motion, brushing against my legs, its soft fabric caressing my skin mid thigh, with a silver lace trim along the bottom edge. There's silver lace trim on the neckline, sleeves and along the corset trims as well.

This is way too intricate of a dress for a casual lunch. What the hell was he thinking getting me fancy dresses like this? Even with the built in shorts, it doesn't seem like a dress you would wear to live, hunt and most likely fight in the woods. I would feel horrible if I spilled on it or got into a fight and it tore.

Before I can change, the flap of my tent flies open again and I spin around. "I told you to wait outside! I could have been naked!"

Ryat laughs, looking me up and down. "I can hear you muttering about the dress being too fancy. I knew you were dressed, or at least I guessed you were and was willing to risk it." He laughs again. "It's not too fancy and you look beautiful. Now let's go get lunch before they eat both of our portions."

He grabs my hand and pulls me out of the tent before I can respond. I can feel the warmth of the flames on my skin as we make our way past the fire, towards where everyone is sitting around a large wooden table. Which is probably a good thing, because my response may not have been very kind. I also realize that in my haste, I forgot to attach my blade to my hip and without it I feel strangely bare.

He interlocked our fingers this time, like I've seen my parents do. It feels nice and his hand is warm. As we get closer, a few people wave and say hello. I wave with the hand Ryat is not holding (captive). The emotions at the table are a mix of surprise, confusion, excitement, and contentment. I assume the contentment being from the food filling their wooden bowls. Ryat sits down at the far edge of the bench, across from a copper haired man with one brown and one green eye. He pulls me down next to him, close enough that our thighs are touching under the table. There are bowls in front of us filled with what looks to be a stew, and my stomach growls as I smell the spices in the air.

Looking at me, Ryat gestures to the man across from us, "princess, this is Fenor, he's our Foxe shifter and our cook."

Smiling, I look over at Fenor. "It's a pleasure to meet

you. Thank you for the meal." Fenor gives me a toothy grin, both canines sparking in the sun. "Darlin, the pleasure is all mine."

He looks over at where me and Ryats arms are brushing and then looks back at me with a cocked eyebrow and the same grin but a bit wider. "I know our group can get rowdy, but we're all good folk. You'll see."

I smile shyly, feeling a blush working up my neck, "So far you all seem lovely, though I am not used to being around this many people, so it is taking some adjusting." I look around the table and see that people have already started to eat their stew, so I pick up my Spork and grab a potato.

Fenor laughs, "honey, you were also locked up in a cell for over a month, so I'm sure adjusting is a light word for what you need. But you have time and we have patience." He smiles at me kindly, taking a bite of his own stew. His emotions are quite calm, mostly contentment and a bit of intrigue.

I take a bite, my taste buds instantly noticing the

potent blend of garlic, rosemary, and a surprising hint of nutmeg. The flavors combined are quite nice and the rabbit meat he used is tender, making it very soft and easy to eat. The potatoes are not charred, though that is unsurprising.

Looking over at Ryat, I ask, "Where are Arden and the others?" I had noted there were only seven of us at the table, meaning there were six people not here.

"They went out to hunt. Arden has been missed. He has gotten quite good with a bow and we were running low on meat, so they went out to see what they could find." That makes me smile. I enjoy knowing that even in his short time here, he had found a place and a job. Friends and people to spend time with. Though I was alone in the cavern, Arden had a lot of friends in the village, and I know he likes to be around other people.

Ryat gestures to the woman sitting a chair over from Fenor, "This is Eira. She's our Water Elemental, and she handles all of our laundry and cleanup."

Eira is a small woman, with blonde hair and bright

green eyes. She has lovely green freckles along her face and shoulders. Her emotions are much mellower than the others, but just as friendly. I smile at her and give her a small wave, "Hello Eira, I'm Emory."

"I know, Adren has told me a lot about you, and I'm excited for us to get to know each other." She has a kind smile, and she seems genuine.

I take another bite of my stew as she points to the man a couple of seats down from her. "This is Nox. Don't let the scary fire tattoo on his neck scare you. He's a real softy." Nox turns to look at us and gives me a lopsided grin, the same way Arden does. His skin is a rich shade of deep brown, and his eyes are a vibrant hue of bright orange that perfectly matches the coloring in the tattoo on his neck.

"I'll show you soft the next time we fight in training Eira," he teases as he looks over at her with the same lopsided grin. He has a playful energy around him and I can tell they are close. He looks across the table at me and his smile softens, "it's nice to meet you, Emory. Arden has been a great addition to the party, and I'm sure you'll fit in just the same."

A deeper voice speaks up from beside him, "You'll be busting our balls just like Miss Eira here in no time, only louder, I can already tell!" He's laughing a deep belly laugh, looking at me with his deep blue eyes that seem to hold something much darker in them than I've seen before. He looks over at the man seated across from him and then back at me before speaking again. "I'm Vor. I'm a Warrior and I'm in charge of the meat they get during their hunts. The man across from me is Vulcan. He's our Scribe, but he doesn't speak much, so don't expect him to hold much of a conversation with you."

Vor's dark brown hair, combined with his olive skin and piercing blue eyes, creates a striking contrast that leaves me in awe of how a Warrior can be so pretty and so friendly. Vulcan has a ghostly pale complexion with jet black hair and eyes. Not only that, but he also has a smattering of black freckles along the bridge of his nose. There's a large contrast among these three males, yet these seem to be quite close. The energy flowing between them holds a lot of trust and admiration.

I set my Spork down after swallowing my bite and make eye contact briefly with each of them. "It's very nice to meet each of you. I'm very thankful you've allowed me to join your party. It may take me some time to get used to all the people, but I will catch on as quickly as I can." I smile, thinking to myself that I had finally said something I thought made a lick of sense.

"Princess, you can take as much time as you need. We've all had to unlearn past lessons and grow into who we are now." Ryat says from beside me.

He has been quiet until now, though I could feel his gaze on me through the introductions. Resting below the table, his hand finds its way to my knee, and the heat radiating from his palm and fingers creates a comforting sensation that tickles my skin. I do my best not to react, but I can feel warmth spreading across my cheeks. I had just got it to go away from when Fenor had noticed us touching and now it's back. I do hope I will learn to blush less around him or this is going to be quite embarrassing.

"So, princess, why don't you-" Ryat is cut off by a loud scream.

"HELP, WE NEED THE MED TENT NOW!"

There is a large group of people coming out of the woods to the left of the camp, and my eyes widen in shock as the first thing that comes into view is a chilling sight - a vivid crimson stain splattered across the makeshift stretcher they carry. It looks to be made of large branches and vines tied together, and the amount of blood pouring from the bottom of the body within it is quite alarming. The emotions in the air shift to worry, anger and fear as our lunch is forgotten. The men at the table spring into action, abandoning their seats in a flurry of movement to run towards the man in the stretcher. Eira rushes to my side of the table, her hand gripping mine tightly. The rush of adrenaline courses through my veins as she forcefully pulls me out of my chair.

I feel her shake my arm and look over at her. "Emory. I need you to help me get the med tent ready and we need to move quickly. Can you do that?"

Shaking my head quickly to clear the fog, I look back at the group and see them moving towards the tents in a rush. I look back to Eira and stutter, "yyes, I can help. Just tell me what to do."

Eira and I sprint towards the tents, the pounding of our footsteps resonating in my ears. The scent of smoke from the crackling fire fills the air as we enter a tent on the opposite side. The interior reveals a simple setup, with a cot positioned in the center and storage shelves lining the edges, the musty smell of fabric lingering in the confined space. Eira rushes to the back of the tent, her hurried movements causing a faint rustling sound.

With urgency in her voice, she tosses a bundle of linens towards me, the fabric swishing through the air. "Hurry," she exclaims, "put the linens on the cot and come here so I can hand you the supplies!"

I quickly put the linens on the bed, tucking the corners in tightly as I assume whoever is injured will thrash around and I do not want them to come undone.

As I finish securing the last corner, I dash to the back of the tent, the sound of my footsteps muffled on the ground. Reaching the back, I grab the piles of bandages and supplies that Eira has set out. The scent of sterile materials wafts through the air, mingling with the subtle metallic tang of the scissors and suture supplies. I set the first piles of bandages on the closest shelf to the cot, thinking that would be easiest for whoever will be tending to the wounds, and set the medical taping next to it along with scissors and suture supplies.

Suddenly, the tent entrance bursts open, the sound of fabric flapping violently. My eyes widen as a tall man is carried in by Ryat and Hellion. The sound of his strained breathing fills the tent, mixed with the faint hum of pain. I've never seen him before, but he is very tall with bright blonde hair. Ryat and Hellion lift him out of the stretcher and lay him on the cot. My gaze follows the deep wound running across his torso, from his left nipple to his hip, and it is bleeding rapidly, but also faintly glowing.

"We have to get the shrapnel out of him before it

closes. He can't stop the healing, so we'll have to be quick. EIRA! I need a large, sharp knife. NOW!" Hellios yells.

I have never heard anyone yell like this, and my heart feels like it may pound right out of my chest. I take a fast step back in panic and crash into another body. Without turning or looking, I can tell that it's Ryat. I still as my body goes warm, and he places his hand on my hip to pull me into him. I watch as Eira hands Hellios a terrifyingly sharp knife.

Without a moment of hesitation, Hellion sticks the blade into the wound on the blond man's body and cuts. I feel my body flinch, and Ryat must too as he starts rubbing circles on my hip and pulls my head back to rest on his chest with his other hand. I do not fight him as I watch Hellion dig sharp and angry looking pieces of metal out of the man's wound. The man is groaning painfully and his face seems to be contoured, as if he's trying to concentrate. The emotions in the room are heavy with determination and anger from Hellion, along with the confusion seeping from Ryat. It reminds me that while Hellion knows what happened, Ryat does not.

The man's legs kick with each piece of metal pulled from his body and with each clang of them hitting the floor, I feel my body flinch as well. This goes on for what feels like an eternity, but is actually only the course of a few minutes before Hellion stops and sets the knife down.

The man's body goes still and the glow of his wound glows brighter as Hellion looks up at Ryat and hoarsely speaks, "brother, this is war."

CHAPTER EIGHT

I am sitting in my tent with Arden now. After Hellion's statement about war, Ryat tapped my hip and softly told me to go to my brother. He said that he would be speaking to the group shortly and everyone should wait in their tents until then. I had just nodded and walked out of the tent to find Arden waiting outside, his face paler than I had ever seen it before. Though I felt like I was in a fog, I told him what Hellion had done and what Ryat said. He told everyone else to go to their tents and then walked to mine.

Arden speaks the moment he secures the flap on my tent, his voice low but urgent. "It was just a normal hunt. We were tracking a deer in the woods, not even a mile out, the scent of pine and damp earth still filling the air around us. We were close to taking the shot when suddenly we heard a rustling in the underbrush. Azrael and Hazel had split off to find larger prey, leaving just me, Hellion, Teirney, and Fenris on the deer's trail.

I activated my Warrior ability, the familiar surge coursing through me, heightening my senses until every rustle of leaves and distant chirp of birds felt amplified. I motioned for the others to fall in behind me and Hellion, my instincts kicking in. The noise was coming from the front, sharp and unsettling, and I could feel that it wasn't just a single creature—it was multiple gifted.

When they emerged from the brush, four men stepped into the clearing, their silhouettes dark. My instincts screamed at me; I could sense that two of them were shifters, their energies crackling with a wild, untamed power. but that's all I could tell."

He stops for a moment, closing his eyes and sitting down on my cot. Speaking again, he whispers, "One of them asked what a Fire Elemental would be doing with a Null."

My breath catches. I did not think it was possible to pick out a Null from any other gifted. I had been told my entire life that we were just like everyone else in looks and senses. I sit next to him on the cot. "How did he know?" I ask, fear rising in me faster than I ever thought possible.

Arden shifts back to lay his upper body on the bed, legs hanging over the edge. "I don't know. I didn't have time to ask before Hellion spoke up. He told them that who he spends his time with is his business and if they had a problem with that, he was happy to fight about it."

That sounds like something a Fire Elemental would say. They tend to be hot headed and short-tempered. With Hellion's fiery red hair and eyes, I'm sure he was gifted with a large amount of flame to match his temper.

I lay back on the bed next to Arden, practically holding my breath, wondering how it could have led to Fenris being injured. And to be injured in that way, with metal in his body and a gaping wound across his chest.

"They said they were not looking for a fight today, but instead were there to give us a warning. They said war is coming and we are on the wrong side. Then they read us a prophecy."

What Arden says next, low as if he wishes he did not have to speak it at all, shakes me to the core.

When the skies weep and the winds hold their breath,

A woman of lunar light shall rise, her hair as silver as the moon who watches.

She shall stand before the gods with love, her wish a whisper woven with sorrow.

To save her lands, they will demand a sacrifice.

A price of blood, or bone, or soul.

And though her fate is veiled in shadows deep,

The lands will flourish in her wake,

For from her sacrifice, life shall bloom once more.

"They read us the prophecy and told us that if we wanted to live, we were to give them the silver-haired woman in our camp." Arden's voice trembles, a sorrowful weight laced with fear, anger, and guilt that hangs heavily in the air.

I shake my head, trying to deny the reality creeping in. "The prophecy must be speaking of someone else, Arden. It cannot be me." My whisper barely escapes, a fragile hope against the tide of dread.

"Emory, we both know it is speaking of you. There's no use in denying it." His eyes flash with intensity, and I can feel his desperation radiating toward me. "I should have never made you leave the Wishing Tree. We need to go back immediately, so they cannot take you. It's rare enough to be born with silver hair, but to also possess the blessing of wishing upon the gods? It's you, and I will not let them take you." His voice rises, echoing in my tent, filled with a fierce protectiveness.

The tent feels suffocating, the silence amplified by the echoing emptiness that surrounds us. "I do not want to be alone again, Arden." The weight of my words hits hard, and tears well up in my eyes, blurring my vision. They spill over, tracing cold paths down my flushed cheeks.

"Why don't we wait to see what the party's plan is and go from there? I'm sure they will have thought of something." I grasp for any semblance of hope, willing to beg for a chance at freedom, for companionship.

Arden sighs softly, the tension easing just a fraction as he meets my gaze. "If that is what you want, then that is what we will do, Emory. But if things go bad, you being safe is my only priority." His resolve is unwavering, and in that moment, I can see the boy I grew up with—the protector who has always been there, steadfast against the storms of our lives.

Changing the subject, I wipe my tears and ask, "What happened in the fight, Arden? How was Fenris hurt the way he was?"

He shifts on the cot, the weight of his memories evident in his posture. "We had the upper hand, and

I thought they were close to retreating when suddenly another man charged out from behind us and threw a homemade explosive. Fenris was the closest, and it hit him first. They filled it with nails and other sharp objects. Teirney managed to dig some of them out when Fenris was healing her wounds." His voice falters for a moment, and I can see the horror playing out in his mind.

"But while Hellion and I were still fighting with the original four men, another attacker came from the same direction and slashed his sword down Fenris' torso." The words spill from him like a confession, heavy and raw. "After that, all the men retreated, but not before they threw another explosive as Fenris lay there, splayed open like a deer being prepared for butchering. He passed out, and his body tried to heal itself, but we knew we had to get him back before he healed completely. Teirney had to run as far from us as possible to keep from boosting his healing, while Hellion and I started carrying him back. Azrael and Haven found us soon after—they said they smelled the blood and helped us run the rest of the way."

The sorrow in his voice envelops us, intertwining with my own fear and grief, creating a suffocating atmosphere in the small tent. I can feel the weight of our emotions swirling around us, thick as fog, echoing from the other tents where the rest of the party is grappling with their own emotions. I wipe the tears from my cheeks and temples, but the flood doesn't stop; they continue to spill down my face as I fight to hold it together.

Arden remains composed, a stark contrast to my turmoil, but I recall the anger and determination radiating from Hellion in the med tent. It makes sense now why he had been yelling the way he did. This kind of grief and pain is the stuff of nightmares—something you hope to avoid at all costs. Yet in Alblasia, it's a brutal reality, where friends can be torn to shreds before your very eyes. I realize with a pang that I've never experienced this before.

Before we can say anything more, a loud whistle cuts through the tension outside the tent, followed by Ryat's voice calling for everyone to meet at the table.

CHAPTER NINE

R yat and Fenor sit at the far right edge of the table when we arrive, which I can now see is made from a solid oak tree, its surface polished and coated with a protective sealer that catches the soft light. Next to Fenor is Arden, followed by Eira, Hellion, Nox, and Vor. On our side, Ryat occupies his usual spot, then it's me, Haven, Azrael, Teirney and Vulcan. The emotional weight at this table feels almost suffocating, a turbulent sea of sorrow and anger that swirls around us like a storm. Tears roll down my cheeks, and nobody but Ardon even knows why. The rest of the party doesn't know about the gifts I've taken; they just think I'm overly emotional about a man I don't know.

Ryat sits beside me, though not as close as he usually does. Still, his hand rests on my thigh, tracing gentle circles that send a wave of comfort through me, rather than the blush of embarrassment I expected. I had never realized that a simple touch could evoke so many feelings, and that thought sends me spiraling into confusion.

Ryat's voice cuts through the tension, soft but firm enough to command attention. He glances around the table, meeting each gaze. "This was not a random event. This was a personal attack on our party."

A shockwave ripples through the group, quickly replaced by a rising tide of anger. Hellion sits silently, his gaze dark and intense, a deadly look etched onto his face. Arden's expression, however, betrays a flicker of guilt.

Vor mutters, his voice low but fierce, "We should confront them. I'm done with the hiding and waiting."

Azrael's voice cuts through the tension, louder, almost vibrating with fury. "If they show their faces again, I'll tear them to pieces," he snarls, clenching his fists.

Hellion's eyes remain fixed ahead, unblinking.

I remain silent, tears still streaming down my cheeks, feeling Ryat's hand continue its gentle, reassuring motion on my thigh.

With a sharp look, Ryat silences the group, his gaze fierce. "They spoke of a prophecy that has come to light. It speaks of a silver-haired woman whose wish to the gods and sacrifice will save the lands." His voice wavers slightly, tinged with a mix of sorrow and desperation. I feel everyone's eyes turn to look at me, but I do not stop looking at Ryat. I do not want to see the fear, anger or any of the other emotions I am currently sensing written on their faces as they look at me. It is bad enough having to feel it all swirling in the surrounding air.

Ryat continues when nobody says anything, "we have been told that if we do not turn Emory over we will all be killed." With this soft statement, he looks me in the eye. "We will do no such thing."

There are very mixed emotions at the table. Relief from some, anger from others. Confusion, resentment and despair are mixed in as well. I can only imagine what people are thinking. They just met me and if my life could save them all, why should they have to risk everything to save me? They have people they love and care for, people they are still trying to find, and all of this will halt that. Ryat must be able to sense where my mind is going. At some point I dropped my chin, and I am now looking at the table between us. He reaches down and lifts my chin to look at him, and I hear a couple of small gasps from around the table.

"You are part of our party and we do not give up on each other, no matter what." He says, his voice full of unwavering confidence and compassion.

The rest of the group speaks up in agreement, fists beating on the oak table and I feel Arden's hand as he reaches over to squeeze my shoulder. I look down at the shaking table at the people I have just met, and those I have not met at all. "Thank you," I say, with tears still rolling down my cheeks and a quivering voice.

"Fenris was injured during the fight that happened after their declaration. They had homemade explosives with shrapnel inside them and based on when they threw it, it would seem they knew about his ability to heal himself. We will need to be extra cautious since they seem to know a lot about our gifts." Ryats' voice is hard and full of anger when he says this, and I can feel the guilt flowing from him too.

He speaks again after a slight pause. "Me, Hazel, Arden, Teirney and Vor are leaving right away. We are going to search the lands for more information on the prophecy, the war and see what is affecting the lands to cause it to need saving. The rest of you will remain here and set up a guard shift, with someone always on watch."

This shocks me. I did not think anyone would leave except possibly me and Arden. But definitely not the leader of the party, and Arden, along with him.

Looking back at me, he adds, "Emory, you will be in

charge of caring for Fenris as he heals himself. This will take him time and we also need to ensure you are both the most guarded at all times, so this kills both birds with one stone."

Before I truly process this anymore, he stands, grabs my hand, and pulls me up with him. I catch a surprised widening of the eyes from Hazel and wonder if I should be concerned. I do not sense any ill will or negative emotions as Ryat looks over the table again. "My team, get packed. Everyone else, when I get back, you better all be alive."

I turn from the table and walk with Ryat, feeling the cool breeze brush against my face. He takes hold of my hand again, our fingers interlocked tightly, as we move forward. The sounds of leaves rustling under our feet mix with the distant chirping of birds, creating a soothing melody in my ears. His pace is brisk, forcing me to take twice as many steps to match his long strides. The exertion sends a tingling sensation through my legs, a reminder that I need to work on my endurance. I am extremely grateful when he gets to the tents. If this is how he always walks, I will need to begin leg exercises right away. When he strides past my tent, I shoot him a confused look and he just smiles at me in response. He continues walking, past Ardens and the one behind his which I now know to be Hellions. At the very end of all the tents, there is one that is set slightly farther out from the fire than the rest. Approaching the front of the tent, I feel the texture of the fabric under my fingertips, smooth yet sturdy. He opens the tent flap and steps in, pulling me in behind him.

Looking around, I see the tent has the same setup as my own, aside from a much larger cot and furs of black wolfer instead of my copper foxe furs. There is a black shirt just like the one he is wearing tossed over the bottom end of the cot and that is the final clue as to this being his tent. I hear him securing the tent flap closed behind me as I run my hand over the soft Wolfer fur and look around, wondering if he may have anything personal in here.

Not that I would snoop, of course.

"I am not sure how long we will be gone on our

journey," Ryat says and he pulls me back into him by my hip. I feel my body warm as it does every time, feel his strong chest behind me and the powerful muscles in his arm along my side. It is interesting to me how I seem to have gotten so comfortable with him touching me so quickly after having never touched another person like this before.

I sigh, leaning my head back and to the side so I can look up at him, "you are leaving and taking Arden with you, yet I do not know when the only two people I know, mostly, will be back. That is enough to drive a woman mad. And I'm not even sure if I like you yet."

He laughs, loudly, "oh, princess, you like me. I can tell."

I roll my eyes. What an infuriating man, "how can you tell if I'm not even sure yet? I know nothing about you." I mean, sure, I was comfortable around him and he made me feel safe, but I knew nothing of his past or his morals. What if he killed sleeping children, so they didn't grow up to one day kill him? Okay, that's extreme, but I don't know. How could I? We haven't even had time to speak, let alone learn about each other.

He laughs softly, "what would you like to know princess?"

I look up at him, smiling down at me, and think. It is nice that he is willing to speak about himself, but there is so much I wish to know about him and so little time. Shifting a bit against him, I settle on the first thoughts that pop into my head, "how about your past, what was it like? Do you know what God Blessed you? Is your sister blessed? Do you touch all women the way you touch me? Is it normal to touch women this way? I don't see Fenor holding me or anyone else." I am out of breath when I finish and Ryat is full on grinning now, dimples and all. I have said and asked too much, just like I was worried about.

Stupid.

Ryat takes a step back, causing me to lose my balance. I feel his strong hands firmly gripping my hips, steadying me. The scent of him lingers in the air as he guides me to sit on his cot. Climbing on and leaning back against the pillows he has set up, he motions for me to come to him, but I am not sure what he is meaning for me to do. He laughs again and I am so confused.

Are all males this confusing?

"Here," he pats the spot between where he has his legs open, "come sit here and lean back against me."

My cheeks heat and I shake my head. "I asked you a question."

"I'm going to answer your questions, plural, but I wanted to be comfortable while doing so. So, come here, princess," he says, his voice deep and smooth as he pats the space in front of him, between his legs, again.

Against my better judgment, I cautiously crawl over and settle between his legs, the cot uneven beneath my knees as I try to position myself. However, I've obviously never done this before and I don't know how. As I sit down facing forward, a wave of embarrassment washes over me, causing my cheeks to flush with warmth. Our faces are so close that I can almost feel his breath against my skin. Determined to find a better position, I spin around, knocking my knees into his in the process (which he apparently thinks is hilarious). But, finally, after some adjusting, I am facing away from him. His chest presses against my back as he adjusts me, and his touch sends a shiver down my spine. Gently, he reaches up and guides my head back, resting it against his chest..

"Alright, so to start, me and Teirney grew up in Naboo on a Spring Bonnet farm. They are the most treasured flower in Naboo, a beautiful purple and blue flower that only grows in certain villages within the nation. It was very peaceful for the first ten years. We were raised by our mother, Millia and our father, Roz, and even went to the local school. But there had been some bad trade deals, I guess, and our village was raided by Arrakis one night. I was taken and put into a work camp with all the other children they had taken from the village. I had hidden Teirney when I heard the shouting, and she stayed hidden until she made her way to our grandparents' home once the raiders were all gone, where she stayed, thinking I was dead until I returned to get her. I got back to her at Nineteen and started this party half a year later to help other people find the people they had lost and were searching for." He stops to chuckle, still looking down at me. "I can see the curiosity on your face, but I promise I'll tell you more about that on a different day."

I'm sure there is more than curiosity showing on my face. My father had heard the whispering of the children taken to Arrakis and nothing he heard was pleasant.

My mouth emits a low sound of pleasure as his fingers glide through my hair, creating a delightful sensation. I sense he has that warm emotion again, though I still do not know what it is. But I do not ask what it is, I just let him continue.

"I am blessed by Riven, The God of War. My sister is not blessed by any gods." He says, still stroking my head, still playing with my hair.

He continues, "As for your other questions, no. I do not touch other women this way and it is not considered normal to do so. When I am touching you, it is like my mind stills and the world quiets. I like to touch you and I believe you like it when I do so, so that's why I am. But if it ever made you uncomfortable, you would just have to say so and I would immediately stop."

I close my eyes, thinking about all he has now told me. "I do like it when you touch me. It makes me feel warm, and I have been cold for a long time."

We sit in silence for a bit, with him lightly stroking my head and hair. Knowing he will be leaving soon, I feel a sense of sadness, as I won't have the opportunity to get to know him better until he returns. There is so much I would like to know about him, and it feels like I am meant to learn it all. But, I am also incredibly nervous for him, my brother and the others.

Ryat speaks quietly, "it is time for me to go, and time for you to say goodbye to your brother. I will bring him back and we will have more information, but in the meantime, if Fenor tries to touch you, let him know I'll come for his head." He says the last part with a laugh and I join him, though I am not sure what he means by that. I make a quick mental note to ask somebody from the party once I have gotten closer to them.

Getting out of his cot, we both exit the tent and he walks me back to mine, holding my hand again. When we get there, he lets my hand go and walks off toward his tent again. When I enter my tent, I see Arden sitting on my cot with his bag packed next to him.

"Do you mind if I take your Wishing Tree blanket with me?" He asks.

I smile, glad I packed it, "of course not. I hope it keeps you warm in the woods. I will miss you while you're gone, but I'm glad you've found your place within the party."

Arden smiles up at me from his seat on my cot, barely shorter even while sitting. He laughs, "If I had known getting good at hunting would separate us, I may have picked a different skill to learn."

Sitting next to him, I laugh with him, thinking of all the times he wished to join father on his hunting journeys as a boy. "No, you wouldn't have. This is what you were meant to do."

"I'm not sure I agree, but it's time for me to go. You'll be safe here and we'll be back soon with more information. We've known a war was brewing between the nations. We just didn't know when it would hit our lands. I guess now we do." He stands up, pulling me up with him and then in for a hug.

"Hey, before you go. I don't have to hug people like you do, right? With the back hitting and stuff?" I see amusement in his eyes as he tries to hold back a laugh and fails.

"No, that's just a guy thing, sis. You're safe," he says, still laughing.

I punch his arm as we walk out of the tent and towards the group huddled together by the table. But, I am really glad it's just a guy thing. It really does look like it would hurt.

I hear Hellion speaking as we approach, "alright everyone, they're off. We know our jobs and they're going to be fucking fine. No need for more tears and soppy goodbyes. They'll be back soon, and we'll be ready for whatever they find on their journey."

Everyone breaks off and goes back to the tents, leaving just Hellion, Ryat, Haven, Azrael, Vor, Arden, Teirney and I. I give Arden another hug, squeezing him extra tight and relishing in the closeness for a moment. Reluctantly, I release my grip and step back, the heaviness of the emotions in the air weighing on me. Tears have already stained my cheeks, leaving my face swollen and tender. I attempt to suppress the urge to cry, diverting my attention towards Teirney and Ryat engrossed in an animated conversation. Their gestures are bold and exaggerated, their heads inclined towards each other in deep concentration. As their conversation ends, they laugh as they hug.

Ryat walks towards me, at an unhurried pace, so different from the quick steps from just a while ago. "I'll be back soon, princess. You won't have to wait too long." I nod and my heart flutters as he gently squeezes my hip, then turns and starts the path into the woods. Arden, Haven, Teirney and Vor follow beyond him and soon enough I can't see any of them at all.

CHAPTER TEN

The hours after they left were full of scrambled planning, shuffling of tents and hurried conversations about camp responsibilities. I had stood at the entrance of the woods, watching the spot they had entered the trees, until Azrael had come to get me for the discussions. I had missed little, only learning that my things have now been moved to the tent next to the med tent, and Hellions is now directly behind the two.

In the next topic, it was decided that Hellion was taking over as interim leader for Ryat. Azrael would prepare the meats after hunts in place of Vor and Vulcan is going to help with wounds until Fenris is healed. Eira was now also in charge of finding fruits and vegetables, on top of her other tasks, and helping me with Fenris. It was decided that since Arden had told them of my love for cooking, I would take over that responsibility so Fenor could join the Hunting team with Fenor, Nox and Azrael.

I tried not to be too excited, as the reason this job became mine was no reason for celebration. I failed. Thinking of all the herbs, spices and combinations I could try had occupied my thoughts during the conversations I was not a part of. Imagining the sizzling stews, succulent roasts, comforting soups, flaky pastries, and even the intriguing casserole my father once described, I couldn't help but feel a surge of anticipation. I learned how to cook from my mother and gained skill from the books of recipes my father found me on his journeys. Being in the kitchen has always calmed me, and I feared I would need that in the time that Arden, Ryat, and the others were gone.

But, on the bright side, everyone had divided up the jobs and taken the extra easily and with no fight. It was a relief to me, as I had only read in my books, that people were selfish creatures by nature and did not take on extra responsibilities lightly. I had said as much to Eira and her eyes lit up with excitement, confusing me.

"You read too!" She all but yelled, her emotions shifting from sorrow to excitement.

"I do. My parents could barely find enough books to keep up when I was growing up." I had always read through them so quickly, never wanting to put them down or miss what may happen next.

She squeals, a high pitched, happy sound (which matches the joy she is practically throwing at me through her emotions now), "oh my gods! What type of book is your favorite?"

I feel the blush grow on my cheeks and wonder if I should lie. What if she is a history reader, or worse, she only reads of the religions and I shock her? I did not want her to think me impure. "Romance." I say quietly, hoping that she will not judge me.

A large smile overtakes her face, showing off her

pretty white teeth and making her eyes sparkle. She grabs my hand, sending a shock through me that she would touch me so casually. "Me too! I love romance! I have some books here that I have already read if you would like to borrow them. You will be spending lots of time in these tents or the woods, so you'll need something to pass the time!" I could sense that she was excited to share this with me and I could feel the excitement growing in me as well.

My smile grew to the point that my cheeks hurt a bit as I thought of being able to read again. I squeezed her hands softly as I replied, "I would absolutely love that! Thank you so much!"

She released my hands, popping her left hand on her hip. "Quick question though, when you read your romance books, did they ever have any spice to them?" I can see a gleam in her eye and sense some mischief swirling in her emotions. I do not know what she means by "spice". How can a book be spicy?

"No..?" I say, dragging out the word as a question. "I'm not sure what you mean by that."

She smiles again; the mischief growing in the air and I tilt my head a bit in confusion. "I'll start you off with a light one, then. We can work our way up! I'll explain everything as you read, cause I'm sure you'll have plenty of questions."

I think she may be a bit batty, but I think I like her that way. "Alright, I'll come to you with anything I do not understand and we can go from there." I had decided not to question it further. If she enjoys these romances, I am sure I will as well.

Once we had finished discussing books, Eira had told me we needed to go to the bathing tent. I had asked why and she had told me it was a surprise. I have always been apprehensive of surprises, never quite knowing how to react or why so many things needed to be such. This surprise is no different. As we step inside the tent, I notice a generously sized bucket filled with plump elderberries, accompanied by a collection of towels laying beside the tub.

"Are we cleaning berries?" I ask, not sure why this

would be a surprise.

"No, silly! We're going to dye your hair so it doesn't draw so much attention while Ryat and the others are gone. Isn't it genius! I sent Azrael out to get these right after they left so we could do it while I'm still able to touch you." She got a goofy smile on her face and I know she is really excited about this, but I am not. I love my hair.

"You want me to dye my hair with berries? How long does that last? I love my hair. I don't want to mess it up and never have the same color or something. What if it dyes too much and never comes out? I don't think-" She cuts me off.

"I've done this dozens of times to my hair, Emory. It only lasts a couple of weeks and comes out completely. Your hair will be totally fine and I think you'll look beautiful with pink hair!"

I am still apprehensive. I've never seen myself with anything but silver hair. I know it would be safer this way, for me and everyone else, but it seems like a lot to ask. My hair is one of the few things me and Arden have left of our father and I am terrified of no longer having that piece of him to see each day. I look Eira in the eyes and sense no ill will. She is only trying to help me. I straighten my shoulders and release a deep breath. I know I need to do this.

"Okay," I say softly. "How would you like to do this?"

Eira walks the couple steps over to the basket of berries and lifts them by the handle, walking over to the tub. Setting them down next to it, she places a folded towel on the ground in front of the tub and an unfolded one along the edge. "Just sit back against the tub with your hair in it, and I will take care of the rest."

I walk over to sit on the fluffy towel, feeling its warmth against my skin. I pull my hair up, feeling the weight of it in my hands, and drop it into the porcelain tub. As I lean back against the smooth side, I can sense the plushness of the towel against my back. With delicate movements, she brushes her fingers through my hair, sending tingles down my scalp. The air is filled with the sweet, intoxicating scent of the bright berries.

With each stroke, I feel the coolness of the berries being worked into my hair, starting from the ends and gradually making their way to my roots.

My anxiety grows and I worry I will not look nice with pink hair. What if it makes my eyes look scary instead of just startling? She works in silence as I debate this. No sound except for the occasional muttering of how she wished she had such long hair. This makes me smile, and I'm glad I have not entertained my thoughts of chopping it short. My mother had always told me of her mother and how she had hair to her ankles. I had decided at a young age that I would do the same, in honor of the woman I had never met, but was grateful to for the love she had shown my mother.

After what feels like hours, Eira slides the bucket away from the tub with her foot and speaks softly, "I'm going to rinse you now. Don't be shocked by the pressure of my water."

Though I had been prepared and taken her warning seriously, I had never met a Water Elemental with the type of gift she had. She could conjure water like any other, but her water was powerful and seemed to have no limits. The pressure she had warned me about was that of a waterfall on the side of a cliff, the pressure stunning and overwhelming. It roared in my ears, drowning out all other sounds. She tilted my head back farther with the hand she was not using for water and sprayed my scalp, the cold droplets trickling down my forehead. It felt like tiny icy needles pricking my skin, sending a shiver down my spine. I kinda felt like I was being waterboarded, my breath catching in my throat as I struggled to stay calm. The intense scent of moisture filled the air and I tried to focus on that instead. After a few moments, she went back to the tips of my hair and then I felt the water stop, the sudden absence leaving me feeling damp.

"You're all done and properly pink, my dear." I can hear the smile in her voice and a small part of me iss excited to see the pink hair. Arden had described pink hair to me a dozen times, and it had always sounded so beautiful. Pink hair had always been Ardens favorite, more than the purples or blues he sometimes detailed for me too.

She takes the towel from behind me and dries my hair some before motioning with her hand that I can get up. Standing up, I reach back to pull my damp hair in front of me, and am bewildered by the pink and ruby hues throughout it. It's as if it is glowing with vibrance and I can not help the smile on my face, nor the excited squeal that leaves my mouth.

Hellion approaches us the moment we walk out of the tent, a big smile on his face. He laughs, "well, that makes my job a lot easier. I was getting ready to cloak you up, but now I don't even have to do that."

Cloak me up?

"What?" I ask.

Hellion laughs again, "I need to go to market and since Ryat left me as your guard dog, that means you need to go to market. It'll be much safer now that we don't have to hide all of your hair."

"Market? Like a village market where they have the shopping and vendors?" I ask, excitement pouring off of me in waves. I have never been and I can't believe I am finally going to get the chance. This is amazing! How can a day with such tragedy have so many great things in it?

Eira giggles from beside me. "Yes, they do typically have all of those things at a market. Though we mostly need medications and weapons for the hunting party."

That makes sense, but still! I will get to see it all!

"When do we leave?" I all but yell at hellion, smiling ear to ear and practically shaking with excitement.

"We're leaving right now. Grab your bag. Make sure you have room to carry the medicine, since I'll have the weapons." With that, Hellion starts towards the tents on the other side of the fire and I run to mine for my bags.

CHAPTER ELEVEN

Hellion leads us through the woods and had said it would only be about two hours before we got to the nearest market. He walks in silence and I trail behind him, counting the vegetables and fruits as I normally do. We haven't been walking long before I hear a rustling in the bush next to me and slow my steps, hand reaching for the blade on my hip. Hellion must have heard it as well, because he is now beside me, motioning with his finger against his lips for me to be silent.

As if my own fear isn't already forcing me to do so.

The sound does not sound as though it is coming from a large creature, but that does not mean that it would not be a small and deadly one. These lands have many small creatures who have the strength of beasts three times their size or poison that works faster than you could ever hope to find a healer. I still remember the first time me and my brother had encountered a Tencan in the woods. They are like snakes, but can grow to be over twenty feet long and some have poisonous venom as well. The one we encountered was just a baby, only a few feet long. It had been a bright green color, its scales blending in perfectly with the grass that it had been hiding in. I had stepped on its tail and it had quickly bitten my ankle, right through my boot and the bone. Arden had chopped off its head, later using part of its small skeleton to make a blade that I still keep in that same boot, before carrying me to the wishing tree. We had barely made it in time and the memory of that near death experience will never leave me, not as long as I live.

But thankfully nothing dangerous jumps at us from the brush. In fact, it is quite the opposite!

"I's a Yip!" I squeal and I run forward to pet the

beautiful creature. Yips are a hybrid of foxes and dogs that are sent here from the mainlands, since they are not fans of mixed breeds. They are known to make a yipping sound when they bark, which is how they inherited their name in our lands. I hear Hellions laugh from behind me as I bend over to lift the pale blue Yip up into my arms. The small creature nestles into my chest, emitting a gentle purring sound that vibrates against my skin as I stand. They are known to be very picky animals, only allowing certain gifted to be near them and typically bonding with them for life.

But, when the gods send you a Yip, you do not turn it away.

Overwhelmed with joy, I turn to Hellios, unable to contain my excitement. "Look how precious it is! I think it has picked me Hellios!"

Looking down at the fluffy creature, I hear Hellios from behind me. "I have never seen a Yip in person, only heard stories of them finding their kindred spirits in this way. You have received a blessing from the gods today, girl, and we shall not waste the luck." Laughing, he shakes his head as he turns back to his trail, "bring your Yip and let's carry your luck into our journey."

I hold my Yip in my arms as we continue to walk, petting its soft velvety blue fur and playing with its long pointy ears. It has a long black snout and short black legs, but its tail is a deep blue color. From its size, barely bigger than my palm, I assume that this is a young Yip. I had heard they were around fifteen to twenty pounds full grown and this one was definitely closer to five. My father had told me as much as he could of Yips and the other creatures like them when he learned of them on his travels, and those had been my favorite stories of them all.

Discovering the Yip shifted Hellios' mood a bit. I can now sense that instead of just the anger, determination and guilt he had been feeling, there was also a swirl of awe and amusement now. Speaking up, I ask, "what do you think I should name it?"

Hellios stops and turns back to look at the Yip. I can sense his indifference and care in the air, though none of it showed on his face. I appreciate that he cares enough to make me think he is truly thinking about the decision, that he wants me to believe he is going to be a part of naming the Yip with me. He looks up at me, his face showing contemplation as the indifference still hangs in the air. "What is its gender?" He asks.

I had not even thought to check yet. Lifting the short little leg, I take a quick peek and see that I am holding a female Yip. Smiling, I settle her back against my chest and look up, "she's a girl."

He smiles, "you should give her a strong name. She will need it to keep up in these woods. Especially if those legs stay that short." With one last chuckle, he turns back around and continues walking toward the market. I smile to myself as I follow behind, holding Kalleli close.

CHAPTER TWELVE

Kalleli remains peacefully asleep, cradled in my arms throughout our hike, her soft breaths blending with the rustling of leaves and chirping of birds. She barely stirs from her spot nestled in between my breasts as I reach to adjust her so she is on top of them instead. I hate to risk bothering her but she was exposing more cleavage from my corset top than I would like a bunch of strangers to see exposed. The scent of various spices and fresh produce fills the air, mingling with the faint fragrance of flowers nearby as we walk up to the market of the Southern Woods.

Hellios stops at the entry of the bustling market, a bit

off to the side of a large open arch between two of the wooden cabins. The sights and sounds overwhelm my senses as I take in the scene. The market is alive with vibrant colors, vendors shouting their hands, and the chatter of gifted having conversations. The air is thick with the smell of spices, freshly baked bread, and a hint of smoky fire. From here, the market looks like its a large circular shape. The wooden cabins are so close together that the logs from each touch the one on either side, making it so you cannot see in from anywhere but the arch.

As Hellios looks at me and Kalleli, he speaks quietly, his voice barely audible amidst the noise of the market. "I will find you once I've gotten everything we need at camp. Stay away from the arch once we go in. It's the only entrance or exit, and I don't want there to be a possibility of you getting grabbed." Handing me a small coin purse, he speaks again, his words barely reaching my ears over the noise. "Use this to buy anything you please. It's not much, but it should get you what you'll need for your new pet and a quick bite to eat."

I look at the coin purse in my hand in confusion, feeling the weight of the coins against my palm. The bustling market surrounds me, overwhelming my senses. I decide not to ask what I have done to deserve the coins and reply instead. "I named her Kalleli, and thank you. We will stay away from the arch and be ready to leave once you are."

Hellion turns with a nod, walking under the arch. I follow along behind him, entering through the arch and slowing my steps as I look around the market. The sights, sounds, and smells engulf me as I take in the vibrant scene. I was right about the shape. Some of the cabins are open-faced, allowing glimpses of the things being sold inside. They are all built directly against one another in the shape of a large circle, enclosing the market completely. In the middle of the market, a crackling fire pit is lit and flickers, surrounded by a few smaller cabins with only two sides, allowing easy access from the fire and walkway. I take a right, trying to go with the flow of people walking from cabin to cabin. As I pass, I can't help but admire the names carved into the logs above the doors, each one revealing the type of shop within.

There are SO many shops!

There are shops for clothing, bath supplies, cooking, weaponry, and all kinds of other things! As I walk through the bustling marketplace, my senses come alive with all of the sights, sounds, emotions and smells. The colorful array of shops catches my eye, each one beckoning me in with its own unique label.

I am immediately drawn to a shop labeled "bedding" and step through the creaking front door. From the moment I step in, I am absolutely floored by the sheer amount of things they have in the small cabin. From the front, along all the sides and even the back wall, they have different shades and sizes of furs. I make my way deeper into the cabin, my fingertips itching to explore the softness of the furs and the plushness of the pillows. SO MANY pillows line the shelves, seeming to beg me to sink my hands into their fluff. My gaze goes to the cots, their sizing leaving me in awe. Some seem too large to even be transported!

Though I have no immediate need for bedding, I relish in a moment of petting the soft furs before stepping back out through the front door.

The next shop I enter is wearables, which I had correctly assumed would be weapon holsters, jewelry and things like that. This is where I make my first purchase from the coin purse. I found a small knife holster, adjustable for men and women, and buy it for Kalleli. I plan to use it as a collar, thinking that Hellion should be able to help me meld a name bracket to go where the knife would slide in. It will be adjustable, so I can make it larger as she grows and use it for as long as I need. I walk up to the counter they have set up for payment and smile at the lady behind it. She smiles back and tells me the price, holding out her hand for the coins. Handing them over, she tells me to have a nice day, and that's it. For some reason, I had thought making a purchase would have more steps, but this had been much easier than expected. With a quick wave goodbye, I walk back out of the shop and step onto the walkway.

A few cabins down, I see that there is a cabin labeled "Diners Inn" and I walk towards it. I haven't been able to eat at a diner before, and I wonder briefly if Kalleli will be allowed in with me as I approach. Before I can open the door, there is a hand on my arm and I am turning around to see who has stopped me.

A large male with bright off green hair, a dark black beard and green eyes is standing in front of me and I shake his hand off of my arm as I ask, "hello, is there something I can help you with?"

He's got a light smile on his face and I sense no negative emotions coming from him, which lessens some of the nerves prickling through me. "Sorry sweetheart, I don't think you want to go in there."

Now it's confusion prickling through me. Why wouldn't I want to go into a diner? I start to open my mouth and ask, but before I can he speaks again. "I see that you're confused. That is not a diner, sweetheart, it's just a poorly named brothel, and I can practically smell your innocence from here. You do not want to go in there."

I don't know what a brothel is, but more than anything I don't like that this strange male is telling me what I should and should not do. I straighten my shoulders, tightening my jaw. "I know exactly what I am doing. Now if you will excuse me, I was just going in." Most of that is a lie, and now I'm nervous about what's inside, but I refuse to stand down.

The green-haired male shoots me a cocky grin and I can sense his intrigue in the air. He laughs, "alright sweetheart, let's go on in then." Before I can say anything else, he has grabbed both my arm and the door, pulling me inside with him.

Oh. My. Gods.

As my heart pounds, I can feel the blood surging through my veins, causing my face to flush and my head to throb. My wide eyes take in the scene before me, the room bursting with an array of sights and sounds.The air is heavy with the mingling scents of sweat and arousal permeating the space. There are over two dozen bodies pressed together in different ways throughout the room. Some males have women pressed against the walls, against tables, and one couple is even sprawled out on the floor. There are a few cots in the room, one of them holding a female and TWO males. They are all making different noises. Groans, screams, moans and whines I believe to be from pleasure resonating through the air. Overwhelmed by the sensory overload, I can almost taste the intoxicating mixture of bliss, desire, elation, and excitement that radiates from these gifted, and the feeling is unsettling.

I hear a laugh from beside me, jumping as I remember I had not entered alone. Glancing in his direction, I notice him still grinning at me. "See sweetheart, I told you that you didn't want to come in here." I could tell from half a mile away you'd never seen or experienced anything like this before."

I shake my head, trying to clear the thoughts racing through it, "you're wrong, it's just that the one back in my village was different." I lie. I don't know why I'm still lying, when I should probably run out the door right now. Pulling Kalleli closer to my chest, I look him in the eye and watch as his grin grows.

"Well, if I was wrong, why don't you and I go grab a cot? I have a feeling you'll be distracting for the others, so the back one should do us fine." He starts to pull me farther into my room, surely attempting to call my bluff, and I dig my heels into the ground, feeling the sturdiness of the hardwood floor beneath me.

"No, no. You're right. I'm sorry. I'm ready to go. Can we go now?" I all but beg. As I apologize, I can feel my heart pounding in my chest. My words carry genuine remorse. I'm ready to leave, the emotions in the air making me feel crazy. I can't help but tug against his firm grip, a sense of urgency pulsating through my body, my gaze bouncing around the room in fear. He nods, his grin falling off of his face as he pulls me to the front door with him, our steps echoing in my ears. With a final step outside, I notice a slight breeze caressing my skin, carrying with it the scent of freshly cut wood.

I settle against the side of the cabin, tilting my head down to kiss Kallelis' fur as she nuzzles between my breasts again. I do not have the energy to move her as I try to catch my breath and calm my racing heart. As the male settles next to me against the cabin, I lift my head to look over at him.

"They were just out in the open, surrounded by others," I mumble. I don't know what I expect him to say, or if I expect him to say anything at all.

But he does.

"Brothels are a place for people to fuck freely, with no judgement. Most nations allow males the freedom to engage in such activities without judgment, while females are punished for doing the same. Brothels such as these are based on the secrecy of other patrons, making it easier for ladies to do as they please without the fear of repercussions." I can sense that he has a respect for this, but that there is also some disgust swirling within him at the thought. I assume he is not a patron.

"All I wanted was a meal in an actual diner. I've never had one before. I cannot believe I was going to walk in there by myself," I say softly, anxiety rising at the ideas that may have bloomed in the male's minds.

"I will take you to a proper diner, one where they allow pets. It's the least I can do for not being able to convince you to stay outside." I sense guilt now, and feel horrible for having put it there with my stubbornness.

I smile lightly as I say, "no, I will take you to the diner. Once you show me where it is, of course."

Standing up from where he was leaned back against the cabin, he smiles at me and nods. He tilts his head to the right, so I follow. The sound of our footsteps echoes on the worn path as we make our way down the walkway. Finally, we arrive at a cabin labeled "food," and my anticipation fills the air as I feel my stomach flutter with excitement..

The male, whose name I still do not know, opens the door and holds it open for me to enter. The inside is simple, with three rows of four tables, four chairs at each. I smell a subtle hint of cleanliness, mingled with the faint aroma of freshly brewed tea as he walks to the table farthest from the door and takes a seat against the wall, facing the door. That is where Arden would have sat as well, never wanting his back to an entryway or possible enemies. I miss him already and he has only been gone a few hours. But, with the reminder that he is gone comes the reminder that so is Ryat. I hope that Hellion is done soon, because this male touches me a lot and I don't know when the traveling group will decide to make a camp for rest.

How quickly I've gotten used to the feeling of being touched after so long with no contact. I will be sad to see my gifts return, and I really hope it happens when I have already gotten back to camp. My mind continues with thoughts like these as we sit and soon get interrupted by the presence of a petite woman. She approaches our table, her light brown hair cascading around her face, and her golden eyes are bright and kind. A gentle smile graces her lips as she places a piece of paper on the table in front of me..

"What can I get the two of you to drink?" She asks, a thick accent pouring from her lips that makes me wonder where she's originally from.

"I'll take a tea, cold." He sounds confident in this decision, so I look at her with a smile and tell her, "I'll take the same."

She nods and walks toward the far side of the cabin, and into a side room that I assume to be their kitchen. I look down at the paper she put in front of me and see that there are five different food options on it, the one on the bottom of the page being a dessert. Looking between the options, I decided I will get a sheep's pie. It's a recipe my father had gotten me once, though I had not had the chance to try it yet, and the thought of tasting it now is incredibly exciting.

Looking up, I see the male is still looking at the items on his menu. "What is your name? I have been calling you Green Haired Male in my head and though it suits you, I don't think it's right," I joke.

He looks up at me with a quick laugh. "My name is Ryar, and most consider my hair to be Teal, not quite green." I pause, looking at him a bit closer. As I look at him, my curiosity surges and I can't help but tilt my head.

"The only male I've ever heard of being named that is the God of Luck," I say quietly. I do not drop eye contact as his seem to sparkle.

Smiling a bit wider, he whispers, "that makes sense considering I am the only male to be named that, Emory."

Shock overwhelms me as my eyes widen, and I feel a rush of anxiety coursing through my veins. It is not often that gifted are visited by the gods and if they are; it is typically a message delivered over the course of a few moments. But I have been with this god for much longer and I am not sure what this could mean. Ryar is known to be a kind god, though not one to frequent our lands or socialize often. With Kalleri nestled in my arms, I feel the softness of her fur beneath my fingertips, the gentle rhythm of her breathing against my skin. The sound of her purring, a soft and sweet sound, provides a soothing contrast to the whirlwind of emotions within me. I look down at her and am thankful once again for the gift. "I named her Kalleli. I am very thankful that you sent her to me."

Ryar is looking at his menu again as he responds, "I know you will care for her in the way she deserves, and she you. But she is not why I have come to see you today and you know it, Emory."

He's right, I had guessed he wouldn't visit over the gifting of a pet. Letting out a sigh, I ask, "Do you have a message for me regarding the war?""

"That's right, sweetheart. Your group will return in a few days, another god will provide them with more information than I have. But, the information I have for you could change the tides if you can follow the right path." He's determined now, a bit anxious, but mostly proud. I wonder where all the emotions come from, but I don't have the courage to ask.

"What path am I supposed to follow?" I nervously lower my gaze to the table, unable to meet his determined eyes that seem to bore into my soul.

"Your group will return with information that

speaks of two nations. You need to go to Eldevand and it is okay if you tell the other it was me who told you so. The journey will be long and hard, but you must push forward. Limit your wishes and stick with your gods. They will protect you." My gods? Does he mean not to lose my faith in them? They have blessed me all of my life, protected me in times I had thought impossible. I will stick with my faith until I am no longer on this plane of existence.

"Can you tell me anything else? Can you explain what you mean by stick with my gods? My faith has never wavered." I look up again, but all he does is smile before vanishing into thin air, leaving the chair in front of me empty.

When the server returns with only my drink and doesn't ask where the male has gone, I know that nobody else would remember seeing him. I order my sheep's pie, feeding small bites to Kalleli as I eat and then I pay. The Pie was perfectly flaky (though I would adjust the seasoning when I made it myself) and the tea was sweet and delicious, just as you would expect as a favorite of the gods. But even as my thoughts are fleeting at best, I know it is time to find Hellion. We need to get back to the camp so I can think in the solitude of my own tent.

The restaurant has gotten loud, and I never thought I would crave silence again as I am now.

CHAPTER

THIRTEEN

I find Hellion on the other side of the market, in a cabin labeled "healers". He turns his head as I enter and nods at me before turning back to the man he is currently speaking with. The man looks at me as I approach, but only briefly before refocusing on his conversation with Hellion.

"You are asking for too much friend, I have already given more than the fair share for your camp." The man has a nervous energy surrounding him and you can see a glint in his dark eyes. He has a string of admiration and care for Hellion, so I know he is telling the truth when he says this. The dark skin around his eyes crinkle as he smiles, and he shakes his head. "There is no more I can give, but if you find your way back here, I will provide as you wish."

Hellion sighs softly, "thank you for what you have already given. You have always been good to me, Elron. When I find my father, you will be the first to know." With that, Hellion gives him a soft hug (the way I am used to seeing hugs be done) and turns to me. "Are you ready to return to camp?"

I nod, trying to force a real looking smile onto my face. It must be close enough because Hellion just removes my bag from my shoulders, careful not to disturb Kalleli, and fills it with the medications. He slides it back on me as I adjust her in my arms to put them through the straps, and then he walks toward the door. We do not speak as we pass the shops, exit through the arch or start our hike.

I find that this is one of the few times I am grateful that I am not expected to hold conversations.

We pass a few Bundra on the hike home and each time Hellion stops to shoot them with the new bow. By the time we arrive back at camp, he has five of the two headed rabbits stringed up on his hip. I know that this means I will be preparing a lot of rabbit dishes in the next few days, but this is still not enough to pull me out of my thoughts. I think of the brothel, what I saw there. What I heard there. I think about Ryar and his message. I also think of what Hellios had said in the shop about finding his father. I had not known who he was searching for, and I hope to one day help him succeed.

If I live long enough to do so.

We enter back into the camp, and I see everyone is sitting around the fire. As we approach, Vulcan is playing a soft melody on a tongue drum, the beat consistent and steady as if he has played it a million times before. The vibrations of the music pulse through me, making me think of simpler times and dancing in the rain under my autumn trees. The melody does not stop when he notices our arrival, his photographic memory surely making it simple for him to know where each indent is on the drum. Looking up at us, he smiles, though he does not speak, just nods his head low.

"How was the market?" I hear Eira ask. We have gotten close enough now that before I can reply, I hear a surprised gasp from her and then another one of her excited squeals. "Oh, my gods! You've been gifted a Yip! You must tell us everything of your journey!"

I laugh as Kalleli lifts her little head to look around; the noise having woken her. Smiling, I take a seat on the log next to Eiras' stump and look at the fire. "This is Kalleli. She was gifted to me just as we started our hike. She was a sign of luck."

Hellios takes a seat next to me on the hog, his weight causing it to shift slightly. "Our journey was quite lucky indeed. I was able to negotiate for all the weapons and medications well under the amount we had allotted, and I even killed five Bundra on the hike home." I can hear the smile in his voice and feel one start to grow on my face as well.

I set Kalleli down on the ground in front of me,

watching as she sniffs around everyone's feet before settling back down on the ground beside me. My heart warms as I see her choose to be near me, knowing that in the time of me feeling alone I was gifted something to make it so I never had to be alone again. I look up from Kalleli, looking over at Hellion. He is already looking at me and I can tell that he knows I have something to say about my time at the market. The curiosity is flowing from him as much as the others.

"I met a male while I was in the market," I say with a sigh. I feel everyone's eyes on me and the curiosity is growing into fear. "I was getting ready to go into what I believed to be a diner and he stopped me. He told me I should not enter, and I was too stubborn to listen, not knowing what he was talking about because of my limited experience in the real world. Thankfully, he went in with me and I now know what a brothel is." I hear a mix of gasps and laughs from around the fire as my cheeks heat again, thinking of the brothel. "He brought me out and explained what it was before taking me to an actual diner for food. I had not known his name up to this point and I was curious, so I asked him and he told me he was called Ryar."

Vulcan stands, tongue drum forgotten on the ground in front of him, and speaks for the first time since my arrival. "You have been visited by the God of Luck himself." He says this in a deep, gravely voice that is clearly hard to use. Though I am shocked to hear him speak, and it seems everyone else is as well, I am most surprised by his knowledge of the Gods and their true names. Most gifted do not care to learn them all. Ryar is one of the lesser known gods, out of the total nineteen gods and goddesses of old.

"Yes," I say. "And he has allowed me to speak of the warning he has given me."

Eira reaches over, grabbing my hand in her own and giving me a kind smile. "We are here for you and you can tell us anything."

Giving her hand a light squeeze, I look over at the rest of the party. Making brief eye contact with each person, I begin. Though, I had decided right away I would not be trying to explain the things I saw inside the brothel itself.

"Ryar tells me that the party in search of information will be back in only a few days, as another god will give them most of their answers along the journey. He said that this god will know more than he did, but that the information will not be pertaining to me. The information they will be given will be of two lands, and Ryar says we are to go to Eldevand. He states the journey will be a hard one but that we must not give up. Before he disappeared, he told me to be careful with my wishes to the gods, but to trust in them as they will protect me. And then he was gone." I feel the anxiety, shock, and uncertainty in the air. But, I can also feel the determination growing as well and that gives me hope.

I feel Azrael's gaze on me and look over to meet his eyes., "Did he say if the party would return unharmed and whole?" He asks this softly and I can tell that Hazel is heavy on his mind.

"He did not tell me of their conditions, just that they would be returning in a few days. The gods are known to sometimes speak in riddles and give as little information as possible so they do not disrupt the fates." I look over to see that the sun has almost completely set now, and I let go of Eira's hand. "It is probably best if nobody touches me from this point forward. We do not know when Ryat will choose to rest."

I hear the muttering of agreeance from Eira and the others as I look back at the fire. I can tell that everyone here is deep in thought, pondering what will come next and remembering what today has already held. After almost forty days of doing absolutely nothing and being trapped in a cell, I never would have guessed how busy today would become.

I decide after a few minutes it is time for me to return to my tent. Standing up, I tell everyone goodnight and bend over to grab Kalleli. She nestles into my armpit as I walk to the med tent and peek in the check on Fenris. He is still deadly still on the table, his breathing and the pale yellow glow of his wound are my only clues that he is still alive. Being a Loric with the gift to heal is a beautiful blessing that is doing him wonders right now.

Any normal male would have died long and from the wounds inflicted upon his body. But he still laid here. His body softly glowing as the wound stitches itself back together and his blood somehow replenishes.

I close the tent flap behind me, the soft rustle of the fabric filling the air, and walk over to my tent next door. As I step inside, the scent of fresh earth and pine greets me. Setting my bags down on the floor and removing my boots, I feel the coolness of the ground beneath my feet. I carefully place Kalleli on the cot, the softness of the fabric against my fingertips. With my hands now empty, I walk back to the front of the tent and secure the flap closed, the sound of the velcro echoing in the stillness of the night. Getting undressed, I feel the crispness of the air against my skin as I climb into my cot. I slide under the furs, and pull Kalleli into my arms, feeling her soft fur against my cheek.

As I close my eyes I hear the sounds of nature outside, the distant hoot of an owl and the gentle rustling of leaves. Hoping for some cuddles and to borrow Kallelis warmth, I drift into a peaceful sleep.

CHAPTER

FOURTEEN

I wake up to the sound of rain hitting my tent. Soft droplets, like the sky is just preparing us for the day ahead. Kalleli is snuggled up in my arms and purring softly in her sleep and I smile to myself at the cuteness. For the first few moments of being awake, I forget about yesterday's events, forget even about the cell and the war. It is nice to forget for a moment. Things almost feel normal, the buzzing back beneath my skin and my gift in full force within me.

Deciding not to put off the start of my day, I stretch my arms above my head, feeling my fingertips graze the tent behind me. I crawl over Kalleli as softly and quietly as I can, trying not to disturb her, and stand next to my cot. Wiggling my toes and stretching my neck to both sides, I decide to look in the wardrobe for an outfit. Walking over, I open it up and look through the frilly dresses for one a bit more on the simple side. I decide on a black dress with silver bows. The first bow sits right between my breasts and the other lands right above my ass.

Of course they do.

I decide to ignore it, as it is the least frilly one I see in the wardrobe (even with its scandalously placed bows). Walking back to the front of the tent, I look over to see that Kalleli is now awake and watching me, her little head resting on her two front paws. I lean over to give her a kiss on the head. "Come on Kalleli, it's time to check on Fenris."

Walking out of the tent, Kalleli follows as I walk next door to the med tent and open the flap. I walk in and secure the flap behind us, wiping the rain droplets off my face, and turn to check on Fenris. When I look over, expecting to see the same sight as last night, I do not. Fenris is sitting up in his cot, reading a book. I gasp, "oh my gods, you're awake! How are you feeling?"

Fenris looks up briefly before looking back down at his book. "I feel as if I was blown up and torn open with knives and swords. But that is to be expected, I suppose." He looks up at me again with a smile. "Eira left this book for you. I saw it sitting on the shelf with a note saying your name and I stole it. I've always asked to borrow one, and she has never allowed me, so I had to take the chance while I had one."

I laugh, "if you are willing to steal them, her books must be lovely."

A grin is on his face now, though mixed with a wince of pain as well. "You have no idea how fascinating the contents of this book really are. Once I have finished it, I will return it for your use."

I look at him and smile, glad that he is awake. "I am very glad you're awake. I have been around little magic and the others were unsure how long you would be unconscious for the healing to take place."

Eira had guessed that he would wake up tonight and Azrael had guessed next week. The others all guessed some number in between, not knowing or having anything to go off of. But, after my visit with the God of Luck, I suppose his waking would make sense. The gods spend little time around the gifted because we pull the energy from them. It does not drain them or hurt them in any way, but it can be an unfair advantage for a favored. I am probably still seeping a bit of luck.

"How healed are you? Do you know how long until it is fully?" I wasn't sure how much he knew of the speed or full power of his gift.

"I am around halfway healed, and in around four days I will be back at full health. Though it will take me a few more to restore my energy and be able to heal others again." He looks back down at his book again, which I take as a signal that he wants to read and not conversate. I understand that.

Smiling, I walk toward the tent opening. "I will come

back in a bit to check on you. In the meantime, I will be making breakfast. Would you like some?"

He just nods, fully concentrated on the lives playing out within his pages.

I turn and exit the tent, seeing that the rain has now stopped. Kalleli and I walk to the area used for cooking and I began to set up. It's a simple area, two long tables with a fire pit and a wood-burning stove. They have knives lined up along one table and bowls lined up along the other. I start the fire for the stove and pull a few handfuls of blueberries, strawberries and sweetberries from the bucket sitting next to the table. I get to work crushing them into a paste, making sure to mix them together thoroughly. Once I have completed that, I begin working on a pastry crust, mixing the dough with my hands and stretching it out to the large size I need for this many people. I cut the dough into twelve squares, putting the fruit paste in the middle and folding the dough over the top to fully cover it. I squeeze the edges to create a seal and put some oil on the tops, along with a sprinkling of black sugars I found on the shelves. Putting them on the metal sheet clearly welded together by Hellion, I slide them in the wood-burning stove and wait until they are golden brown to pull them out.

I put two pastries into each of the seven bowls and carry them all over to the gathering table, setting them down in the places I remember everyone sitting at the last meeting. I take Fenris his, which he takes with a quick thank you before returning to his book and then I call out to the rest of the party that it's time for breakfast.

I hear a groan behind me and turn in my seat to see Nox walking to the table. He looks at the table with confusion, "we do not typically get served breakfast."

"Breakfast is the most important meal of the day, so I will be serving it. Good morning." I can see that I woke him up and I do feel bad. I am used to waking up with the sun, but I suppose this party may be one that sleeps in.

"Good morning," he says. He sits down in his seat,

picks up his pastry, and takes a bite. With a loud groan, he drops his head to the table and lays it down, keeping his hand with the pastry in it next to his mouth. "Alright, this is worth you waking me up at the ass crack of dawn."

I laugh. It is not the ass crack of dawn. I have made Arden get up much earlier than this. He continues to eat his pastry, eyes closed and head laying on the table, as the others (also half asleep) stumble out of their tents.

Hellios is the only person who sits at the table and doesn't look as if he wants to kill me for waking him. He gives me a smile, looking mostly awake, "good morning, Emory. I guess we should have told you we enjoy sleeping around here."

I laugh as Nox speaks again from his slouched position on the table. "Brother, it's worth it. Eat the pastry and shut up. If you or anyone else ruins this for me, I will come for your heads."

There's that saying again!

"What does that mean," I ask, "that you'll come for

their heads?"

Hellios laughs as he looks back over at me, "it's just a saying. He isn't actually going to hurt anyone. It is just him saying that this is something that matters to him and he will fight for it."

I lower my voice a bit. "Can I ask you something?"

He nods, leaning in. I lean in a bit too. "Before Ryat left, I asked him if it was normal for a male to be touching a woman as much as he touched me and mentioned that I hadn't seen Fenor holding me or anyone else. He said it wasn't, but if he heard Fenor had been touching me while he was away, he would come for his head. Why would that matter to him? I don't understand."

I can tell Hellios is trying to hold back a smile or laugh, and that only confuses me more. He clears his throat, seeming to get himself under control. His emotions are a mix of amusement, bewilderment and humor as he responds. "My brother has accepted you as his, and males are known to be quite territorial with their mates."

Mates? I do not think that he is understanding the situation properly because there is no way that we are mates.

I have been reading and hearing about mates all my life. They are two souls fated to be together, and there is little you can do to change their destiny. The telltale sign of a mate is that when they have accepted the bond, they will have a dark black marking appear on their arm. It signifies the permanence of this decision and can never be undone.

I shift in my chair, confusion evident in my voice as I speak. "We are not mates. He doesn't have the mark."

"Are you positive about that? Have you seen him without his shirt, because I have." Hellios says nothing more after this, leaving me to ponder this on my own.

I sit at the edge of my chair, absently pushing my pastry around in its bowl. It's still warm, but I've lost my appetite. My mind keeps circling back to what Hellion said. That me and Ryat were mates.

Mates.

It doesn't feel real. Not yet. The idea that Ryat and I are bound by fate, that he bears a mate mark tying us together, is almost too much to process. I glance down at my bowl, but all I see is the swirl of thoughts racing through my mind, tangled like the lines of fate that supposedly connect us.

Could it really be true? That Ryat is my mate?

I think about him—his steady presence, the way he looks at me with those steady eyes, the way his touch warms and lingers on my skin. I have felt a pull to be close to him since we met. But a mate bond? That's something else entirely. That's not just a pull—it's a force. It's destiny.

I'm not sure I even know what it means to have a mate, to be bound to someone like that. It's not just a choice, it's a fate written into our very being. Ryat would be mine, and I would be his. Forever.

I push my pastry around the bowl again, my

thoughts heavy. What would it be like to have a mate? To share every part of my life, every fear, every joy, with one person? To have someone who knows me, truly knows me, at a soul-deep level? The idea is both comforting and terrifying.

I think about what I've heard of mates—the stories passed down about how they are inseparable, how the bond between them is so strong it can't be broken, even in death. It's supposed to be beautiful, this connection, but also intense.

Overwhelming.

A bond that could either strengthen me or completely unravel me.

I've spent so long alone, never letting anyone get too close. How can I even open up enough to accept something like this?

And Ryat... How does he feel about all of this? If he has the mark then he already knows, deep down, and he's accepted it. Accepted me. I think back to the way he looks at me, the way his hand lingers on mine when we touch, and I wonder if he's always known more than I have. In the stories it is said that some feel the bond snap in place immediately and for some it takes time and acceptance.

I set my bowl down, staring out into the woods. My mind keeps spinning, but one truth keeps pulling me back. If Ryat truly is my mate, if this bond is real, then everything will change. My future, my choices—it will all shift.

I take a deep breath, trying to steady myself. I don't know if I'm ready for this, but I can't deny that something about it feels... right. There's a warmth in the idea of having a mate, of not being alone anymore. Of having someone who will stand beside me, no matter what.

But it's still so much. Too much to process all at once. I look down at my hands, tracing the harsh scars along my palms.

If I'm truly his mate, then what does that mean for us?

For me?

The next few days fly by in a blur. The camp gets better about breakfast, not wanting to miss whatever I will have made for the day, and I find a steady flow between cooking and checking on Fenris. I learn he has a preference for deer, claiming that the meat helps with healing. I do not ask around to see if this information is fully truthful. I just ask the hunting party to find me a deer and they do. We eat that over the next few days and the wound seems to heal quite quickly (though that could just be the gift healing as it normally does).

Kalleli follows me around, eating and sleeping when I do and seems to grow another five pounds almost overnight. She has started to trust Eira, letting her scratch her soft ears or rub her tummy by the fire and things are much more mild than I had grown to expect. My thoughts still drift to the conversations of the last few days during our evening chats around the fire and the times I am alone. The talk of mates with Hellion is most heavy on my mind. I had always dreamed of finding my mate and it would explain the ease I feel in his presence, the comfortability I have at his touch. But then I worry that if I get my hopes up and let myself believe it could be, it will break my heart if it is not the case.

CHAPTER FIFTEEN

I wake suddenly, startled, and jump up to sit. At first I do not know what woke me until I hear the screams.

"MED TENT! NOW!"

I throw my furs off of my body and jump out of bed, starting Kalleli as she jumps up as well. Throwing on the first dress I can grab, a sage green one (with silver lace along the front corset, of course) and hurry out of my tent. I think to myself that I am thankful I had bathed yesterday before going to sleep for the night, and that it had been an early night as well. I run into the one next door, seeing that instead of Fenris on the cot, it is now Ryat.

My blood runs cold as my mind goes blank and everything in me freezes. They say that in a moment of panic your choices are flight or fight, but everyone always forgets about freeze. It feels as if I cannot move, as if I am no longer in control of my limbs, though all I wish to do is to move toward the cot. Closing my eyes, I hold my breath in and release it. My father always told me that fear is normal. It helps you survive, but you cannot let it control you.

"Give yourself five seconds, my love". That's what he would tell me. "Take five seconds, and then let it all go. Get back to work."

I breathe in for two seconds, and then I let it go. Three seconds of exhale, just as I was taught.

Opening my eyes, I walk to the cot and feel my body zone back into the present. Ryat is on the table, but he is awake. His eyes are open and he's looking straight at me. "Princess, you may not want to watch this. They're going to have to cauterize my wound, and it will not be pretty." I see the pain in his eyes and I can feel his worry in the air. Worry for me, not himself.

"I want to stay if that's okay," I say quietly, stepping up to be beside him. He nods and then looks at Fenris, who has a blade in his hand, fire red from where Hellion had just been burning it with his fire. I feel Ryat grab my hand, feel the buzzing in my body still, as Fenris lowers the blade to Ryats hip. He has a gash there that is roughly four inches long and half as deep. Fenris presses the blade's flat edge against his wound. I hear the sizzling of blood and flesh, I smell the burning and somehow Ryats grip does not tighten. When I look over, I see he is just looking at me, that he does not seem to have ever looked away. He is not flinching, or even wincing in pain. I look down again at his hip, and then up to his torso. My gaze traces the hard panes of his abdomen and the scars littering his skin there. Rises to his chest, also dusted in scars of different sizes and textures. I know then, remember then, the stories I had been told of Arrakis and the children taken there. This is why he had not reacted. He was used to the pain. The pain I saw in his eyes earlier had not been for himself, but for me having to see this.

My eyes pause at his arms, large and strong, with no marks but a solid black line around his left bicep. My eyes fly up to his, and I know immediately that he is my mate. I feel the magic tingling my skin as the band traces along my left arm, and a smile traces his lips.

CHAPTER SIXTEEN

"**A**nyone wanna tell me where the Yip came from?" I hear from behind me. Turning to look, I see Hazel standing at the tent entrance with blood covering the middle of her dress.

"Are you injured?" I ask.

She answers before I can make my way to her. "No, the blood is from your mate. I helped him walk the rest of the way home so Arden could carry Vor. They knocked him out, but he is fine. Arden took him to his tent and then posted himself outside until Ryat had been treated." She is still looking at Kalleli, who has now taken a seat in between my legs on the floor.

"This is Kalleli," I say. "She was gifted to me by Ryar, the God of Luck. We have quite a lot to tell your group, as you do us."

Hazel nods, looking up at Ryat and me. "I am glad they got the bleeding to stop. I am going to go take a bath and rest for a few hours before breakfast. I have been told nobody is allowed to miss it and it is at first light, so I will need to go now. Teirney went straight to the baths, but she should be finished by the time I arrive."

I smile, "you will not be sorry to have joined, and I will prepare extra to make it worth your while. Enjoy your bath and tell Teirney I said hello."

Hazel exits the tent, as do Fenris and Hellios, and Ryat speaks from beside me, "we do breakfast now, princess?"

I laugh, looking back at him and smiling at the amusement wafting off of him. "We do, and it has been quite appreciated. Nox said he would come for heads if it was taken from him."

As Ryat tips his head back in laughter, the tent flap opens again and Arden walks in. Before he has taken more than three steps, I have dashed towards him, feeling the rush of anticipation in my chest. I throw myself at him, embracing him tightly, the warmth of his presence enveloping me. The scent of him lingers in the air, a mix of musk and sandalwood. His grip is firm, maybe a tad too forceful, but I do not complain, feeling a slight pressure against my ribs.

"I don't think I'll ever get used to missing you," he says through a laugh.

"Neither will I, little brother, neither will I." His emotions are full of love, pride, and hope. I feel them seep into me, just as his emotions always have, and I know that as long as we are together, it will all be okay.

Arden pulls back, laughing a bit. "I have been told breakfast is at the ass crack of dawn. I'm assuming they do not know the meaning of the term and figured I should ask you what time of day I will be woken." Humor swirls in the air and I laugh.

"No, they truly do not. I have been waking them at sunrise and they act as if the world may be ending." I say with a smile, knowing Arden will understand that for me, sunrise is sleeping in.

"I will get up at dusk and help you prepare then, goodnight Emory. I love you," he says with his silly boyish grin. I repeat the sentiment back and turn back to Ryat, where he is now holding Kalleri and petting her snout.

Of course, she would also trust him immediately.

"You should get some rest before breakfast, and Fenris will need his cot back." I do not know where we go from here or what I am supposed to say. We both know we are mates and we will need to discuss it, but I do not think now is the proper time. He had already accepted the bond, so I know he wants this, me, but I do not know what that means.

Ryat smiles softly, "will you join me?"

Confused, I tilt my head to the side, "join you where?"

"In my tent. I would like for you to stay with me from now on. You are my mate and I wish to stay close to you." He says this, still smiling, with full confidence. There is no waiver, only determination, along with a flutter of excitement and that warm feeling.

I do not overthink the decision. In fact, I do not think at all before I agree with a quick nod of my head. An anxious breath leaves my lips as he grabs my hand and stands from the cot, Kalleli still in his other arm. With one more quick smile, he walks out of the tent, calling out to Fenris, who is sitting by the fire, that it's all his.

I follow Ryat to his tent, our hands intertwined and his steps less hurried than the last time we made the walk. My brain has now decided to think. A lot. What if he wants me to do the things I saw in the brothel? I am not ready for that and I don't even know what some of it was. I feel my face heat as I remember. And I usually sleep in the nude, as I do not have any pajamas. What will I wear to sleep in his cot? Where will I change? Will he wait outside? Should he have to? I am his mate, after all. And he is injured! By the time we are entering his tent, I am a ball of anxiety, a shaken jar of bees and my brain is scrambled by all the questions.

Ryat secures the tent flap, sets Kalleli down and turns me by the hips to face him. Looking up, I see him smiling down at me. "You do not need to be anxious. I have no expectations except for that you sleep in my cot and let me hold you."

I feel my anxiety release from me like a breath of air and nod my head. "What will I sleep in?" I ask.

Ryat guides me back by the hips and moves me to sit on the cot before walking over to his wardrobe and pulling out a large undershirt. Tossing it to me, he says, "you can wear my clothes. They'll be large on you and you should find them comfortable. I am going to go take a quick bath while you change and then we will sleep."

I smile and nod at him, thankful that he had thought of everything I was nervous about. Once he has exited the tent, I secure the flap again and remove the dress I had thrown on. I am thankful it had not gotten dirty, as I had no clothes in his tent and would need to wear it again in the morning. I slide the undershirt on and note that it falls halfway down my thighs, reminding me again how large Ryat really is. I decide to go ahead and crawl into the cot, sliding under his black furs. Kalleri jumps up to curl up on my chest and I lean down to kiss her small forehead.

When Ryat returns, he simply secures the tent flap and slides into the cot. He pulls me into him, settling my head on his chest, and falls asleep while playing with my hair. I lay awake like that, feeling his fingers in my hair and his heartbeat under my ear, for far longer than I should.

CHAPTER

SEVENTEEN

I wake slowly, noticing the warmth that has spread through my body and seems to have seeped into the very core of my being. I contribute this to the arms wrapped around me and the very male body pressed against my back. We must have rolled in our sleep, as we are both now on our sides. Kalleli is nestled in my arms, a soft and sweet purr coming from her in waves. I decide that his idea to sleep together may have been my favorite idea of all.

I relish in the warmth for a moment before attempting to detach myself from Ryats grip. As I shift my body to the side, his arms grow tighter and I feel a low growl leave his lips. I feel the vibration of the growl in his chest and smile to myself. I like that even asleep; he does not want to let me go. We haven't had the chance to get to know each other well, but he is my mate and I like that he wishes to keep me close. However, I need to make breakfast and cannot do that from this bed. I go to pull away again (a bit harder this time) and feel his arms release as a sleepy groan leaves his lips, and he rolls onto his back.

Crawling slowly out of the bed, I turn away and remove the undershirt he gave me. With quick peeks over my shoulder to ensure he is still asleep, I quickly step into the green dress and tighten the straps on my shoulders. Once I'm dressed, I take one more quick look at Ryats' sleeping form and smile to myself at how peaceful he looks lying there with a sweet Yip pup at his side. His pale skin is littered with scars, healed wounds of all textures and sizes along each piece of skin that I can see. Which is a lot as he is only wearing his undergarments and the furs are laying haphazardly over his torso and legs. I know he will one day tell me how he received the scars, and it hurts to think of the young version of him going through such pain. Though his body heat is surely enough to keep him warm, I still take a moment to pull the furs back up before turning and exiting the tent.

I make the quick walk over to the cooking station and see that Arden is not here yet. He has always been slower to rise, his sleep having not fully left him yet. Making quick work of lighting the torches, I set to start prepping. Fenor had told me of the oats he had not known what to do with, and they would be the main base for today's breakfast. I start to chop them so they will be a finer texture and have almost finished when Arden walks up to the table.

"Good morning. I see you're prepping for oat cakes?" He says this with a large smile (as I knew he would, since they are his favorite). I have been making oat cakes for many years now and they've always been a dish he would wake early for.

Laughing lightly, I reply, "I sure am. When Fenor told me he had oats and no use for them, I knew they would make a good breakfast for your return. I remember how much you love them."

"You've always been too good for me, Emory. The fates gave you to me as a gift, and I will forever be thankful." He says this with the same smile as he takes over the chopping of the oats. He has said this many times over the years and, like always, I laugh.

"You were the gift, dear brother. Now watch the knife. You don't want them to be too small and you know it."

We work in silence, the only sounds being the gentle rustling of ingredients and the occasional crack of autumn nut shells. I chop apples into small cubes, smash the auburn nuts into small pieces, and whisk eggs Eira had found in the woods. The earthy aroma of the nuts mingles with the sweetness of the apples in the air around us, bringing a smile to my face. When Arden has finished, I mix all the ingredients together and add in my spices as he goes to prepare the wood stove and his footsteps echo in the early morning silence. The scent of burning logs adding a hint of smokiness to the air.

With a steady hand, I begin to pour my batter in small circles onto the pastry tray. Once the first batch is poured, I pull out another bowl and begin making syrup.

"What type of syrup are you making today?" Arden asks. I know he is hoping for maple, which is exactly what I have started to prepare. I lift my eyebrow as I look at him and see as he realizes that's exactly what he'll be getting. "It's maple isn't it! I know it is!"

Smiling, I look back at the bowl and continue to whisk my ingredients together. "Sure is, baby brother." With a quick look over my shoulder, I see that the fire looks to be ready. "Can you put in the first tray?"

A few flips and tray switches later, we have a large stack of oat cakes ready to go. I grab a larger serving spoon for the syrup as Arden gets plates and silverware. We walk over to the table as Arden tells me about the beginning of their travels and set up the table for all eleven of us.

"Overall, everything was pretty normal. We walked until well after nightfall on the first day. Ryat wanted to make sure you had as much time as possible before getting your gift back. It was weird, by the way, finding out you were mated before you did."

I laugh and look over at him. "I bet it was. It was pretty shocking for me, too."

He laughs, "but that was good news considering everything else we learned. The second day was the same as the first, walking and chatting on our way to the next town over. We camped that night and told stories of our first fights. You should ask Haven about hers sometimes. It's quite the tale." He laughs before continuing. "We got into town on day three and that's when it got interesting. We split up, and each asked around about different things, not wanting the market to know that we had a group asking about all the topics at once. I was to get more information on the current Null situation." He sighs. "I got little. Other than that we were still being executed. There was no mention of anyone being able to tell a Null from one look. I asked around the entire market, speaking with anyone who would so much as gossip but heard nothing worthwhile." I can tell this makes him worry, feel the anxiety in him. "The others gained much more than I did, thankfully. They're going to tell everyone at breakfast and we'll have to leave camp pretty quickly."

Arden's emotions are a heavy mix. Anxiety, hopefulness, love, determination, fear. There are smaller emotions, too. A waft of guilt, a seed of spite, and a light dusting of excitement. I guess the excitement is for the oak cakes, but I do not try to distinguish the rest. I have long since learned that sometimes even the person feeling the emotions is unsure of where they're all rooted.

I hear a tent flap and look over to see Teirney walking towards us. I give her a smile and call out, "good morning!"

Smiling back, she replies, "good morning, my new sister." This shocks me. I am her brother's mate, but I had thought little about it yet. I didn't have a chance last night to think about who all knows or how she would feel about the situation. I find myself smiling, glad that she seems to have accepted me already. We haven't yet officially met, though that will change in a few moments, as she is almost at the table now.

When she gets to the table, she walks over to me and pulls me into a tight hug. So tight, in fact, that I can feel her heartbeat against my temple. I had forgotten how tall she was, almost as tall as Ryat and he is well over six feet. "We shall chat later, but for now you should go wake my brother. I do not believe he will enjoy waking up to you absent on your first morning with the marked bond."

I laugh, smiling, "you are probably right. I'll go wake him. Can you give us a few and then call for the others?"

"You bet I can. I love yelling at the folks in this camp." She says this with a dimpled grin and mischief swirling in the air.

I turn with a laugh and head across camp to Ryats' tent. I hear some rustling with tents as I pass and smile to myself, happy that some people are already getting used to waking for breakfast. I open the tent flap when I get there and close it behind me, looking over to see Ryat laying as I left him. The blanket is back to being draped over his feet, but it seems as if nothing else has changed. Kalleli opens her eyes and yawns, her long ears twitching as she wakes up. I squat down beside the cot and run my fingers over Ryats' marking. The dark line is around an inch thick and goes all the way around his bicep, just as mine does. I feel the muscle in his arm twitch and look up to see his eyes open, now looking at me from my position next to him. He gives me a soft smile, his eyes traveling across the parts of my body he can see from his position on the cot.

Looking back up to meet my eyes, he speaks softly, "I knew you would look lovely in the mornings." Hope, admiration, and awe fill the surrounding space.

I feel my cheeks heat, not yet used to the kindness spilling from his lips. I smile, laughing softly, "you have put me in quite beautiful clothing. I was a bit worried the pink in my hair would clash with the soft green of the dress."

I hear Teirney call out for breakfast as Ryat reaches a hand towards me, twisting his body on the cot to get closer to my face. He sets his palm on my cheek, looking me in the eye, "I bought you the clothing because you deserve to be in beautiful clothes. You deserve to feel beautiful, but you do not need them to be so. You would be beautiful to me in rags, and your soul is more beautiful to me than you could ever begin to understand." He leans in to kiss my forehead, thankfully not commenting on the tears that have formed in my eyes. "Now let's go see what you've cooked up for our breakfast, princess."

Ryat pulls back just enough to rise out of the cot, pulling me up into a stand with the hand on my cheek. Kalleli stands as well, leaning into a stretch and softly pawing at the linens. I sniffle a bit as I work to control the tears attempting to leave my eyes and smile up at Ryat. He smiles back as we exit and the hand on my cheek lowers to intertwine with my fingers.

CHAPTER

EIGHTEEN

K alleli eagerly follows behind me, her paws softly padding against the ground as we make our way towards the table. Although she has grown larger than expected, her short legs have not grown any longer.

As we settle down, the table comes alive with the murmurs of sleepy voices saying good morning. The aroma of the freshly cooked oat cakes fill the air, mingling with the sweet scent of syrup being poured onto each stack by Arden. Nox, is in his usual position, slumped over with his head resting heavily on the table, his eyes closed. Everyone else is sitting in various positions, each reflecting their own level of weariness. Haven sits upright, as if she has been awake for hours, gently rubbing Azrael's back as he rests with his forehead against her lap. Eira leans her head on Vor's shoulder, a serene smile on her lips as he engages in lighthearted banter with Hellion across the table. The party emanates a palpable sense of exhaustion, yet even with the fatigue, there are subtle waves of contentment and love flowing between everyone gathered around the table.

I smile as I look around the table and pick up my Spork. Ryats' hand is once again on my thigh and I can feel the same love and contentment coming from him as I cut the first bite out of my oat cake. I feel the others' emotions as they take their first bites, hear the groans of passion, and smile a bit wider. There's just something about the feeling you get when people enjoy your cooking. It's always been one of my favorite feelings, knowing that something I made was bringing someone else pleasure. So much of my life I had been remembering the terror people felt as I left them as

Plains, and there was little that shook the feeling from memory. I tried to fill the space with the positives I felt from others. That has gotten much easier since joining this party.

Looking around the group, I see everyone is now sitting up to eat and looking much more alert. Nox has almost finished his stack in just a few bites, and is currently reaching for more. I smile and decide that there is no better time than the present to start the conversation.

"Much has happened since we last saw each other. If your group would like to start, I'm sure there's a lot to do once we're all caught up." I can feel the group that left shifting their attention toward me, emotions swirling around—waves of determination, fear, and hope wash over me.

Ryat gives my thigh a gentle squeeze, and I glance over to meet his eyes. He smiles and nods. "Good idea. We have much to do indeed." He looks around the group and begins, "We hiked for the first two and a half days without incident. When we reached the main market in Kons, we split up to gather information. Arden was tasked with learning more about the current Null situation. He asked if anything had changed about their presence in the lands, if there were ways to spot them, and any other pertinent details."

Ryat turns to Arden, who speaks up, his gaze sweeping the table. "I spoke with anyone I could find, asking questions and trading gossip. Unfortunately, the situation with the Nulls hasn't improved. We are still to be executed if found. Nobody had heard of any ways to identify us, either; most just laughed it off." He sighs. "No matter who I spoke with, there was no new information." As he finishes, I continue to eat my breakfast, pondering his words.

"Teirney was searching for information on the prophecy," Ryat says, looking over at her.

Teirney nods in acknowledgment before adding, "my information came much quicker, as it seems everyone has now heard the prophecy. They all spoke the same words in the same order. It never changed, no matter who I spoke with. Some had heard more than others regarding the prophecy. I heard from a woman in a flower shop that the woman was known to have once been trapped but was now free." She laughs at this, looking at me with a twinkle in her eye and taking another bite before continuing. "An elemental in an herbal store told me he had heard that she was traveling with a god, and another said he heard she herself was a god as well. I heard many tales, mostly gossip. The main information I gained was that nobody knew who the woman was, where she came from or anything of her minus the silver hair." She looks at me, smiling. "The pink hair looks lovely, and should help us a lot on our journey." With that, she looks to Ryat beside me and nods that she is done.

"Haven gathered information on the lands," Ryat continues, gesturing to her.

Haven takes a breath before diving in. "I heard of many blights affecting the lands, though they haven't reached Mygreen yet. Travelers spoke of diseases spreading from tree to tree in Frontasia, wiping out parts of the woods completely. There's been an influx of Cayman in Kiasta, breaching their usual bounds and causing havoc." I sense a wave of disgust and fear ripple through the group. The Cayman, giant crocodiles over forty feet long with razor-sharp teeth, are one of the more dangerous creatures sent here from the mainlands. She exhales. "I collected dozens of stories about new creatures appearing, lakes drying up, and villages burning to the ground. I barely made it through a few stands before hours had passed and we were preparing to return."

As she finishes, I see Azrael take her hand and press a quick kiss to her palm. Their connection radiates love, respect, and admiration.

Ryat breaks the momentary silence, glancing around the table. I notice that no one from our group has spoken up yet; curiosity and focus line their faces. "Vor uncovered information about who's responsible for the new war and their motives."

Vor's voice drops to a lower tone than I've heard him use, a stark reminder that beneath his beauty lies the heart of a Warrior. "We're in for an uphill battle. The

God of Revenge himself has claimed this war. It's said that Ymir visited many of the most powerful gifted in the lands, warning them not to interfere or face his wrath. Not much is known about his plans, but it seems his goal is to wipe out all life here." He pauses, glancing around as if gauging our reactions. "Nobody could confirm whether the mainlands or other provinces are involved, though many speculate they are not. Given what we learned about the blight, it appears Pack Alpha Tyrak of Kiasta didn't join him, nor did Lord Grayson of Mygreen, Lord Zephus and Lady Emeir of Frontasia, Lady Alvara of Eldevand, or Lord Dorian and Lady Vala of Ulopia. Haven didn't hear anything about the other lands, so it's unclear whether they've joined him or if word of their blights has simply not spread yet." His emotions, while harder to read, pulse with intensity— determination and anger flowing down the table and into me.

Ryat lightly traces circles on my thigh as he speaks again. Now that we've all finished our oatcakes, everyone's full attention is on him. "I was searching for information on where the war might be fought when

I was visited by Riven—the god who blessed me. And, being the God of War, he gave me information on what he knew so far." There are gasps around the table. Shock fills the air, and I feel it rise through the entire table. Based on the reactions I guess that me and Teirney are the only ones who knew of his favor from the god.

"He said that the gods have become divided since the end of the Dark War, angered by the New Gods being hidden by those within the group. He revealed that when the Dark War ended, it was sealed with a prophecy much like this one. However, the man who brokered the deal with the gods was a liar. He hid the existence of a child, and when he sacrificed himself to end the war and save the lands, he left behind the power of the Fated." Ryat turns to me, his voice softening. "This child was your mother. When she had you, she passed down that power."

A jolt of shock courses through the table, electrifying the air. I feel the weight of the moment, my heartbeat echoing in my ears. Pain radiates from Arden at the news he'd already heard. My body feels strangely disconnected from the world around me. My mother had rarely spoken of her father, saying only that he passed when she was young. Her mother had raised her, doing everything she could to give her the life she deserved, in a land that was very hard on unmarried ladies. I can't help but wonder if my mother—or her mother—knew of this power.

They must have.

The world was full of gifted but powers had been lost long ago. To be born with powers was dangerous. To be born a Null was life threatening, if not extremely careful. To be born with both was a death sentence. I had never been allowed around people, not for even a moment. I steal a glance at Arden, his eyes filled with a mix of sadness and understanding.

"She must have known." I say softly. "To have kept me locked away all those years, to never be allowed out, even when we had guests."

Arden nods slowly. "I believe she did. I tried for years to get you out, even for just a moment. She always said the same thing." He mimics her voice, slightly off-pitch but endearing. "'My dear boy, we can never let anyone see our gift. They would take her, and she would never fulfill the destiny given to her by the fates. We must protect her, even if it means keeping her locked away with only us to love her for now.'" His gaze drops to the table as he speaks softly. "I've always believed you were destined for something great. I just never thought it would be this. I never considered the implications of those words."

Tears trail down my cheeks as I sniffle. Ryat's hand comes up to wipe them away, his voice steady as he continues. "Riven said we must stay together as a party and protect the Fated until she can protect herself. Now that the prophecy has been found, there will be no way to evade or slow down the war; not truly. He mentioned two possible paths for the war, though he didn't specify which we were to follow."

Looking up at him, I gather my thoughts. "I know the path we're meant to take, but please, finish first. I'll share my information afterward."

Ryat nods, his trust bolstering my spirits. "Riven said the final battle will take place in either Promental or Eldevand. We need to arrive there within two weeks and be prepared to woo and to fight. He couldn't divulge more, but we should expect many gods to be present at the final battle—both old and new."

CHAPTER

NINETEEN

The news vibrates through me, a shockwave of realization. I had known that the prophecy must be about me, despite my hopes to deny it. My conversation in the Diner had confirmed my place in the final battle, but I had not expected to have the gods be there as well.

The gods were all equal in strength, yet their powers differed greatly. The God of Love, for instance, would never engage in a fistfight. I wonder who will be on my side, and if they will help me or just watch as I sacrifice myself for the lands.

Do I want to sacrifice myself for these lands? These lands have hunted me, kept me prisoner in a cell and are now trying to tear me from the only freedom I had ever known. It does not seem fair that I am to be set free and have it all stripped away in such a short time.

But, the lands have never been fair.

Especially to me.

"Did your group hear if any of the other gods have picked sides in this war?" Azrael's voice cuts through my thoughts, tense and focused on Ryat.

Ryat shakes his head. "No, aside from Riven, we haven't heard from any other gods about the war. If we didn't have such a strict timeline, we would have sought more information, but we'll have to gather it as we journey to whichever nation we decide upon."

I take a deep breath, gathering my courage. "We have heard from another god." My voice is soft, but I lift my gaze, feeling my tears begin to dry as I straighten my spine. "While you were away, I was visited by the God of

Luck, Ryar."

I sense the attention of Ryat, Teirney, Hazel, and Vor shift to me. "Hellion took me to the market the day your group left. It was a strange encounter with a god, so I'll start from the beginning." Nods of understanding come from around the table as Ryat leans closer, his hand moving to my hip and tracing gentle circles.

"After we started walking to the market, I was gifted Kalleli, my Yip. She found us in the woods and has been with us since." I feel her shift beneath my feet at the mention of her name, her energy a comforting presence. "We split up when we got to the market so Hellion could get the supplies and I could visit the shops. I spent some time in a few before noticing what I had thought was a diner and going towards it. I had never been to one before, so I was really excited. That is when I met Ryar, though I did not know that at the time and wouldn't for a while."

Vor clears his throat, "you were with a god and he didn't immediately tell you his purpose for the visit?"

I nod. "Yes, he stopped me before I could enter the cabin. He told me I should not enter, and I was too stubborn to listen. He tried to convince me, but I continued pushing back, not wanting to be told what I could not do. He went in with me when he realized I would not back down, though I did not know what I was entering into, as he had used words unbeknownst to me at the time. I quickly learned what the word 'brothel' meant. I do not recommend entering one." Heat floods my cheeks, a mix of embarrassment and discomfort, and I can feel Ryat's hand freeze on my hip, his tension palpable.

Ryat's voice turns low and fierce, filled with a protective edge. "He took you into a brothel?"

Looking into his eyes, I offer a soft smile, hoping to calm him. "No, he went in with me and when I realized what I had done, he quickly got me out. He was very kind to have done so."

Looking over, I see Arden looks just as angry. I do not want to know if they have been to a brothel such as that one or taken part in the things I saw happening within. I decide not to mention him calling my bluff while inside, either. Shaking my head to clear the thoughts, I continue.

"Once we had exited, I had him lead me to a proper diner, and he sat down with me to have a meal. That is when I asked him for his name and he told me it was Ryar. I knew immediately that I was sitting with a god, that I had now been with one for who knew how long. That is when he gave me the message and warning he was there to deliver."

I stop picking through the emotions at the table, so many now that I am becoming distracted by them all. Ryats' shoulders are tense beside me and I can tell that we will probably be discussing this more when we are alone. I am not used to having a mate, so I am not sure how that will go. Is he mad at me for being in the brothel, or for being in a brothel with another male? Is he mad at me at all or is it the situation that has anger wafting from him as thick as a brush fire? I start to feel my anxiety rise, realizing that I do not like being unsure if he is angry with me. I must make some kind of noise or facial expression, as I feel his hand begin moving again on my hip and he leans in to give me a quick kiss on the side of my head.

Clearing my throat, I try not to think about that right now, knowing we have much more important topics than my crazy emotions.

"Ryar said that we need to go to Eldevand. He said the journey will be long and hard, but we must not give up. He cautioned me to be careful with my wishes as we travel but assured me that if I remain faithful to my gods, we will be protected. He didn't know much else, except that your group would receive additional guidance from another god."

Ryat nods from beside me, "then we shall go to Eldevand. We were told to be there in two weeks' time almost three days ago, so the journey will have little time for rest." He looks over at Fenris, "brother, do you believe you can begin the journey now or do you need another day?"

"One more day will have me at full health and that would be best for us all if we are going to encounter new creatures within the lands. We can leave tomorrow at first light." Fenris says this and then looks at me, "that is, if we can have deer for dinner again tonight. I will need the additional strength."

I smile and a laugh bursts out of me, "then deer it is."

I feel the confusion coming from Ryat and look over to shake my head at him, smiling.

Vor speaks now, in the same low voice. "To get to Everand, we will need to cross through Ulopia, Frontasia and Kiasta. We cannot risk going through Promental since they've expanded the Null Grounds."

I see Nox nod, "you're right. That would make the most sense, though it will make for a difficult journey indeed. If the Cayman have moved past their boundaries, we will need to be heavily armed. Or we will need to find ourselves a Cayman shifter. They will not attack one of their own."

I feel Arden's gaze on me, a cold wave of apprehension washing over me. "We already have one," I blurt out before I can stop myself. My eyes drop to the table, the wood grain blurring under the weight of nine curious stares.

"What do you mean, we already have one?" Vulcan's question is soft from disuse yet probing, though I sense he already suspects the answer.

"I'm a Cayman shifter. It's a gift I stole during an attempted raid many years ago. I can't use the gift to its full extent, but I can manage a shift." My voice is barely a whisper, and as I speak, I feel my body sag deeper into my seat, shame heavy in my chest. Ryat's hand continues to trace circles on my hip, a comforting reminder of his presence, and I wonder if he's already guessed.

Eira speaks softly from her seat, "why did you not tell us before this? Do you not trust us?"

I feel my heart shatter into a thousand pieces, the jagged edges piercing through my chest. It's as if the entire world has shifted under me at her words. I had been so worried they would hate me for the information; I had never truly thought to look at it from their perspective.

"I thought you would hate me in the beginning." I say hoarsely, my voice trembling. "I thought you would think I was a monster for having stolen the gift the way I did. I have grown to think of you all as friends in my time here, and I did not wish to lose you."

"In this world you do what you must to survive and people will love you for having the guts to do so." Eiras' voice is stronger now, passion flowing into her words. "You survived, Emory. I would have it no other way."

Haven stands, walking towards her tent with Azrael behind her, but stops briefly to call out. "You are part of us now, Emory, and we will teach you to embrace your gifts. Find us when you are ready."

Vulcan, Vor and Nox follow with a quick smile my way. Fenor stands, looking me in the eye, "you'll accept yourself as we have one day, but we will hold you up until you can do so for yourself."

Soon, the table is empty and the tears flow freely from my eyes once again. Ryat's gentle hand wipes away the warm tears as they fall, but they do not stop as my shoulders shake and the feeling of my chest tightening makes it hard to breathe.

I sob for the me that was terrified she would never have friends or love.

I sob for the me that was forced to steal gifts to survive.

I sob for the me that knows what I will inevitably do when the final battle comes.

CHAPTER

TWENTY

I feel Arden's arms go around me and I turn my head and rest it gently on his broad, sturdy shoulder. I did not hear him get up from his chair on the other side of the table through the raw sobs that have been wracking my body. He has taken the seat next to me and is leaning over to reach my hunched over frame. Ryats' hand moves from my hip to my back and he has not stopped rubbing his comforting circles. I have run out of tears, leaving only dry, heaving sobs that reverberate through my entire being. The pain is tangible, etching itself into my throat, leaving it parched and scratchy. My eyes burn from the tears that have already spilled. I feel the same hollow emotions pouring into me from my brother, and I know he wishes more than anything he could change the fates.

But it was not he who was born with the ability to wish upon the gods. Nor was he born with the destiny to die for the ones he loves. I know that this is harder on him than anything else, that this was the fate given to me by birthright. That had he been the eldest, it would be him. Arden has always wanted to fight my battles for me, and I fear now that him doing so is what allowed me to stay so weak. I had not wanted to accept the gifts I stole, so he had. He had worked on them day and night to master the forms and elements, working to ensure he could keep me safe. Arden had the gifts of two shifters. He could transform and fight as a Tencan, flee as a Bundra. He had fire, which took him months to control, working daily to tame the flames. He could do so much more, and I could do so little. He had always borne the burden when he could, and now I know it is time for me to face my own battles.

He would be by my side until the end, but he could

not win the final battle for me. I would be the only one able to complete the prophecy and save the lands. Save him.

I would need to get stronger. Quickly.

I could not risk going into the final battle as I was now, weak and full of fear.

I had people I now called friends and a mate, along with the brother I had sworn to always protect.

There was no room in survival for crying.

Not now.

Maybe after.

If there was an after for me to cry in, that is.

I take a shaky breath, trying to calm my racing heart. I feel Ryat lean further into my other side, feel the heat from his skin as he leans his head towards my own. He speaks softly, his voice full of compassion and his emotions engrossed in pain. "Let's go back to the tent for a bit, princess. Let me hold you for a while, please."

I nod against Arden's shoulder, pulling my body up.

Slowly.

Painfully.

Arden drops his arms, sitting up in his chair. "I will burn the world to ashes before I let you go, Emory. You will not die in this war. I will not allow it."

His voice is hard, his eyes seemingly made of steel. I nod at him too, nothing left in me able to form words. I know, though, that this is my burden to carry and I will let him do no such thing. Arden stands, puts a hand on my head to ruffle my hair, and then turns to walk back to the tents.

Ryat pulls me into a stand, holding my body weight in his strong hold. I feel as though I have cried out my very existence.

Will the people of this camp, my parents and the god themselves, be the only ones to ever know that I existed?

If I am to sacrifice blood, bone, or soul, will anyone remember me at all? Or will it be as it was in the diner with Ryar? One moment he orders a tea, and the next nobody remembers he was ever there at all.

I do not want to have never truly existed. I believe that may be my biggest fear of all.

To be forgotten as well.

I realize that we've been walking, or more likely shuffling, as it seems my legs do not want to work in the way they are meant to. They are wobbling as newborn fawns' long legs do when they take their first steps. It feels as though these are my first steps into a new life. In this life I must be strong, but first I must let out the weakness.

It will not help me on the journey.

Ryat must decide that this walk/shuffle thing we're doing is pointless. I feel his arms against my lower thigh and shoulders moments before he has lifted me into his arms and the warmth seeps into me once more. When he holds me like this, my head on his chest and his arms around me, it almost feels like he is the entire world. He has grown to be a safe place for me in a world full of danger and I thank the gods for the gift of a mate, even if I only get to experience the beauty for a short time. It will have been worth it, I can already tell.

Ryat gently carries me into his tent, the dim light of the morning filtering through the thin fabric. He lays me on the soft cot, its surface cool against my skin. As he turns to close the flap behind Kalleli, I can hear the faint rustling of the fabric, sealing us off from the outside world. I sense Kalleli's presence before I see her, her concern palpable in the air. With a graceful leap, she joins us on the cot, her paws lightly padding against the fabric. As she approaches me, her warm breath tickles my neck, carrying a faint scent of the woods. I feel her gentle nuzzle, her nose pressing against my skin, emitting a soft whine that resonates in my ears. Curled up on my side, I huddle into a ball, the chill in the air causing my body to shiver. Without the heat provided by my mate, I long for warmth. Kalleli settles against me, her body radiating a light heat. I can feel her weight against me, her head resting on my neck, and her body pressed as close to my chest as possible. I gaze up and see a soft smile on Ryats' face.

His eyes, filled with tenderness, meet mine as he walks to the cot, crawling over my body and settling in behind me. He pulls the fur up to cover our bodies and pulls me into his warmth. "She worries for you. More than I thought possible for an animal to care for another being, one not in their own species."

I nod again, snuggling closer to him, and feel the heat and comfort of the bond return to my body. We lay like this for hours before I fall into a soft sleep and thankfully; I do not dream.

CHAPTER

TWENTY-ONE

I wake to the soft sensation of gentle kisses brushing against my still puffy face. My heart races as I recognize the lips—only one person has ever kissed me, so I know they belong to him. Ryats lips glide across my left cheek, warm and tender, leaving a trail of warmth that ignites my skin. The sensation sends shivers down my spine, each kiss igniting a spark of comfort and safety I desperately crave. He moves to my chin, the pressure light yet electrifying, as if he's trying to convey all the unspoken words between us. When his lips find my nose, it's a delicate touch that feels almost playful, a sweet reminder of the intimacy we share. Then, he brushes against my right eyelid, his kiss feather-light, like a whisper of affection that seems to wrap around my heart. The wisps of his hair tickle my forehead, mingling with the warmth of his kisses, and a small smile lifts onto my lips. "Hello, mate."

"Hello." He continues his light kisses along my face, never reaching my lips. I open my eyes and see that he is hovering above me. His brown eyes are full of passion, and his emotions are soft and warm.

Licking my lips, I look at him. "You have not actually kissed me yet, not on my lips."

Ryat smiles, dimples in full display, and my heart seems to skip a beat within my chest. "Would you like me to kiss you, mate?" I hear the teasing tone in his voice, but I can sense the hope in his emotions. He wants this as much as I do.

"Please kiss me Ryat, please."

"You never have to beg for a kiss princess, I would never say no." He says this softly as he smiles that big, beautiful dimpled smile. He lowers his head towards my own and my stomach flutters. He closes his eyes and I follow suit. I can feel the soft brush of his breath against my skin and I feel goosebumps rise the moment his lips touch mine, feeling the softness, but also the intensity of his emotions. He starts softly, as he had been kissing my face, before he gains intensity within the kiss. His lips press against mine, hard and seemingly impatient. His tongue is tracing the seam of my lips, as if asking for permission to enter, and I do not hesitate to open them. At that moment, everything changes. He traces his tongue along mine and though I do not know what I am supposed to do, it does not matter. My skin buzzes, the fluttering in my stomach now an earthquake within me. Every nerve in my body tingles, as if electric currents are surging just beneath my skin. I enjoy the feeling of his lips, his tongue, and his breath in sync with my own. The cot beneath me shifts and I feel his left hand leave the cot and come up to cup my cheek tenderly, tilting my head back as he dives deeper into my very soul. Into the very core of my being.

Before I know it, he is pulling away and I am panting for air.

I look up at him, a large smile on my face. "I did not know that is what kissing was like. I hope you plan to do that way more often." I say this as a breathy joke (mostly), but I see his eyes darken at the words.

Leaning closer to me, I sense the warm emotion I do not know emitting from him again. "We can kiss, and do more, whenever you please. My body, my heart, and my soul belong to you. I will always want to be with you in any way you would like."

Oh. I had forgotten for a moment about the more.

I speak softly, feeling my cheeks flush with embarrassment at my lack of knowledge. "I know very little about the things that are a part of being mated. You will have to tell me things, explain them to me, teach me." I shift my head to the side, unable to meet his intense gaze.

Ryat gently tilts my chin up with one hand on my cheek, his touch sending shivers down my spine. "I will teach you everything and anything you could ever wish to learn, princess," he says, his voice tender and reassuring. "We will discover the joys and trials of matehood together."

Ryat's lips meet mine again, soft and warm, like velvet petals brushing against my skin. The world around us fades away, leaving only the gentle pressure of his mouth and the comforting weight of his arms around me. I inhale deeply, breathing in his scent – a heady mixture of pine, cinnamon, and something uniquely Ryat. It fills my senses, intoxicating and grounding all at once.

My hands, trembling slightly, find their way to his chest. I can feel the steady rhythm of his heartbeat beneath my fingertips, a soothing cadence that matches the pulse thrumming in my own veins. As we kiss, time seems to slow, each second stretching into an eternity.

Ryat's fingers thread through my hair, cradling the back of my head with tenderness. His other hand traces a path down my spine, leaving a trail of tingling warmth in its wake. I shiver, pressing closer to him, craving more of his touch.

Our lips part for a moment, and I gaze up into Ryat's eyes. They're dark, like the depths of an ancient lake. Flecks of gold seem to dance in their honey depths, reminding me of sunlight filtering through fall leaves. His breath fans across my face, warm and sweet, carrying the faintest hint of wild berries.

"You're trembling," he murmurs, his voice a low rumble that I feel more than hear. His arms tighten around me protectively, as if he can shield me from the world.

"I'm not afraid," I whisper.

I smile up at him, feeling the joy rise in me at knowing I'm not alone.

I lower my voice a bit, "though, I am sorry I fell apart this morning." I feel stronger now, and I am glad I had the chance to let it all out. Though, I am sorry that the camp had to witness it. That I could not be stronger.

Ryat leans down and places a soft kiss against my lips. "You never have to be sorry for feeling your emotions, Emory. You are one of us and we are here for you through the tears and we will be here even in the battles."

Ryat shifts, moving over me to lie on his back. I feel his arm snake under me as he pulls me to lie on his chest. Laying my head on him, I settle at the sound of his steady heartbeat. "We will be leaving out early tomorrow morning, and the first stop will be the main market you went to with Hellion. We need to get horses if we are to make it in the timeframe we were given." I feel determination, fear and hope in him. These are the main ones he emits and they make me feel steady as well, knowing that in everything he is consistent in his fears and hopes.

"I understand. I will do whatever is needed to help, but I have no gifts that will be of much use. The most I can do is tell you the emotions someone is feeling, but I cannot tell you where they come from." I say this, forgetting that I have not told him I have this gift yet. "I have the gifts of a Celtic. It's the only gift I have mastered, since I cannot turn it off as I can shift between the others."

Ryat nods, "I had guessed you sensed emotions in some way. You always seem to be assessing people within the camp. That may come to be quite useful along the journey as we cross potential enemies." He pauses, as if he is thinking about what to say next. "What other gifts do you have?"

"I have the Celtic Empathy, the Cayman Spirit, a Foxe spirit and some minor Lakin abilities." I feel the shock move through him at the last gift. Lakin are an indigenous group of gifted born in Athas. The nation is home to only their families and spans multiple generations. They are known to travel rarely and dislike visitors, so my crossing one is quite a shock, I'm sure.

Ryat runs his fingers through my hair as he asks, "Lakin are known to have the gift of Illusion, it's said that they can bend the very ground you stand on within your mind's eye. Do you know which family tree your gift is descended from?"

I have wondered about this and even spoke with

Arden about it multiple times in the days after. "No, I do not. I happened upon the Lakin on my way to my mother's burial. In a crowd full of people, she chose to pickpocket me and grazed my arm. Everything after that happened so quickly, I had no time for questions. Arden had grabbed me as she screamed in terror for the guardsman and we had run. That was just days before I was captured and taken to the Null Grounds." I remember the deep pain I had felt that day from my mother's passing. But I also remembered being elated. As Arden had told me he thought nobody would notice if I went to the village to watch the burial ceremony. I had missed fathers, as mother thought it still too dangerous for me to be around other people. She had been right. I, however, had been the danger. "I have only attempted to use it once since stealing it, and it appeared it would be moderately powerful with training. Arden said I had shifted the lake in front of us to show pale pink waters instead of their seedy green."

Ryat continues to run his fingers through my hair and clears his throat. "I am sorry you weren't able to see your parents' ceremony. I missed my own parents, but

Teirney said it helped her with the grieving and I wish you had the opportunity."

I did too, more than anything. I nod against his chest. "Will we have a Mating Ceremony?" I ask, my voice soft.

Ryat laughs lightly, his chest vibrating under me. "Yes, my mate. We will have a mating ceremony. Before the final battle, if I can find us a rabbi within the villages along our journey. I do not wish to enter a war without being tied to you in both life and death."

Mating Ceremonies are an oath to the fates, tying your souls together and ensuring that you would be together in the afterlife as well. They were sacred within all lands and could only be performed by a rabbi who had been blessed by the fates themselves. I smile, thinking of him joining me in the afterlife, knowing that I have that to look forward to, even if the war steals my time with him in life. "I would like that very much."

I feel Ryats' stomach rumble with a growl and laugh. "I guess I should go and prepare lunch. It seems I am not keeping you satisfi-"

Before I have even finished my sentence, Ryat has flipped me onto my back and is once again hovering over me on the cot. "You keep me more than satisfied, and Fenor has already started lunch. You are going to lie here and kiss me until it's ready, mate."

His voice is a deep velvety purr, sending shivers down my spine. As I gaze into his eyes, they shimmer like pools of liquid honey. A rush of warmth floods my body, igniting sensations in places I never knew existed, like a flame flickering to life. The air around us seems to vibrate with the intensity of our bond, causing my heart to thud in my chest like a drum. My eyes wander, tracing the chiseled contours of his jaw, the softness of his lips, before returning to meet his darkened gaze. It feels as if an invisible current passes between us, fueling the growing pulse within me, like a powerful heartbeat.

"What is this feeling? It's hot and I can feel my pulse everywhere?" I ask, barely able to get the sentence out through my sharp breaths.

Ryat's gaze moves from my parted lips to my eyes,

a smoldering fire burning in his. "You're turned on, princess, It seems you like being told what to do." His lips curl into a charmingly crooked grin, revealing his left dimple. "That will be useful information for a later date, but for now, just know that it's completely normal. I feel it as well and have for quite a while now, as I'm sure you can tell." He leans in to press a gentle kiss against the tip of my nose, pulling a giggle from my lips.

My heart races as I lock eyes with him, feeling like electricity is coursing through my veins. "Will you kiss me again now?" I ask, knowing there is nothing I want more at this moment than his lips on mine again.

He obliges, pressing his soft lips against mine once more. As we kiss, the line between myself and Ryat blurs until there is no distinction between the two of us at all. It's just us, with the Yip pup peacefully asleep at our feet.

CHAPTER

TWENTY-TWO

We had eaten lunch in our tent earlier, soaking in as much time together as we could before separating for baths and agreeing to meet for dinner. I told him of my childhood, recalled stories of a young Arden and listened as he recalled his time living at his parents' home. We stayed on light topics, both knowing we would have plenty of dark ones in the days to come.

And we kissed. Oh my gods, did we kiss. I was beginning to believe the fates had been unfair to all other females in giving him to me, because his kisses could probably restart your heart after death.

But now, as twilight settles over our camp, I feel a bittersweet heaviness fill my chest. This is our last dinner here, and I want it to be special. I make a rich deer stew, simmering with carrots and potatoes, just for Fenris. For Vulcan, I bake soft rolls, having noticed his habit of snatching a few whenever I make them. And for Nox, with his sweet tooth, I whip up some sweetberry cookies, the aroma mingling in the soft air.

As we gather around the table, the crackling campfire mingles with the distant chirping of birds, creating a comforting backdrop. I pass down the bowl of biscuits, and Vulcan meets my gaze with that soft smile and nod of appreciation that warms my heart. At the other end of the table, I hear Hellion and Arden engaged in a spirited debate over whether we should carry swords versus bows for our upcoming journey. Their differing opinions clash like blades, each trying to assert their point amidst the laughter, and I can't help but smile at their enthusiasm.

Eira is at it again, her voice rising in mock

exasperation as she whisper yells at Fenris for stealing the book she left for me. "Those words aren't meant for male eyes!" she exclaims, a mix of indignation and humor coloring her tone. I stifle a laugh as Fenris teases back, claiming that if a male had been present during its creation, the descriptions might have been more accurate.

Haven and Teirney are deep in discussion about tomorrow's market visit, planning which shops to explore while the men trade for horses. I sit back, absorbing the lively atmosphere, a smile spreading across my face. It feels so good to be part of something so wild yet so tightly knit. I never know what will come out of Nox's mouth, Haven speaks mostly of shopping and Vulcan barely speaks at all. They are all so different but so close, having chosen each other either way.

I feel Ryats' gaze move to me and look over to see that he and Fenor are both looking at me expectantly. I must have missed something. "Hi!" I say, my voice squeaking a bit.

Fenor laughs, "I didn't think you heard me." His eyes

and teeth twinkle in the light. Part of me wonders how some people are born with such sharp canines. "I said the cookies are fantastic. I have never thought to use spices in the ways you do."

I smile a tad wider, "thank you! I have always loved playing with different herbs and spices."

I barely get the sentence out before Arden shifts in his chair, the wooden seat creaking softly beneath him. "Just be happy you got the properly seasoned cookies. Her experimental recipes probably took a dozen years off my life. I can still taste the paprika she added to my oatcakes that almost killed me," he says, his face contorting into an exaggerated grimace, followed by a dramatic shudder. The faint smell of smoke from the campfire mingles with the scent of our meal, a comforting backdrop to his antics.

I laugh, the sound bubbling up as I shake my head. "You did not almost die! You just had a red tongue for a while. It wasn't that bad!" I can still picture his tongue— a bright, shocking red that had made him the center of attention at school. It's hard not to giggle at the thought of the bewildered looks he must have gotten.

"Tell that to the nine-year-old me who lost his crush and had to use the guest chambers that week because of the red tongue and red defecations! It was quite the week for me, and you thought it was hilarious!" Arden's laughter echoes through the warm evening air, and I can't help but join in.

Hellion bursts out laughing beside him, his voice loud and contagious. "You had red shits, brother? That is hilarious!" He reaches over, putting his hand up toward me. Confusion washes over me, but Ryat must sense it; he lifts my arm and gently slaps my palm into Hellion's.

I look over at Ryat, confused, the cool air brushing against my skin.

Ryat chuckles, a rich sound that warms me from the inside. "That's a high five, princess. It's not super common in Mygreen, but it is in other lands. It's like saying congratulations or way to go."

Interesting.

Hellion is now doubled over, belly laughing and slapping the table, the wooden surface vibrating with each slap. The laughter draws the attention of everyone around us, and I feel my cheeks flush as Nox leans in, eyebrows raised. "What the hell is so funny?"

Blushing fiercely, I lower my eyes, the warm glow of the campfire flickering against my skin. "When I was twelve, I accidentally turned Arden's tongue and... well, his defecations, red. Hellion thought that was hilarious and tried to give me a high five, but I didn't know what that was, so Ryat had to explain it to me." I say everything quickly, hoping they do not think I am silly.

Laughter erupts around the table and Azrael roars, his voice booming, "You turned his shit red. Gods, that is hilarious!" The sound fills the air and Haven playfully slaps him on the top of the head, laughing as she tells him to shut up.

"I have since learned what spices should be used and in what amounts," I mumble, feeling slightly embarrassed but also relieved by the laughter. Ryat pulls me toward him, his hand warm on my head as he kisses my forehead. I can feel the soft brush of his lips and the vibration of his laughter through the kiss, sending a ripple of joy through me, and I can't help but laugh again.

After a few more moments of laughter, the table quiets down, a comfortable silence settling over us. Conversations fade and I see the smiles left in their wake. "I am so glad your party found Arden and invited us to join you," I say, looking around at the people I'm growing to call friends—my brother and my mate. Kalleli is asleep in my lap, her soft breaths a soothing rhythm, and for the first time, I truly feel free.

Vor speaks up, his voice carrying a blend of warmth and resolve. "We are glad to have found you both. The journey ahead will be deadly, but together we will make it through." His emotions are a mix of determination and hope, grounding me in the moment. The flickering firelight dances in his eyes, and I feel a surge of warmth at his words.

Arden clears his throat from across the table and

we all turn to him. "We have been together for some time now, but I fear this journey will reveal a new side to us all. We must be prepared to see the fighters, the protectors, and the gifts within everyone around us." He looks around the table, his eyes hard. "We can no longer hide away our gifts and the darker parts of ourselves. To survive, we may need every bit of that darkness and more."

Nods and words of agreement go around the table before Ryat replies. "We are all going to fight with everything we have until the very end. No one should fear rejection within the party, or worry that they will be feared for doing what is needed to protect the ones they love. We all have each other's backs through this and we can all survive, but that is the only way we will all make it out of this alive." He pauses, looking over at me before looking back at the rest of the table. "Now, everyone who hasn't, please get a bath, pack and rest. We leave at first light, and the camp needs to be completely empty when we depart."

CHAPTER

TWENTY-THREE

y senses slowly come to life as I awaken to Kalleli's soft nudging on my arm. My eyes flutter open, adjusting to the darkness inside of our tent. Kalleli's face is inches from mine and for a moment, I am startled and feel my body flinch back. But then she leans in to give my cheek a gentle lick and whines softly, her message clear - she needs to use the restroom. I smile at her before turning to whisper to Ryat that I'll be right back. He mumbles something unintelligible in his sleep and I chuckle softly as I slip out of his arms.

Peeking outside, the air is cool and crisp, hinting at the lingering darkness that still envelops the world. In my half-awake state, I don't bother putting on my dress and instead just grab Ryats' oversized pants, tying the waist as tightly as possible. The fabric pools at my feet but I just hold it up as I step out into the night. The ground is damp beneath my bare feet, dewy with moisture from the night.

Kalleli immediately makes her way towards the trees, eagerly sniffing around as she always does. As she sniffs and wanders, I take a moment to look around and appreciate my surroundings. It's still quite early, a few hours left until the sun rises and chases away the darkness. The sky above me is a vast canvas, painted with countless twinkling stars that seem to stretch on forever. The rustling leaves of the trees above me only add to the beauty.

The air is filled with a mix of fragrances - the sweet scent of nature blending with the earthy aroma of the ground beneath my bare feet. I take a deep breath, letting myself relish in the tranquility of the stars for just a moment. Above me, the moon shines brightly, casting a silvery glow that adds an extra layer of magic to the night. It occurs to me that I should do this more often - take a few moments to marvel at the beauty of the night sky and get lost in its wonder. Despite the chaos and busyness of everyday life, there is still so much beauty and magic all around me and I'd like to appreciate it more often.

Looking back to where Kalleli is sniffing, I see I am no longer alone. There is a woman leaned down and petting my small Yips head. She is an older woman, wrinkles having formed on her tan skin and a full head of soft gray hair. She is wearing a pale pink dress long enough to trail behind her in the grass. Though I know Yips do not trust those with ill intentions, I feel my anxiety rise just the same.

I approach the woman slowly. "Hello. I see you have met Kalleli."

She stands up gracefully and turns to face me, her hair cascading down her back in soft curls. The moonlight filters through the trees, casting a silver glow on her delicate features. My eyes are drawn to the pink freckles adorning her nose and cheeks, each one shaped like a tiny heart and adding to her ethereal beauty. With a start, I realize who she is - Dyra, the Goddess of Love.

"It is a pleasure to make your acquaintance, Dyra," I say with a bow. "I have long loved the stories of the God of Love and am grateful for your visit."

A pleased smile spreads across Dyra's face and I can see the twinkle in her eye as she responds, "Hello dear Emory, I have been waiting my turn to meet you. Ryar had only wonderful things to say about the woman you have become. I am glad he was not mistaken. You are truly lovely." Her compliments make my cheeks flush with warmth, both from her words and the thought of Ryar speaking of me to other gods.

"I hope to live up to the example set by the woman who raised me. Thank you," I reply softly.

Dyra steps closer to me, leaving only inches between our bodies. "I am here to deliver a message, dear," she says softly. "Your party will depart tomorrow morning for the market. When you arrive, go straight to the cabin labeled 'Tailor'. Inside, you will find a man named Athius. Tell him Ava sent you. He will have ten horses prepared for your group, along with other necessities for your journey. And ensure that Ryat drinks the green potion - it will allow him to control which gift he takes from you at will." My gasp betrays my surprise; I had no idea such a thing was possible.

Before I can even voice my question, Dyra shakes her head and speaks quickly. "I cannot explain, for it would anger the fates. Just make sure Ryat drinks the potion, and only him. And know that Athius and his party will be moving into this camp, as part of the deal made for the horses. You cannot return here."

I nod, understanding the gravity of her words. "Thank you," I say sincerely.

Dyra's smile warms even more, her emotions radiating love and kindness. "Of course, my dear. Now I must go, but please know that we are watching over you and will do all we can to aid you on this journey."

I smile back as she disappears. Kalleli yips at me from her tree and I look over at her. "I know, sweet girl, let's go back to bed."

My eyes flutter open to the gentle sensation of Ryat's lips pressing soft kisses all over my face. I can't help but smile as I take in his handsome face, illuminated by the soft light seeping through the tent flaps.

I speak softly, still basking in the peaceful moment. "I took Kalleli out to use the restroom while you were sleeping and was visited by Dyra, the God of Love."

Ryat blinks as he sits up on the cot, stretching his long arms above his head. His tousled hair falls perfectly in place as he looks down at me and I sense curiosity in his emotions. "Did she tell you more information to help with our journey or the war?"

I nod, "yes. She told me who we have to see for the horses while at the market. She traded the camp for ten horses and other things she said we will need along our travels. Though she also said we cannot return here, that the horses and supplies will be more important."

I can feel some tension in him, most likely from someone else trading away a camp he worked so hard to build. "If that is what the gods deem necessary, then that is what will be. We will have to build a new camp after the war.

I do not mention that I may not be there to build the new camp, and neither does he. Though, I can feel the anxiety within him at the thought.

I get out of the cot and turn towards the outfits we had laid out last night for today's travels. I have a soft dress made of a stretchy gray material. It is plainer than the outfits Ryat prefers, having no frills or bows at all. I turn to see Ryat closing the flap behind him as he exits the tent, and then I remove his undershirt from my body. I step into my dress, pull the straps over my shoulders, and braid my hair. I finish the braid and put an elastic at the end, thankful Haven had some in her tent and that she was willing to give me one. Now completely dressed, I follow Ryat out of the tent with Kalleli behind me and walk to the table. We will eat at the market so I did not prepare breakfast today. This meeting is just to discuss today's plans.

I hear Ryat speaking as I approach and know that he is speaking of my visit, even though I missed part of his words. "-a deal to secure us horses and supplies." I see him look up at me and sit next to him with a quick smile around the table. He speaks up again. "Emory. Can you tell us all of what Dyra told you this morning?"

I nod. "Dyra told me that when we get to the market, we must go to the cabin labeled "Tailor" and find a man named Athius. She said he has ten horses and our supplies ready, but that we must tell him a woman named Ava sent us. To secure the deal, Dyra traded this camp and said that we cannot return. She also said that with the other prepared supplies, there will be a green potion that Ryat must drink and only Ryat. She said this will give him the ability to choose which gifts he cancels out with his touch instead of it canceling them all." I feel the shock pulse through the table.

Eira speaks, "how is that possible?"

I shake my head. "I do not know. She said if she told

me, it would only anger the fates."

I speak again, "she said that there were many gods watching over us and they would aid us as much as they could, but that is all I was told before she was gone."

Fenor grunts, saying, "Even the God of Love speaks in riddles and veils her words in mystery. I'm guessing we'll have a lot of unanswered questions during this trip to Eldevand and this war." He laughs, shanking his head to himself.

Ryat laughs from beside me, "that we will, brother. Now let's move out. We have horses to acquire."

CHAPTER

TWENTY-FOUR

As we walk through the dense woods, the sunlight filters through the leaves, casting dappled patterns on the forest floor. The air is rich with the scent of damp earth and wildflowers, and the sound of rustling leaves creates a soothing backdrop to our chatter. Kalleli darts ahead, her excitement palpable as she sniffs at everything in her path.

Ryat walks beside me, his hand intertwined with mine, and I feel a warmth radiating from him that makes me smile. The trees stand tall and proud around us, their trunks sturdy and covered in vibrant moss. I can hear the distant chatter of our party behind us, filled with laughter and lighthearted teasing, but as we venture deeper into the woods, the atmosphere shifts subtly.

A tension hangs in the air, prickling at the back of my neck. I glance at Ryat, whose expression has grown serious. "Do you feel that?" I murmur, anxiety creeping into my chest.

He nods, his jaw tightening. "Yeah. Stay close."

Suddenly, a deep growl reverberates through the trees, making the ground tremble beneath our feet. My heart races as I turn to see a massive black creature emerge from the underbrush. It stands easily over seven feet tall, its sleek body coiling like a shadow. Its head is a grotesque deer skeleton, and its hollow eye sockets glow a menacing red. Panic surges through me, and I instinctively take a step back.

"Get back!" Ryat shouts, his voice cutting through the shock. He pushes me toward Teirney and Eira, who stand ready, their expressions filled with determination and fear.

Kalleli, sensing the tension, races back to my side, her small body trembling. I scoop her up, clutching her against me as the creature lunges forward. Haven and Azrael shift into Wolfers, their forms large and powerful. The transformation is almost mesmerizing, and I can feel the air thrum with energy as they take defensive stances. Hellion steps forward, flames flickering to life in his hands, illuminating the area with a fierce light that contrasts against the creature's dark presence.

"Emory, stay with Teirney and Eira," Ryat insists, his grip on my hand tightening before he releases it.

I nod, fear knotting in my stomach as I watch him join the others. The creature lunges, its jaws snapping at Hellion, who sidesteps and unleashes a torrent of flames that lick at the beast's side. It howls, a bone-chilling sound that echoes through the trees, rattling my bones.

Arden stands back with a bow drawn, releasing an arrow that strikes the creature's shoulder. It barely flinches, its focus shifting toward Arden with a sinister growl.

"Watch out!" I shout, my heart pounding as I see the creature charge toward him.

Before I can move, Fenris steps in front of Arden, a soft yellow glow emanating from his hands as he prepares to heal any injuries. The air feels electric, and I can sense the tension building. Vor, Vulcan, and Fenor rush in with their swords drawn, their expressions fierce as they attack the creature from different angles, slashing at its flank.

Hellion continues to hurl flames, but they seem to have little effect on the creature's thick hide. It lunges again, this time at Haven, who is fast but not fast enough. The beast catches her side, and she lets out a pained growl, seeming to shift her focus to retaliate.

Eira stands beside me, her body tense and ready, though she doesn't summon her water gifts just yet.

I can see the determination in her emotions, a silent promise that she'll act if needed.

Just as I think the creature will overpower Arden, Ryat charges forward with fierce determination. He drives his sword deep into the creature's flank, and it lets out a deafening roar that reverberates through the trees.

In the chaos, Arden makes a swift decision. He shifts into a giant Tencan, his form massive and coiling, eyes glinting with purpose. With a hiss, he lunges at the creature, and sinks his long fangs into its thick hide to deliver his poison.

The beast stumbles back, momentarily dazed, and Haven takes her chance. She lunges, jaws snapping around the creature's neck, and with a powerful shake, she brings it down.

I hold my breath as it crashes to the ground, lifeless. The forest feels eerily quiet as the echoes of the battle fade, leaving us in a stunned silence. My heart pounds in my chest, and I clutch Kalleli tighter, feeling the warmth of her tiny body against my trembling hands.

"What was that thing?" I ask, my voice trembling as I step forward, taking in the unsettling sight of the creature sprawled before us.

Ryat approaches, his brow furrowed with concern as he glances between me and the fallen beast. "I don't know," he admits, shaking his head. "But we need to be careful. It's not something I've encountered before."

Nox groans, and I look to see him on the ground, a pained expression on his face. Fenris kneels beside him, hands glowing with a soft yellow light as he works to heal the injuries Nox sustained while fighting.

As the weight of what just happened settles over us, I cling to Ryat's side, grateful for his presence as we stand together, surveying the aftermath of the fight. The woods feel different now, the shadows deeper, the air thicker with an ominous tension.

Fenris had finished healing Haven and Nox and after everyone shifted back to their normal forms we had begun the silent walk once again. The rest of the hike to the market takes a little over two hours and as we approach the arch, the group splits into two. Half of us go for the horses, while the other half collects supplies for the next place we will camp on the way to Eldevand. Me, Ryat, Hellion, and Arden walk to the cabin labeled 'Tailor' and go inside through the front door.

When we get inside, I notice the cabin is mostly empty, aside from a few racks of clothing along the walls. The clothing adds a touch of color to the otherwise minimalist space. The only sound within the cabin is the steady rotation of a fan beside the door, blowing air around the large area. There is a subtle scent of freshly washed linens mingling with a hint of wood from the cabin's walls. There is only one man in the cabin, and Hellion steps in front of me to approach him.

"Hello, are you Athius?" He asks. The dark-haired man nods and Hellios continues, "Ava has sent me to get ten horses and other supplies from you."

"No, you weren't sent for anything." the man shakes his head as he looks from Hellion to the rest of us. HIs gaze settles on me and he points his long finger my way, "she was."

I startle. I had not known Dyra told him it would be me looking for the horses, though I now do not know what all she had told him to begin with. Does he know who I am? Does he know what he is doing by giving us these horses in the trade?

""You're right," I say, trying to inject steel into my shaky voice. "Ava sent me for the horses, and we are here to collect them. Where are they?"

Athius smiles, the fine lines of age creasing his face. "The horses are all set in the stables, ready for you to embark on your journey." He reaches down and lifts a brown leather bag off the floor, tossing it to Hellion. "These are the rest of your items. Now follow me. I will take you to your horses."

As we follow Athius out of the cabin, the sun bathes the market in a golden hue. I sense no ill will from him, only a steady calm and determination that puts me at ease.

The stables come into view—six large cabins

interlinked by sturdy gates and solid walls. Inside, twelve majestic horses stand, their coats a dazzling array of rich browns, creamy whites, pitch blacks, and shimmering speckles of gold. As we approach, the rhythmic beat of their hooves resonates through the air, accompanied by the sounds of their neighs and the gentle rustling of their large frames. The warm scent of hay and fresh earth wafts toward me, mingling with the soft breeze.

Athius approaches the first horse in the stable on the left side, reaching out to pet its long tan snout. "This is Lana. She is the horse Ava has appointed for Emory and Ryat. You have the freedom to choose the rest within your group, but she stated Lana must go to Emory, as she has a personal attachment to it." He gives me a quick smile before continuing. "I must be going now, but you will find everything in order for your departure. The last two horses on the right are not for your group, so please leave them."

I nod, offering him a small smile. "Thank you for the horses and the help." He smiles back but says nothing else before turning and walking away.

I turn my attention to the tan horse, Lana, her coat gleaming under the warm sunlight. As I approach her, I feel the soft breeze brushing against my skin, carrying the faint scent of hay and earth. With cautious anticipation, I extend my trembling hand toward her snout. In this moment of uncertainty, I sense Ryat's reassuring presence beside me.

"They are very gentle creatures," he says, his voice soothing and soft. "Very loving. I'm sure you will grow to love her as you have Kalleli."

Speaking of Kalleli, my heart aches a little. She went with Eira to avoid raising questions at the Tailor's cabin, but I'm not used to being away from her, and I find I don't prefer it. I lay my palm on Lana's soft nose, feeling the warmth radiate from her. As she exhales, a gentle puff of breath tickles my hand. "I think it's time to go. Do you think they got everything else we need?" I glance over at Ryat, who is watching my hand on Lana's nose, a small smile playing on his lips.

He looks up and meets my eyes, his expression thoughtful. "I'm sure they've had time. Let's go to the Pastry cabin and see if they are there yet."

We had agreed to meet at the Pastry cabin after we finished our tasks and grab a quick bite before leaving. Hopefully, they found everything, and we can get started on our journey. We only have ten days left to reach Eldevand and can't afford to waste any time.

Fortunately, after a brief walk to the Pastry cabin, I feel a wave of relief wash over me as we find the rest of our party already there, animatedly discussing their haul. The rich scent of baked goods fills the air, making my stomach rumble with anticipation. We waste no time placing our orders and quickly eat our breakfast, savoring the warm pastries before heading back to the stables to saddle up.

When we arrive, the energy is electric as everyone eagerly chooses their horses and prepares for the journey ahead. Yet, nerves churn in my stomach. Ryat, sensing my unease, pulls Lana from the stable and begins to guide me through mounting her.

He points to a leather loop hanging down her side from the saddle. "You will put your foot in this loop here," he instructs, his voice steady. "Then, put your hand on the saddle and throw your leg over to the other side. I will hold her steady and assist you with your positioning before I get on."

My gaze shifts from the loop to the saddle, then back to Ryat. Doubt fills me. "I'm not sure that's something I can do. That seems difficult."

Ryat chuckles softly, a sound that eases some of my tension. "Okay, princess. But next time, you mount the horse correctly." As I start to inquire about his comment, he swiftly lifts me up, and suddenly, I find myself sitting on the horse. It takes a moment to sink in.

I am actually on a horse. Oh, my gods.

Oh, my gods.

I am so high in the air; I feel like I could touch the clouds themselves if I wasn't too afraid to move my arms from where they are currently gripping the handle of the saddle.

Ryat gently places Kalleli in my lap, her warm body nestled against my legs. I observe in awe as he confidently steps into the worn loop; the leather creaking softly under his weight. The sound of his boots brushing against the saddle echoes in the air. With a quick and fluid motion, he swings his leg over to the other side, his body smoothly sliding into the saddle and pressing against me. I can feel the warmth of his chest as he settles into the saddle. My thoughts of how complicated it would be seem silly as I witness the ease with which he accomplishes this simple task.

I feel Ryat's hands find mine, gently pulling them from their death grip on the saddle. He lays them to rest on his hard thighs instead, leaning into me from behind. As he presses a kiss to the back of my head, a shiver runs down my spine, and I can't help but smile. He grabs the leather reins, and his voice carries over to the rest of our party. "Is everyone ready to go?"

The resounding chorus of agreement from everyone

meets my ears, and in that moment, I feel the gentle motion of the horse as it starts moving beneath me, causing me to draw in a shaky breath.

Lana's coat is a soft tan, shining like polished wood in the sunlight. I reach down to stroke her neck, marveling at how warm and inviting she feels beneath my fingers. The sensation of her soft fur is comforting, and I can't help but smile. It's as if she senses my excitement and nervousness, responding with a calmness that eases my racing heart.

As we make our way through the bustling market, I take a moment to glance at the cabins lining the path. Vibrant fabrics sway gently in the breeze outside the clothing shop, and the sweet aroma of baked goods wafts from the pastry shop, reminding me of our recent visit. My fingers graze the edge of the wooden arch as we pass underneath it, the rough texture grounding me in this moment. It's a simple gesture, but it connects me to the lively spirit of the market, a place filled with laughter and the scent of fresh produce.

Ryat shifts slightly behind me, his presence a steady

anchor. I can feel the warmth of his body pressed against my back, and it brings me a sense of security. It's comforting, knowing that he's here with me, guiding me through this experience. I steal a glance at him over my shoulder, and he offers me a reassuring smile, his eyes filled with warmth and encouragement.

As we pass the trees lining the path, their leaves rustle gently in the breeze, creating a soothing melody that accompanies our ride. Sunlight filters through the branches, casting playful shadows on the ground. I take a deep breath, inhaling the earthy scent of the forest mixed with the sweet smell of blooming flowers. It's invigorating, filling me with a sense of freedom I didn't know I craved.

But then, I remember that today's ride will stretch on for several hours. I wonder how I'll feel by the end of it—whether my legs will ache or if I'll find a rhythm with Lana that makes the time fly. It's both exciting and daunting, and I can't shake the flutter of nerves in my stomach. But for now, I push those worries aside and focus on the beauty surrounding me. The trees stand tall and proud, their bark rugged and ancient, whispering secrets of the past as we ride by.

I look back to Ryat, who seems to be in tune with the rhythm of the ride. "Isn't she beautiful?" I ask, my voice barely louder than a whisper, yet filled with awe.

He nods, a broad smile lighting up his face. "She's a true companion. You'll grow to love her even more as the days pass." He replies, his voice soft.

"I already do," I reply, my heart swelling with affection for this gentle creature beneath me.

CHAPTER

TWENTY FIVE

As I looked ahead, the woods seemed to go on forever; oak and autumn trees towering overhead. The fading light of the afternoon sun is casting narrow beams through the canopy above my head, and I can smell the heavy scent of earth and moss around us. The soft rustle of leaves, Kallelis soft purring from my lap and the steady rhythm of our horses' hooves on the path are the only sounds that break the silence.

I'm still sitting at the front of the saddle and my hands are back to resting on Ryats' thighs, but my attention keeps drifting past the path and into the woods. Every rustle in the underbrush, every shift in the wind, seemed to remind me of the threat of creatures lurking just out of sight. Haven had told us of the stories she heard from the travelers of the blights and new creatures that roamed these woods. The way the trees seemed to grow thinner only made my anxiety worse. A knot of worry settles in my stomach, and I can't shake the sense that something is watching us from inside the woods.

Ryat's arm wraps around my waist, his chest pressing firmly against my back. I sense the gentle rhythm of his breath, steady and calm, in contrast to my own restless and rapid ones. His warmth envelops me, as though his presence alone can keep me grounded.

"There isn't anything out there right now," Ryat murmurs against my ear, his voice low. "One of us would sense if someone or something was approaching."

His words are simple, but I can sense the truth in them. I let out a slow breath, leaning back into him, allowing his warmth to seep further into my body. His arms tighten around me. I marvel at how effortlessly he can ease my fears, even though he has only been with me for such a short time.

"I know," I softly reply, though the knot of worry remains lodged in my throat. "It's just... the woods feel different here. Like something is watching us."

Ryat's fingers trace lazy circles on my hip, his touch a gentle distraction. "It is different here," he said, the faintest hint of a smile in his voice. "But everything will be alright and we will make camp for the night soon."

I manage a small smile at his confidence. I glance over my shoulder, seeing the rest of our party trailing behind us. Everyone is riding at a respectful distance, their eyes scanning the woods with the same wariness I've been feeling. Despite our numbers, the woods seem to swallow the sound of our progress, leaving only the faint echo of hooves and the occasional snort of the horses.

Ahead, the path winds deeper into the woods; the

trees growing closer, their branches thick and twisted together, as though the land itself is closing in on us. I can't help but imagine what might be hiding in those shadows—creatures born of darkness and ancient magic, waiting for the perfect moment to strike.

Ryat must sense my growing tension because he leans closer once again, his lips brushing against the top of my ear. "Emory," he whispers, his voice a low rumble, "you're not alone in this. Whatever comes, we face it together."

I turn my head slightly, catching his gaze. His brown eyes are steady. "Together," I echo softly, my voice sounding more certain now.

The horse snorts beneath us, its ears flicking nervously as we enter a darker stretch of the woods. My heart quickens and my eyes scan the thick undergrowth for any sign of movement. Ryat's hand slips from my waist to meet his other hand on the reins.

"We're almost through the worst of it," he says, his voice calm, but I feel the subtle shift in his posture —

more alert, ready. Even as he reassures me, I know he is prepared for whatever might come. For a moment, I close my eyes, allowing myself to simply feel him. The warmth of his chest against my back, the steady rhythm of his breathing, the strength in the way he's holding me.

I try not to look into the woods for the rest of our ride and am mostly successful.

We stop right after nightfall and Ryat gets off of the horse. He reaches up and grabs me by the waist, pulling me and Kalleli off of her as well, before leading her to where everyone is tying their horses to the trees. Ryat, Arden, Hallion and Nox put together our makeshift tents. To ensure everyone's safety during the night, we will sleep in pairs or groups in the tents. While they do that, me and Fenor put together a quick dinner of Bundra and wild rice for dinner. Eira has set up a small bucket of water with rags for a quick wipe off before bed and the rest of the party is setting up logs next to the firepit Hellion started so we can be warm while we eat.

Though the days in Mygreen are quite warm, the

nights get a tad chilly and it will be nice to have the fire after such a long ride. It will also be very nice to sleep, as I am sore in places I was not aware could be sore from the ride.

The crackle of the fire fills the night, its warm glow casting flickering shadows on the party. The air is cool but not biting, the kind of chill that makes the heat of the flames even more comforting. Ryat sits by my side on a log, our sides touching and his hand tracing circles on my thigh. He had drunk the green potion earlier and I could feel my gifts stirring inside me, even as we touched. We had spoken little of the matebond, but I can feel the mark tugging at me as well. Having him near seems to be the only thing that soothes the bond, and I quite like these moments between us.

Our friends are sitting in a loose circle around the fire—Haven sits cross-legged, her sharp golden eyes reflecting the flames as she pokes at the embers with a stick. Hellion lounges back on his elbows, his red hair falling over his brow as he smirks at something Arden is saying. Arden lounges on the grass as well, propping himself up on his elbows while kicking up his long legs against a tree. The firelight dances, and creates a sense of security, as if the shadows beyond the circle are unable to reach us here.

My fingers idly trace the edge of my boot as I listen, though my mind keeps drifting back to Ryat. His quiet presence has a way of distracting me. He hasn't said much tonight, but I can feel the same quiet intensity that always radiates from him.

"So," Haven says suddenly, breaking the quiet sizzling of the fire. "Who wants to share their first shift story? I'll start."

I smile as Haven leans forward, her expression and emotions mischievous. She is always full of energy, and her stories never fail to entertain from what Arden has told me.

"The first time I shifted into a Wolfer," Haven begins, grinning, "I was five. Didn't even see it coming. One minute I was running through the woods, attempting to chase down a deer with my brothers, and the next

—bam!—fur everywhere. Ears, paws, the whole thing. Scared the life out of me."

Arden snickers. "Bet the deer had a heart attack."

"More like my brothers," Haven shoots back, laughing. "They were halfway up a tree before they realized the wolfer chasing them was me. They thought I was some rogue pack member in their first shift. Took them a solid five minutes to stop throwing stones at me." She shakes her head lightly, still smiling at the memory. "It was chaos. I couldn't control it yet, so I kept shifting back and forth. One minute I had paws, the next I was standing there naked in the middle of the woods, trying to figure out what the hell just happened."

Hellion chuckles, his deep voice rumbling. "Sounds about right. Shifting for the first time is always messy."

I glance at Ryat, catching the smile tugging at his lips. I turn back to Haven, who is grinning like she has just won the best-story award. Most gifted came into their shifts or abilities at about that age, so I wondered how common that type of awakening was.

"That's nothing," Hellion cuts in, sitting up straighter. "My parents were both Sand Elementals, so the first time I figured out I was a Fire Elemental, I almost burned down my family's cabin."

Nox lets out a snort. "This I've gotta hear."

Hellion's grin is wicked as he begins. "I was eight, thought I was just a late bloomer—no signs of gifts yet. But one day, I got pissed off at my brother. Can't even remember what it was about now. Some stupid shit, probably. But I was mad—really mad for an eight-year-old—and the next thing I know, my hands are on fire. Not just a little flicker, either. Full-on flames. I freaked out, tried to put it out by flinging my hands around, which, of course, just spread the fire everywhere. Caught the curtains, then the furs. My brother was screaming like a feral Yip, running around with a bucket, trying to throw water on everything. It didn't help. By the time my parents came in, the whole place was up in smoke."

"And your family?" I asked, raising an eyebrow. "They just… accepted it?"

"In due time," Hellion replies, shrugging. "After we rebuilt the cabin. Turns out we've got a long line of Fire Elementals on my mom's side, though they could've given me a little heads-up before I almost roasted us alive."

Laughter ripples around the fire, Ryat chuckling softly from beside me, his deep voice blending with the warmth of the moment. I catch his eye, and for a heartbeat, everything else fades. There is something in the way he looks at me. Something unspoken but undeniable. I can feel the bond between us stirring again, a quiet, persistent tug in my chest.

Arden clears his throat, breaking the moment between us. "Okay, okay," he says, sitting up and holding up his hands. "You think that was bad? Let me tell you about the first time I shifted into a Bundra."

Hellion raises an eyebrow. "Into a Bundra?"

Arden gives a swift nod. "That's right. I was just a child, around ten, and I was being chased by a Wolfe pack in the Northern Woods. I was racing through the woods, sidestepping trees, when suddenly I slam face first into one of the Wolfe shifters and realize I'm about two feet tall and covered in fur. Didn't even realize I'd stolen their gift or shifted until I looked down and saw my paws. It was... not my proudest moment."

Haven laughs. "And the rest of the pack?"

"Didn't see me at all," Arden says, grinning. "I was small, fast, and I knew those woods better than they did. They were too busy sniffing the ground, trying to figure out where I'd gone. I hopped under a bush and hid until they gave up. So, yes, I turned into a bunny, but it saved my life."

"The shifter gift we steal always switches to the form we need most," I tease, my smile widening. "There's something to be said for that."

Arden puffs out his chest, mock pride in his expression. "Exactly. Small but mighty, that's my motto."

More laughter spreads around the fire, and I feel the tension of the day slip away, replaced by the easy camaraderie of our group. The night is peaceful, the fire warm, and despite the dangers we would inevitably face, for now, we are safe.

I glance again at Ryat, feeling the quiet pull of our connection. The firelight dances in his brown eyes, softening the intensity that is always there. Not for the first time, I wonder what Ryat's first story might be— the moment he discovered his strength or the moment he realized he was destined for something more than the life he had been forced into.

But tonight isn't about the weight of the past. Tonight is about warmth, laughter, and the shared stories that bound us together. And for the first time in a long while, I let myself simply be present in the moment, savoring the quiet joy in the air.

Whatever waited for us beyond the firelight, we would face it together, just as we had done today. But for now, this is enough.

CHAPTER

TWENTY-SIX

I wake the next morning to the warmth of Ryats' lips, so familiar to me now, gliding across my chest. The touch of his lips against my skin sends a shiver down my spine. The soft fabric of my tank top brushes against my skin and my blood pulses in my veins, the steady beat of my heart echoing in my ears. Each kiss stirs the fire within me, spreading warmth and desire throughout my body. The sensation only grows as his lips trace the contours of my collarbone, leaving a tingling sensation in their place. He traces the swell of my breast with his nose before moving his lips back up, kissing my left shoulder. My breath catches in my throat as his lips move again, leaving a trail of kisses along my neck and chin. The soft touch of his lips, combined with the emotions flowing from him, fills me with an overwhelming sense of desire and longing.

Ryat smiles against my cheek, laughing lightly as he says, "I know you are awake."

A soft groan leaves my lips. "I did not want you to stop. I'm quite enjoying the kisses."

And I am, a lot.

Maybe too much if the heartbeat filling my entire body is any indicator.

Ryat shifts, the sleeping bag crinkling under me. "We need to be leaving or I would sit here all day, admiring you and tracing every inch of your skin with my lips."

I open my eyes, blinking against the gentle morning light filtering through the top of our tent. Ryat is now sitting, the soft fabric of the sleeping bag pooling around his waist. When he looks at me with a warm, sleepy smile, my heart skips a beat. There's something captivating about the way his eyes glimmer, reflecting the golden rays that dance across his features. In this quiet moment, I'm in awe of his rugged beauty, the kind that feels both fierce and tender all at once. The light accentuates the strong lines of his jaw and the slight stubble that dusts his chin, giving him an air of wildness that matches the woods outside.

"I suppose I will get dressed and go to feed the horses. Kalleli will want to take the time to sniff the entire camp again as well." I say with a light chuckle.

Ryat nods, smiling as well. "I'm going to help Hellion unassemble the tents. We should leave within the hour." He stands with this and closes the tent flap behind him as he leaves.

I lift my arms in a stretch, feeling a satisfying pop from my right shoulder—a reminder of the hard ground beneath me last night. Kalleli, still nestled beside me, stirs as well, letting out a soft yawn that melts into the morning air. She stretches her tiny paws in front of her, her fluffy fur catching the sunlight, then rolls onto her back, exposing her soft belly for a moment before bounding up with newfound energy.

I stand up, shaking off the remnants of sleep, and reach for the dress I've chosen for today. It is a soft pink color with silver bows over the breasts and ass again. Ryat picked this, and I am sure he will enjoy my displeasure at how tight the corset is. I step into it and fix the straps on my shoulders. After pulling on my boots, I take a moment to breathe in the crisp morning air, filled with the fresh scent of dew-kissed grass and the earthy aroma of the surrounding woods.

I step outside the tent, and the camp is slowly waking up, soft voices mingling with the sounds of rustling leaves and distant birds. I glance down to see Kalleli sniffing around with her tiny nose twitching, her long ears perked up in excitement as she explores the path towards the horses. We had carried oats instead of stopping to graze as many times throughout the day and, from what I could tell, the horses enjoyed it. I give them each their serving of oats, which Vulcan had calculated for me the day before. I had not known it was based on the horse's size and had I chosen the amount, they would have surely starved.

Like I said, bad at math if not given over a month to practice the problems.

The rhythmic sound of their chewing mixes with the gentle rustle of the oats. I feel a warm flutter of affection for these magnificent creatures, especially Lana, whose soft, tan coat gleams in the morning light, her gentle eyes watching me with an almost knowing gaze.

With the horses content, I lean back against the sturdy tree they're tied to, the rough bark grounding me in the moment. I take a deep breath, inhaling the rich, earthy scent mingled with the sweet aroma of fresh oats, and reach out to stroke Lana's soft fur. The warmth radiating from her body is soothing, and I feel a bond forming between us. I had grown more comfortable riding her yesterday, but the thought of mounting her again this morning makes my stomach flutter with uncertainty.

"What if I fall?" I whisper to Lana, half-joking. She nudges my hand with her velvety nose, as if reassuring me that she won't let that happen. I laugh softly, the sound mingling with the tranquil morning.

I see Fenor walking up and give him a soft smile, quickly saying, "Good Morning."

He smiles back before leaning on the tree next to me, his large body seeming to tower over me almost as tall as the tree itself. "Good Morning, little chef. I see you are still handling breakfast, even if not for the party members." He says this with a light chuckle, showing off his fangs.

I laugh. "Yes, it looks like I still am. Though I would say that they are appreciating it and are much more alert than the party ever was at breakfast."

He nods from beside me, "that is true." He looks down at me before saying, "I will saddle up the horses this morning. Would you like for me to pack you anything specific for the crossing into Ulopia? It will be hot there and our water stop is halfway through our journey."

I shake my head, "no, I will be fine. Thank you for

thinking of me and my comfort. Though, if you could pack a canteen for Kalleli, that would be lovely."

Fenor nods and straightens before walking to the horses and saddling them. I see him put two canteens into our pack and shake my head with a smile.

Ryat helps me get on the saddle this time and I do so with limited mistakes. Though he had kept me and the horse steady the entire time, Kalleli yipping at us from the ground. He hands her to me once again and I watch as he settles himself in the saddle behind me with the same grace as yesterday.

I wonder how long it will be before I can do the same.

The sun has just started to rise, painting the woods in a gentle, golden hue. A subtle fragrance of the dew on the trees creates a sweet smell in the air, blending with the delicate aroma of tiger blooms that grow by the trees. The horses are alert and everyone in the party is extra lively this morning as they chatter about the market we will be visiting in Ulopia today. Vor, a native of the area, says that the shops are filled with all sorts of things most people would have never seen before and I am excited by the idea.

I have seen so little, but for this to be a first experience for everyone else brings me a sense of relief. I am not the only one who is experiencing things for the first time along this journey. We are all doing this together and I quite like that.

We set a steady pace, alternating between walking and trotting the horses as we travel the winding path. Ryat has one hand on the reins, the other gently resting on Kalleli's back in my lap. She is lightly purring again, fast asleep, her warm body a comforting weight as we ride toward the territory line. I lean back against him, the rhythm of the horse beneath us creating a soothing motion.

But when we trot, I have to shift my body along with the horse's movement, and I find that I much prefer walking.

Trotting is hard.

As we cross the territory line and enter Ulopia, the

terrain shifts dramatically to a harsh landscape of stone and sand. I look around from atop the horse, noting how the sand stretches out as far as I can see. It's the first time I've ever seen sand, having known nothing but the dense woods around our village. The dark orange hue of the sand resembles the sun itself, and I can't help but wonder how hot it might be. I've heard tales that sand can burn your feet under the sun's heat, and the thought of testing that out sends a shiver down my spine.

I glance up at Ryat, catching his gaze. "Is the sand hot? I heard once that it was."

He nods, his expression serious. "Yes, it can be blistering in most parts of Ulopia. Sand is much nicer in other nations. In Promental, it is soft and lines the land by the oceans. That is where the wealthy build their homes and vacation."

Interesting. I knew they had oceans and sand, but I had never considered that the sand could differ so much from place to place.

Vor's voice carries from behind us, breaking my thoughts. "We will be approaching Halis, the city with the lake, soon. Be on alert."

A few miles later, we enter the city, and the air fills with the scents of dust and aged wood. The bustling sounds of gifted moving between cabins create a lively chaos. Some of the buildings appear to be homes, while others look to be shops, but time has clearly taken its toll. The structures creak and groan with each passing breeze, as if they are mourning years of neglect.

As we guide our horses toward the heart of the city, the sound of their hooves clattering against the cracked stone echoes in the air, a stark contrast to the vibrant life around us. But as I look toward where the lake should be, my heart sinks. Instead of water, I see nothing but a large, dry hole. "Is that where the lake was?" I ask, disbelief creeping into my voice.

I feel Ryat's body tense behind me, and he replies quietly, "Yes."

We lead the horses to a sturdy structure meant for

tying them up, and everyone dismounts. Ryat lifts me and Kalleli off again, seemingly deciding now is not the time to teach me how to dismount. He turns to the others, his expression serious. "There is no water here. The lake is dry. I'm sure this is one of the blights we have heard of, and we shall not linger. We will make our way to the main market within Kons, where we can find water and a place to sleep." He pauses, scanning the faces around him. "Does anyone have any issues with that plan or need anything before we continue?"

Everyone replies with a quick "no" or a shake of their heads, their focus shifting back to their horses as they saddle up for the next leg of our journey. I take a moment to absorb the reality of this place—a city once alive with the promise of water, now a ghost of its former self. A feeling of unease settles in my chest, but I push it down, reminding myself that we have a goal, and we must keep moving forward.

CHAPTER

TWENTY-SEVEN

By the time we are renting ten stable slots for the night, it is midday. The rest of the trek from the dried lake took us a few hours, even with the quick pace we had pushed. We had passed a few areas where the sand was almost black, the ground cracking under the horses hooves. Ryat did not remember this from his last travels within these lands so I am assuming this is yet another blight. I walk Lana to her slot and am happy to see that it backs up to a grassed area for her to do some grazing. We had paid the additional coins needed for them to provide two meals and water for all ten horses, but I was glad she would get fresh greenery as well.

Ryat links his fingers with mine as I pet Lanas' soft nose and tell her goodbye for the day. We had agreed that we would stay at an inn within the market tonight and I would not be seeing her until the morning. I turn to look at Ryat and give him a smile. "I'm happy that they will be able to rest and graze until morning. There's no doubt that they need it as much as we do."

Ryat smiles. "I'm sure they will appreciate it." He looks over at the rest of the party, now also done settling their horses into the stable slots. "Let's head into the market and see what wonders we can find inside." He says this with a teasing smile and I roll my eyes.

I am excited, practically vibrating with excitement, actually.

We walk through the stone arch, its rough texture brushing against my fingertips. As we step inside, the vibrant sounds of a musical group flood my ears from a stand to our left. They are singing of the gods, retelling stories passed down in the generations of their powers.

It is a lovely melody, though a tad off tune. This market is much busier than the last. Children dart through the crowd, their laughter ringing like bells, mingling with the joyous sounds of their game of tag. The shops are full of gifted, doors wide open and lines formed at some of the more popular shops.

I walk towards a shop labeled "mates", the excitement building in me even more while I think of the possibilities that may be inside. Ryat walks beside me, gently swinging our intertwined hands and humming along with the music, though I can feel the hope building in him as well.

Stepping into the small cabin feels like stepping into another world. My senses come alive; soft linens adorned with vibrant colors drape the walls like cascading waterfalls of fabric. In the center, a stand displays a dazzling array of rings, each one catching the light in its unique way. The cabin is filled with the delicate scent of lavender and lilies, mingling beautifully with the earthy aroma of the wooden walls, creating an atmosphere that feels both sacred and welcoming.

As I approach the stand with rings, Ryat pulls me into his side, his warmth radiating through the fabric of my dress. "Hello," he says, his voice smooth and inviting.

I glance to my left and see a dark-skinned man kneeling by a statue of Dyna at the back of the room. He looks up at us, smiling, his maroon robe swaying gently.

He bows his head, his voice low and gentle. "Hello. My name is Handi, and I am the Rabbi within this territory. What are you seeking?"

Ryat speaks again, his tone softer now. "We would like to be mate-bonded. Is that a ceremony you can perform?" I feel the hope and anxiety swirling within him, echoing in my own heart.

Please, if the gods are watching, let this man say yes.

Handi smiles as he rises from his position on the floor. "I can, and the gods told me to expect a ceremony within the next few days, so I have everything prepared."

A wave of relief washes over me, releasing the tension that had coiled tightly in my chest. Joy replaces it like sunlight breaking through clouds. "What do you need from us?" I ask, eager for the next steps.

He shakes his head, his expression warm and reassuring. "Nothing, dear. You two may enjoy a few hours with your companions and have a nice dinner. Meet me back here at dusk, and we will perform the ceremony. It is simple and will not take long, so you will have the opportunity afterwards to complete the bond."

Ryat pulls me with him as we exit the stand, my mind buzzing with Handi's words. "What does he mean by completing the bond?" I ask, curiosity piqued.

Ryat leans closer, whispering in my ear. "He means that after the ceremony, it is tradition for the couple to join each other in the flesh."

Heat rushes to my cheeks. "Oh, so we will have... sex after the ceremony?" The words stumble out, and my nerves start to rise at the thought.

He pulls me closer, pressing a gentle kiss to my forehead. "It's the tradition, but you'll never have to do anything you're not ready for, Emory. If you're not ready tonight, we will wait until you are."

I nod, though I can feel the now familiar heat growing in both me and him at the idea. My bond tugs at me and I know that I will be ready tonight. I have only ever wanted to be close to Ryat and this is as close as two gifted, two mated, could get. I steel myself in the decision.

Ryat leads us towards where I can see the rest of our group is huddled. I look at the sign and see that it is the inn we will be staying at tonight and I wonder what it will be like. I've never stayed in one, obviously, so the thoughts of what an inn could look like are circling my mind.

"Hey!" I hear Teirney call out, "there you two are! We had begun to wonder if Emory had found another Yip or something for you to be missing for so long!"

I laugh, scratching Kallalis' ear from her spot in

my arm. "No, but we found a Rabbi and have a Mate Bonding Ceremony scheduled for tonight!" I say, my voice full of excitement and Ryat chuckling from beside me.

Ryat is pulled from me as the males of the group give him their weird hugs and congratulations. Eira runs to me, pulling me and Kalleli into her small embrace as she squeals and Teirney joins the hug from beside me. "I am so happy for you two. I hope to one day find my mate, though I will surely be nowhere as lucky as my brother was when finding you." She says, a smile in her voice and joy flowing from her in waves.

When they release me, I accept a hug from Haven and Fenor, along with a soft smile and nod from Vulcan. My joy is palpable in the air and I can feel it flowing into me from each of the people I have begun to call friends.

Arden pulls me into him, hugging me tightly. I rest my head on his solid chest and soak in his feeling of love and hope. He squeezes me lightly, chuckling, "and you were nervous to join a party. Tomorrow, you will become a full Mated woman, and I am so happy for you," he says, squeezing me lightly and chuckling.

I feel tears well in my eyes as I think of how much we have survived together, alone. Of how much he did and gave up in life to make sure I got to this point. "I love you, Arden, more than anything. I would have nothing at all without you."

As he pats my hair and ruffles it, just as he has since we were young, he says, "You were my gift Emory, I would do nothing differently just for the chance to see this type of joy on your face and to see you be cherished the way you deserve."

We rented our rooms for the night and the males ran our bags upstairs before we set off for dinner. As I sat with my mate, my brother, my yip and our friends, I smiled. I do not know how much time I will get with them, but the time I have is being spent well. I listen as Teirney jokes and Hellion argues, knowing that I would never change a single thing, not even knowing I may die after the experience.

CHAPTER

TWENTY-EIGHT

The light is soft as dusk settles over the small cabin, casting long shadows across the floorboards. The air inside is warm and the scent of lilies and lavender is wafting from the garland hanging around the room. When we entered, it felt as if I had walked into a dream, the fading sunlight giving way to the flicker of candlelight, and the air heavy with anticipation and magic. This is where we will be bound, not just in body, but in spirit—forever.

I'm standing by the wooden table at the center of the cabin, my hands trembling slightly as I run my fingers over the soft blue linens laid out before me. The fabric feels cool under my touch, almost alive with an unknown energy. The linens, woven with threads blessed by the Fates, would soon bind me and Ryat together, a physical symbol of the eternal bond we were about to form.

The rabbi stands behind me, his emotions a wave of calm and affection. The Fates themselves have blessed him, choosing him to perform ceremonies like this one. His robes flow around him, the silver embroidery shining in the flickering light of the candles around the room. He nods softly at me, signaling that it's time to start.

My breath catches in my throat as I look over, my gaze finding Ryat. He's across the table, his presence filling the space with a quiet strength. His brown eyes focus on me, filled with warmth and something else.

Something unspoken but something I understand all the same.

He steps toward me, and the world outside seems to

disappear, leaving only the two of us. "Are you ready?" he asks quietly, his voice steady and sure, though his eyes search mine in question.

I smile, even though my heart is racing and my hands are trembling slightly at my sides. "I've never been more ready for anything."

"Tonight," The rabbi says, gently but firmly, "we gather under the watch of the Fates and the Gods, to witness the binding of two souls who were always meant to find each other," he says as he steps forward, and holds out the long, blue linen between his hands.

I feel my heart swell at the words. The Fates had already written this moment long before either Ryat or I knew it. I glance at the linen, feeling its significance deep in my bones.

Ryat takes my hands in his, and the warmth of his touch sends a shiver through me. His grip is firm, and it grounds me, as if a reminder that no matter what comes after this, he would always be there with me. Together, we place our hands on the blue linen, and the rabbi

---

begins to slowly wrap it around our hands.

"With this knot," the rabbi says, tying the linen around our wrists in a careful loop, "you are bound. Through peace and times of war, in light and darkness, your souls are tied to one another. Nothing in this life or beyond can undo the bond formed tonight."

As he secures the knot around our hands, I feel a pulse of energy rush through my mate mark. I look up into Ryat's eyes and see the same wonder that I'm feeling reflected there. Feel it in the light pulse of awe circling the room as well. It's as if, at this moment, we aren't just two people standing in a small cabin. We are something greater, part of something ancient and eternal.

The rabbi takes a step back, the sound of his footsteps echoing softly in the room. He extends his hand, presenting a small box. As he opens it, a glimmer of silver catches the light, revealing two rings. As I look at them, I see that they are simple but beautiful, made of silver and engraved with the symbols of the gods. One for each of us. Ryat releases my hand just long enough to take my ring from the box, sliding it gently onto my finger, his touch lingering on my skin and leaving a light tingle in their wake.

"With this ring," he says softly, "I give you all that I am, all that I ever will be."

I feel my breath hitch, and I take his ring from the box, my fingers shaking slightly as I slip it onto his hand.

"With this ring," I whisper, "I give you all of me, in this life and all that come after."

For a moment, everything is still. The candlelight flickers, shadows dancing along the walls, and the scent of lilies and lavender seem to grow stronger, filling the cabin with warmth and a wave of peace. The world outside seems distant, like all that exists is this bond, this promise.

The rabbi smiles gently from between us, raising his hands in the air. "The Fates have witnessed your union, the Gods have seen your vows. You are now, in all ways, bound."

We stand here, our hands still tied together with the blue linen, our hearts seeming to beat in perfect rhythm. We both look up at the rabbi, and together, in one voice, we speak words of thanks in voices that do not sound like our own.

"Thank you to the Gods, to the Fates, for guiding us here."

As we speak, the last knot in the linen seems to tighten, and a soft glow surrounds us, as though the cabin itself is responding to the bond we have formed. I can feel it—the warmth of it, the rightness of it.

This is what I had been searching for, what I had been waiting for.

Though I had not known it until this moment.

With the ceremony now complete, I exhale and hear Ryat do the same, the tension of the moment giving way to something softer, something that feels like peace. We untie the linen from our wrists, but the bond remains, a thin gold line now in the middle of our black ones.

Ryat leans down, pressing a soft kiss to my forehead. "We're fully mated now,' he murmurs, his voice low and soft. "I will be with you always, in this life and the next."

The walk to the inn is short and quiet, both of us lost in thoughts of the ceremony and the path that lies ahead. With each step, my certainty grows; the bond we've formed feels like a gentle flame, warming me from the inside out. Still, I can't shake the flutter of nerves that dances in my chest—the kind that seems normal for the first time someone has sex, no matter how much I want this.

When we finally reach the inn, Ryat checks the room to ensure no one else has slipped in before us. I take a moment to absorb the ambiance of the place. The soft crackle of a fire casts a golden glow that dances across the stone walls, creating an intimate atmosphere. I step over to the window, looking out at the stables below, the world outside humming with life. My fingers graze the black and gold bands on my arm—symbols of our matebond, still warm from the ceremony, a reminder of the promise we've made.

Ryat approaches me slowly, his presence a calming force. I can sense the mix of awe and heat radiating from him, a palpable energy that makes my heart race. He's tall and broad, embodying a quiet strength that has always made me feel safe. His hand brushes my arm, his touch both gentle and reverent, as he guides me away from the window and toward the bed. He gazes into my eyes, deep and steady.

Always so steady.

Always so consistent.

"Emory," he murmurs, his voice low, "we don't have to rush. I want you to feel ready."

I feel my heart swell at his words, at the tenderness lying beneath his gruff exterior. I have never doubted his feelings for me, but the vulnerability of the moment makes me feel exposed in ways I hadn't been expecting.

I take a deep breath and give him a quick nod. "I want this, I am ready."

He guides me onto the soft cot, his movements slow

and deliberate. The air between us is humming with electricity and heat, our bond now something tangible, pulsing between us. Ryat's hands are warm and patient as he pulls the straps of my dress down and removes my dress completely. His fingers linger over the soft fabric as it slips from my body. I feel my breath hitch, a flicker of nerves tightening my chest, but Ryat's gaze is soft, almost worshipful as he looks down at me. He leans down, pressing a kiss to my collarbone, and I melt under him. His kiss, like a gentle brushstroke, stirs a fire within me, spreading warmth and desire throughout my entire being. His lips follow the curve of my shoulder, and when he finally looks up at me, I see nothing but adoration in his honey brown eyes.

"You're so beautiful," he whispers against my skin, his voice rough with the warm emotions I feel flowing out of him.

He takes his time, exploring every inch of me with his mouth, his hands, as if committing me to memory. Each touch sends a shiver through me, the slow-burning heat building fiercely in my core. I can feel his restraint, the way he seems to be holding back, allowing me to set the pace. His control is palpable, a silent promise to go as slow as I need.

My fingers tremble as I reach for him, feeling the heat of his skin under my palms as I tug at his shirt. Ryat lets out a soft groan as my hands trace the hard planes of his chest, his muscles rippling under my touch. When our bodies finally press together, skin to skin, I feel our mate mark pulse, deeper, more profound, connecting us in ways words never could.

He hovers over me, his breath hot against my lips. "Are you sure?" he asks softly, his voice barely more than a whisper. "I'll stop if you're not ready."

"I want this," I repeat, my fingers curling into the back of his neck, trying to pull him down into a kiss. "I want you."

Ryat kisses me deeply, slowly, as though he is savoring the moment. He moves with care, his touch gentle as he positions himself above me. I can hear his ragged breath, mixed with the sound of our bodies shifting against the sheets. But his hands are steady, and when he finally enters me, I can tell he is being as tender as the movement will allow. But still, I gasp, my body tensing at the unfamiliar sensation.

Ryat stills, his forehead resting against my own. "Tell me if it's too much," he murmurs, his voice seeming to be strained with the effort of holding back.

I shake my head, my body adjusting to the feel of him. Slowly, he begins to move, each thrust controlled, deliberate, as though he is afraid he might break me. The pain fades into a new kind of pleasure, and I find myself arching into him, my legs wrapping around his waist.

I find myself wanting him to stop holding back, to take me however he wishes to do so.

Our bodies move together in a steady rhythm, the connection between us seeming to grow deeper with every heartbeat we share. Ryat's hand tangles in my long hair, pulling just enough to send a jolt of heat through my body. He growls softly, his breath hot against my ear, and the sound sends a thrill down my spine. I feel tension coiling low in my belly, a tingling sensation that spreads throughout my body and I feel myself tightening around him as the pleasure builds to be overwhelming.

"Emory..." Ryat's voice is rough, almost desperate, as he thrusts harder, deeper, his control finally slipping.

Thank the gods.

His hand tightens in my hair as he buries his face in my neck, his body shuddering against my own.

I feel the tension that had built up start to release and let out a soft cry, my body pulsing around him as the pleasure sweeps through me.

It feels like a million waves crashing against the shore.

It feels as though I have finally learned what true pleasure is.

Ryat follows moments later, his body trembling as he roars out my name, our bond mark glowing bright gold on our arms.

He holds me close as I attempt to catch my breath, his arms wrapped tightly around me, his hand still buried in my hair. His breath is just as ragged as my own, his heart pounding against my chest, but when he finally pulls back to look at me, there is nothing but love and awe in his eyes.

"I'll spend the rest of my life loving you," he whispers, pressing a soft kiss to my forehead.

I smile, my heart full. "And I'll spend mine loving you."

CHAPTER

TWENTY-NINE

The steam of the shower rises in gentle, misty tendrils, caressing my skin as the water cascades down. The shower's warmth envelopes me, but it isn't just the heat of the water that has me feeling so safe. That is mostly due to the steady presence of Ryat behind me, his arms loosely wrapped around my waist, his chest pressed against my back. I let out a slow breath, leaning further into him, trying to hold on to this rare moment of peace before the world demands our time again. We don't have long before we need to leave.

I know that.

But here, in the privacy of the shower, with the water rushing around us and Ryat's hands resting on me, I don't really want to think about anything beyond this moment. It is just the two of us and the bond we share humming quietly, a constant reminder of the connection we have formed.

"We don't have much time," I whisper, though my hands didn't move from his, I don't think I'm willing to move just yet.

"I know," Ryat's voice rumbles in my ear, a low, comforting sound that sends warmth through me. "But we've got a little longer."

I can hear the tension in his voice, the subtle undercurrent of something more—something heavy. He kisses the side of my neck, lingering as his hands trace slow, tender circles on my hips. I close my eyes, melting into the feel of him, into the quiet intimacy of the moment. How quickly I have now gotten used to being nude around him.

"I used to dream about this," Ryat says softly, his voice distant, like he's speaking more to himself than to me.

I open my eyes, shifting in his arms so I can see his face. His expression is thoughtful, shadowed, as if he is somewhere far away. I feel a twinge of pain in my very soul from the pain wafting out of him.

"What did you dream of?" I ask, keeping my voice low and gentle while lacing my fingers through his.

His eyes darken, a flicker of pain crossing his face and filling the air. He blinks, looking away, his gaze fixing on the water trickling over our feet. "Freedom. Warmth. Anything that wasn't cold." I still, my heart aching for him. He had told me of his past, but he had not spoken of it again afterwards. I can hear the roughness in his voice, can feel the hollow agony in his emotions.

"Back in Arrakis," he continues, his voice low, "when I was a labor boy. They worked me to the bone for all nine years, and I was one of the lucky children."

My breath catches in my chest, my mind spinning with the image of a young Ryat—just a boy, forced into a life of slavery and cold. The thought of him, alone in that harsh land, is almost too much to bear. I can't begin to imagine what he had gone through, the coldness of not just the land but the world that had treated him like something less than human. My father had told me stories and I would not wish the recallings on anyone.

"They barely fed us. Barely kept us alive," Ryat goes on, his voice quiet, but I can hear the sharp edge of memory in every word. "The nights were the worst. It wasn't the labor, or the hunger... It was the cold. It would seep into your bones. Sometimes, I thought I'd never feel warm again."

I turn my body fully in his arms, laying my hand on his chest as I look up at him, my heart breaking for the boy he had been, for the man he had become. "Ryat..."

His eyes meet mine, and I can see the vulnerability. I can see that he still carries the weight of those years, even now.

But there is something else too, something gentler.

"I used to dream of warmth," he whispers, his hand coming up to cup my face, his thumb brushing lightly over my cheek. "And I found it. I found it when I found you."

I feel a tear slip down my cheek at his words, and I lean into his touch, my heart full and aching at the same time. I turn my head to press a kiss to his palm, my fingers clutching his hand tightly, as if I could possibly protect him from all the hurt he had known.

"I know that cold," I whisper, my voice scratchy and weak. "I felt it, too... in my cell in the Null Grounds. I never knew what real cold was until they locked me away in that small room." The memory still haunted me. Those days spent trapped in the freezing, lifeless air of the four black walls, when I had thought I might never feel warmth again. Ryat's hand moves to the back of my neck, and he pulls me closer to his body, as if trying to shield me from the memory.

I shake my head gently, needing to say it. "I thought

I'd never feel warm again. I thought that cold would follow me for the rest of my life." I press my hand to his chest, feeling the steady beat of his heart beneath my palm. "But then I found you. And for the first time since that cell, I felt warm again."

His eyes soften as he looks down at me, the pain of the past still there, but now there was something else— an understanding that came from shared experiences, from knowing what it was to face the cold, the darkness, and come out the other side. "You'll never be cold again," Ryat whispers, his voice fierce and tender all at once. "Not while I'm with you."

"And neither will you," I echo, my voice steady. "I'll make sure of it."

We stand under the water of the shower for a long moment, holding each other, the warmth surrounding us. Soaking up every last bit of this time together.

I feel Ryat's lips brush against my forehead as he speaks softly. "We should go."

I sigh, reluctantly pulling back just enough to meet

his gaze. "I know."

But as we stepped out of the shower, hand in hand, I felt the warmth of him lingering on my skin, a reminder that no matter what waited for us outside, we would face it together.

CHAPTER THIRTY

Me and Ryat walk hand in hand to the diner. We had spent the early morning hours with each other while the rest of the party shopped. Kalleli is trotting behind us, her short legs working overtime to keep up, but she did not want to be held this morning so I leave her to her quick pace. She is around fifteen pounds now, close to what I believe is full size, and I am still bewildered by how fast she has grown. It has only been a short time since I got her and she seems to grow more each day.

We walk into the cozy diner cabin and as I pick up Kalleli I smell the scent of syrup, breakfast meats and freshly brewed tea in the air. It's a delightful mix of scents and I feel a smile forming on my face. I have always loved breakfast and I am really growing to love diners as well. As we make our way further inside, I hear our party moments before I see them, the sound of Hellion and Nox arguing about something rising above the noise from the other gifted within the space. As I glanced at the back row of tables, I noticed that our group had taken over the entire area, with each member sitting in a different spot than we normally would. Eira sits with Vor, head resting on his shoulder as she always seems to do to one of them. Haven and Azrael are sitting across from Arden and they all have big goofy grins on their faces, their laughter filling the surrounding space. Vulcan has sat with Fenor and Fenris, likely due to their shared preference for silence. My gaze shifts to Teirney, who is watching us approach from her seat. Although she attempts to smile, I can feel in her emotions as we get closer that she is worried about something.

I smile at Teirney as I settle into one of the empty seats across from her and next to Fenor. A gentle hum of conversation and the soft clinking of silverware fill the room. I set Kalleli down on my lap, feeling the warmth

of her tiny body against mine. "Good morning, Teirney,"
I say, my voice carrying my excitement. "Did you sleep
well?"

She smiles softly, "yes, I did. Though Haven got news
of a friend this morning and she'd like to find her as we
travel. She has been searching for her for a long time,
since they were children. She's an Orange Silken shifter,
which is not very common, so it was quite lucky that
she would catch word of her so close." I can feel the
worry and hope coming from her.

My smile widens. "That's wonderful!" I exclaim. "Is
her friend on our path? We can certainly make a stop for
her."

I feel Ryat shift in the seat beside me. "As long as it
doesn't affect our timeframe," Ryat interjects, his voice
steady, "I don't see any issue in finding her friend."

Teirney's face brightens, and I sense her worry
dissipating into the bustling energy of the room. "She
was told that she was seen in her Silken form not far off
of our path."

Haven, who must have overheard our conversation, gazes over at us. "I was hoping we could just go a bit farther than we originally planned and camp where she was seen so I can try to find her. It will not take long since we had been so close as children. Her scent should stick out to me." The joy and hope coming from her are infectious, and I feel it soaking into me as well.

"I think that's a great idea." I say, feeling the excitement in the air.

Vulcan, Nox and Fenris leave as the rest of us are finishing our breakfast, going to get the horses ready to leave. Ryat discussed the path with Haven and they made a plan. So that has all been settled, and the table has grown much calmer than it was when we came into the diner. We are traveling into Frontasia today, the Land of the Divine. I am not sure what the terrain is like there, having heard little of the lands in my books or even from my father.

I look over to Ryat. "What is it like in Frontasia?" I ask.

GODS BLESSED

He smiles at me, his brown eyes soft and full of love. "It is beautiful. The lands are full of greenery and flowers. They have trees but no true wooded areas like Mygreen. Everything there grows in brighter shades of the colors you're used to seeing, so it can take some adjustment at first. But the weather will be roughly the same as Mygreens was." I can feel the calm peace flowing from him as he tells me this, see the respect he has for the lands in his eyes.

I smile, "it sounds lovely. I'm sure the horses will love the greenery when we stop for their grazing breaks and to use the restroom."

He nods at me, eyes seeming to twinkle in laughter at how much I care for the horses already.

After leaving the diner and getting saddled up on the horses, we had begun our travels to Frontasia. The ride was longer than we originally planned, so we could not take the horses as fast as we had the day prior. We moved at a pace slightly below a trot and stopped to let the horses graze, and use the restroom, around six hours in. We had let them graze, gave them water and chatted about the shops from the market for about an hour before we had continued on our trek. We did not speak of the trees we passed that were shriveled up and dying or the animals that seemed to be withering away. We all knew what it was from, and it only made our journey more important.

Ryat let Haven and Azrael take the lead around twenty minutes ago, as she knew the sights to watch for along the way. We had been riding now, not including our stop, for over ten hours, and my butt was quite sore. I watched as she raised her hand in the air and slowed her horse from in front of us, calling out, "we're here. This is where I was told we should make camp, by the crumbing statue of the Gods next to a pink willow tree."

And the tree is indeed pink, standing tall, its bark a vibrant hot pink. Delicate flowers in various shades of pale blush pink adorned its branches, their scent gently perfuming the air. Dark pink thorns encircled the tree's base, adding a hint of danger to its beauty. Next to the tree, a single dark marble statue stood, contrasting with the tree's vibrant hue. Carved with intricate details, the statue depicted the gods, though they had a covering over their faces to hide their features from the world. Nobody knew what the gods looked like, and if you did, you did not speak of it.

Ryat helps me and Kalleli off of Lana before going and tying her up to the tree with the rest of the horses. We had decided that when we got here, Ryat and Arden would build the tents. Hellion was building the firepit, Eira the bathing station, and I was preparing dinner. We had eaten a brief meal while the horses grazed, but this dinner couldn't come fast enough. Fenor had said he wished to help Haven and Azrael hunt for her friend, Waylo, as he had also once known an Orange Silken and would like to make sure it wasn't the girl he had once known.

We all set about doing our tasks and as I hover over the simmering pot, the aroma of savory broth fills the air. I hear someone walk up beside me and I look over to give Vulcan a smile, nodding hello.

He nods back and motions to the carrots I had

planned to chop next. I assume he is asking if I would like help, so I give him a quick nod and reach down to get him a cutting board and knife from my bags. Handing them to him, a small smile graces his lips as he begins to dice the carrots, each slice falling with a soft thud against the wooden board. The size of the cubes is slightly smaller than I would have preferred, but I choose to appreciate his silent companionship rather than say anything.

When I finish cutting the meat into cubes, I throw them into the broth and turn to Vulcan. "When you have them all chopped, you can put them all into the pot, and then crab the potatoes. They are larger than the ones I usually use, so you can cut them into fours."

He nods at me before continuing his chopping, and I smile. I wonder if cooking takes his mind off of things he'd rather not remember as well.

I start to cut up a few of the vibrantly colored peppers for some spice and see Vulcan put the carrots in the pot. He grabs the potatoes and starts to cut them as I said. I continue cutting the peppers and then move onto the bright red tomatoes. I cube them and then smoosh them a bit with my spoon to bring out the juices before turning to put them and the peppers into the pot. The vibrant colors of the different ingredients are beautiful, and the scent is lovely as it simmers on the fire Hellion had started for me.

Vulcan walks up with his potatoes, dumping them into the mixture, and looks up at me expectantly.

I smile. "That's it for dinner. Would you like to learn how I make rolls and desserts?"

He smiles, much wider than I've ever seen him do before, and in a harsh voice says, "yes, please."

Me and Vulcan carry the rolls and a tray of pastries to the firepit everyone has gathered around once they're all finished cooking, and Arden carries the pot of stew since his hands will not burn from the heat. I take a seat next to Ryat on a log as Arden starts to hand out bows and lean my head onto his shoulder. I feel a pulse in my mate bond at the contact and smile. Haven, Azrael, and Fenor have not returned yet, but everyone else is sitting around the fire. Vulcan has taken a seat next to Fenris, and it seems Eira has given up keeping him from her books, if the one in his hand is any indication.

She had given me one as well, and I had started it on the ride today. It was... Not what I was used to reading. The princess in the book was more worried about her love life than her kingdom and had a growing attraction for a prince in the warring realm. That just spelled disaster if you asked me, but I was enjoying the banter between them, nonetheless. It seemed the rules of contact were different in this book's world as well, because she had even kissed this male. At their first meeting!

I shake my head at the thought. In these lands, that comes with the consequence of being labeled as a ninny. This came with a complete ban on marriage or any form of attachment to a male. And you did not want to be an unwed woman within Alblasia. It is a very difficult place to survive without your family having a male vote in society.

The fire crackles softly, casting a warm glow on

everyone's faces as we sit in a loose circle around it. The night air is cool, but the heat from the flames keep the chill at bay. Kalleli is asleep in my lap, her small body nestled against me, her breaths soft and even. I absently run my fingers through her hair, the repetitive motion calming me. This is one of those rare moments of stillness that I cherish—the calm before whatever chaos awaits us tomorrow.

Ryats shoulder brushes against mine, his warmth seeping into me. I lean into him slightly, appreciating the comfort of his presence without him needing to say anything. Across from us, Teirney leans back on her hands, looking entirely relaxed as she laughs at Hellion's latest story. His eyes sparkle with mischief, the firelight reflecting in his gaze as he recounts some wild dream he's had.

"I swear to the gods, I didn't even know it was a dream at first," Hellion says, his voice animated. "One minute, I'm practicing fire control—just your basic flames, nothing crazy—and then out of nowhere, I'm surrounded by Wolfers. But not just any Wolfers.

Flaming ones. And they're all staring at me like I'm their pack leader."

I can't help but laugh, trying not to disturb Kalleli. "Flaming Wolfers?" I ask, shaking my head. "Only you could dream about being chased by a pack of Wolfers on fire."

Hellion shrugs, grinning. "Well, at first they were chasing me. But then they just… stopped, and I realized they were waiting for me to lead them. And that's when I knew it had to be a dream. Even I'm not that cocky."

Nox, sitting a bit off to the side with a full bowl of food (as usual), snorts. "I don't know, Hellion. Sounds pretty believable to me."

We all laugh, and Hellion throws a piece of kindling in Nox's direction. "At least my dreams don't involve eating the flaming Wolfers."

Ha. Nox does really love to eat.

Vor leans forward, resting his elbows on his knees. "I once had a dream where I was a dragon," he says, his voice deep. "But not just any dragon. I could shift into one, like a regular shifter, but the transformation was slow, like every scale took its time to grow." He looks up at us, a bit of wonder in his emotions. "It felt... powerful. Like I was becoming something ancient."

Eira, sitting next to him with her head leaned on his shoulder, rolls her eyes with a smile. "Vor, you are practically ancient."

"That's not the same thing," he says, chuckling, but I can see the glint of something wistful in his eyes. I wonder if part of him wished that dream had been real.

It would have been a much easier life as a shifter than a warrior, I'm sure.

Teirney pipes up, clearly amused. "Speaking of shifting, I had a dream last night where you, Emory, turned into a phoenix. You know, full-on flaming wings and everything." She gestures dramatically with her hands as if mimicking the wings. "You soared above us, all majestic, and then you just casually dropped Arden into a lake because he wouldn't stop talking."

I laugh softly, still trying not to wake Kalleli as my body shakes. "Honestly, that sounds like something I'd do."

Arden, who has been unusually quiet tonight, chimes in. "I once dreamt I was being chased by a Wolfer pack. But when they finally caught up to me, I shifted into a Bundra." He pauses, looking around at us. "And that's how I escaped."

The group erupts into laughter, and I can see Ryat shaking his head, smiling at Arden's joke.

"You only wish it had been a dream, bunny boy," Hellion says, his deep voice full of amusement.

Arden shrugs. "Hey, worth a try."

I smile. It's these moments that remind me of what we're fighting for—these people, this sense of belonging, of safety, even when everything around us is so uncertain. I glance down at Kalleli, her face peaceful as she sleeps in my lap, and I know that as long as we have nights like this, I can face whatever fate I was destined to have.

From the corner of my eye, I catch Ryat looking at me, a soft expression on his face. I lean my head against his shoulder again, taking in the moment, letting myself feel the weight of his presence.

"Any dreams you want to share?" He asks, his voice low as he glances down at me, a teasing glint in his eyes.

I smile, thinking about the strange dreams I'd had —about gods and creatures, battles and bonds—but I decide to keep those to myself. "Not tonight," I whisper, leaning into him a little more. "Tonight, I just want to listen."

And with that, I let their voices wash over me, feeling the warmth of the fire, the closeness of Ryat, and the soft weight of Kalleli against me.

CHAPTER

THIRTY-ONE

Haven, Azrael and Fenor get back to camp the next morning right after dusk. I see them walking towards me as I'm making breakfast, Vulcan beside me cutting up apples, and notice the copper orange Silken in Fenor's arms.

Why is she still in her shifted form and not her normal form? And why is Fenor holding her?

Haven and Azrael turn off, walking towards Ryat and Hellion, who are putting out the fire, but Fenor stays on course to me and Vulcan. As he gets closer, I see the Silkens' coat is a unique shade that matches his exactly, down to the markings in the strawberry blonde of his highlights from the sun. "Good morning, Fenor. I see you managed to find her! Is she Haven's friend or the girl you knew when you were a child?" I ask.

I don't know why I even ask, I already know the answer.

She has his eyes.

One green, one brown. Both striking, even in her shifted form.

This must be his sister, though he had not told us that was why he wanted to join their search.

He smiles, "this is Raya, my younger sister. She has been missing since I was nine. I caught her scent while we were tracking and knew that she was the Orange Silken we had heard of in the area. I'm afraid Haven was quite sad her friend is still missing, but I know my parents will be ecstatic when they learn that I have found her after all this time."

I smile at him and look back down at the Silken in

his hands. "Why hasn't she shifted back into her normal form?" I ask.

He shakes his head as he looks down at her. "I do not know, and she can't tell anyone from this form so we will just have to travel with her as a Silken until she transitions back or we find a way to help her do so."

Interesting. I sense the same confusion wafting from both him and Vulcan that I feel within myself. I've never heard of a shifter staying in their creature form for extended periods of time. Thankfully for us, Silken are only slightly larger than cats and she would be easy to travel with. She's around the size of Kalleli, who is staring at her from my feet.

"We are making pastries for breakfast. I'll make an additional meal for Raya when I get Kalleli's ready and bring it to you when we bring everything over. Arden is preparing the horses if you want to go and get your bag ready for her as well." I say, looking back down at the dough I've been rolling out.

I look back up and see Fenor nod. "Thank you, I will.

I'll give the horses their morning oats as well."

We finish making the pastries and my mind circles around thoughts of Raya. Why she hasn't shifted, how she went missing, where she could have been since.

I wonder when we will find out, when she will shift back to her regular form.

Me and Vulcan take everyone their pastries and once we've all eaten, we saddle up and begin our travels. Today we will be moving through Frontasia and going to Mazal, a village on the border between Frontasia and Kiasta. This is the next lake and it will be important that we stop here to refill our canteens, and rest the horses.

The air is crisp, filled with the earthy scent of dew-kissed grass and the faint promise of warmth that the sun will soon bring. I sit behind Ryat on Lana this time, my arms wrapped around his waist, Kalleli nestled securely between us. The rhythmic sound of hooves against the packed earth provides a steady backdrop, but my mind drifts far from the comfort of this moment.

The woods around us feel dense and shadowy, even in the gentle morning light. The trees rise tall and imposing, their branches arching overhead like dark sentinels. I find myself drawn to the twisted trunks, many of which are marred by black vines slithering up their bases, giving them an eerie, unnatural appearance. It's as if the forest itself is slowly succumbing to a disease, and the thought sends a chill through me.

"Are you alright?" Ryat's voice breaks through my thoughts, his concern evident as he glances back at me.

"I'm fine," I reply, though even I can hear the tremor in my voice. My gaze drifts back to the trees, their leaves tinged with a sickly hue, and the memory of our encounter with that monstrous creature resurfaces. The deer-headed beast had emerged from the shadows, a horrifying embodiment of the darkness spreading through the land, and I can't shake the fear that it represents.

Ryat notices my distracted state and tightens his grip on the reins. "If you need to stop—"

"No, I don't want to stop," I say, shaking my head. "I just... can't stop thinking about what we saw."

He nods, understanding flickering in his eyes. "The blight is spreading, and we can't ignore it. But we will win this war."

The words hang heavy between us as we ride on. I can't help but wonder how long it would take before the trees are completely gone, the land devoid of life. The dried-up lake we passed earlier flashes in my mind, its cracked surface a cruel reminder of what once thrived there.

"Emory?" Ryat's voice pulls me back to the present. "You're worried."

I nod slowly, my heart sinking. "What if I fail? What if I don't fulfill the prophecy?"

"We'll face it together," he reassures me, his voice steady and comforting. "No matter what. The land needs you and I will find a way to ensure you survive the sacrifice."

His words resonate within me, a flicker of determination igniting despite the weight of doubt. Kalleli stirs slightly, her soft breaths a grounding presence, reminding me of the innocence and hope that still exist in this world.

As we ride further, the path ahead begins to open up, the trees thinning and allowing more light to filter through. I take a deep breath, the cool morning air filling my lungs. The shadows of the forest lift slightly, revealing a clearing bathed in the golden glow of the rising sun.

"Look," Ryat says, pointing ahead. "It's beautiful."

I can't help but smile, feeling my heart swell at the sight. The golden rays dance across the landscape, casting long shadows behind us. For a moment, the darkness that has crept into our world feels distant, and I allow myself to be swept away in the beauty of the morning.

"Promise me," I say softly, squeezing Ryat's waist. "We'll figure this out together."

He glances back at me, his expression fierce and protective. "Always, Emory. Together."

With those words, I take another deep breath, feeling the warmth of hope igniting within me.

We enter the village of Mazal five hours later, having moved at a quick trotting pace for the entire trip. The sound of our horses' hooves echo on the dusty trail, accompanied by the distant chirping of birds.This village is full of beautiful homes and shops, built of sturdy stone, gleaming marble, and richly scented sealed woods. The smell of freshly baked bread drifts from a nearby bakers shop, mingling with the flowers that they've planted in the windowsills. Shop signs, painted an array of bright colors, catch my attention. Their names, elegantly written in fancy print, beckoning me closer. As we approach, the wooden front stoops catch my attention as well. They're lined with meticulously arranged shelves, displaying an array of different clothing and goods.

Ryat leads us away from the shop I was staring at and

I turn my head to see a large stable placed next to the ginormous lake. He pulls Lana into a slot and gets off before lifting me and Kalleli off as he always does.

Turning, he hands the reins to a thin blue haired man, "we will be in the village for a few hours. Can the horses graze while we shop?" He asks him.

The man nods, "yes, we have a large fenced area behind the stables for grazing. I'll put them all out there and keep an eye on them until you return. It is fifty coins for five hours."

Ryat hands him the coins and turns to me, "ready to do some shopping, mate?"

I smile, nodding. "Yes, I saw a lovely bakers shop when we were coming in and it smelled fantastic. I was also hoping we may be able to find an actual collar for Kalleli. This seems like the type of place that may sell them." The leather holster was working but I'd like her to have a proper one if given the opportunity.

We walk to the Bakers shop and I scan the desserts they have lined on the shelf outside. There are cookies, bread, pastries and even muffins! I have always wished for the types of pans needed to make muffins, but they can be difficult to find and would be even harder to travel with. I look at the cookies first, seeing the cocoa chips, sweetberries, cinnamon and other inclusions they've used in the different recipes. The breads are the same, some with brightly colored peppers and some with flakey cheeses or spices on top. I take a longer time studying the fluffy muffins. They've used nuts and apples, berries, cocoa and so many other combinations that my mind spins with all of the possibilities.

I look up at Ryat, who is pretending to be interested in a cookie beside me, "one day I would like to have a shop like this. Or maybe a diner with a Bakers shop attached. I would love to share the joy of cooking and baking with other gifted." I am practically vibrating with excitement, my smile stretching my cheeks.

He laughs, his smile and emotions full of joy. "I will make sure you get the opportunity, princess."

We end up buying a couple loaves of bread made of peppers I have never heard of before, their vibrant colors catching my eye and enticing me. As I hold them in my hands, I can feel their smooth texture and imagine the spicy aroma that must fill the air when they are baked. In addition, we grab a couple of cookies before we make our way out of the shop. As we walk down the path, the sound of our footsteps on the cobblestone echo in my ears. I can hear snippets of conversations, the laughter of children playing nearby, and the distant chirping of birds. My eyes wander and come across the shop's fancy signs, their vibrant colors and intricate designs captivating my attention.

Among them, I see one labeled 'Fortune Teller' and a grin takes over my face. The anticipation builds inside me, and I can't help but turn to Ryat. "We have to go to the fortune teller!!" I exclaim, my voice filled with enthusiasm. "Maybe they can tell us the outcome of the war or when Raya will switch back to her regular form!" I say this with a laugh, the sound carrying a mix of hope and skepticism.

Deep down, I know that the chances of finding a gifted who can predict the future is slim, but the idea still brings me a bit of hope.

He laughs, "alright princess, lead the way."

The air inside the Fortune Teller's shop feels thick, heavy with the scent of smoke in the air—sweet and hearty, almost clinging to my skin. The shelves are crammed with odd trinkets, jars of herbs, and crystals that seem to glow faintly in the dim candlelight. Shadows dance on the walls, and though I expected this place to feel theatrical, like something from a story, there's an unsettling weight to the air that I can't shake.

Ryat's hand rests on the small of my back, a steady warmth that helps ground me. I can feel him watching me, silently checking in, making sure I'm okay. Kalleli is in my lap, shifting slightly as her eyes scan the room. She's quiet, but I can feel her curiosity, the way she's taking it all in.

I can't help but shift in my seat, trying to shake the tension from my shoulders. I came here expecting this to be some kind of joke—a fake, someone who's good at reading gifted but ultimately knows nothing of the future. But as I look at the fortune teller sitting across from me, an older woman with weathered skin and eyes that feel like they're looking straight through me, I realize I might've been wrong.

Her gaze is sharp, too sharp, and it makes my skin prickle. There's something about her that feels real, ancient, like she's been here far longer than I can imagine. I can't explain it, but it unnerves me.

"You thought I'd be a fake," she says suddenly, her voice cutting through the silence like a knife.

I blink, startled. "I didn't say—"

"You didn't have to." She smiles, but there's a knowing glint in her eyes, as if she's amused by me. "Many who come here don't believe until they hear what they already know."

I glance at Ryat, and he just gives me a small, reassuring nod. I'm still not convinced that she can be trusted, but something about this woman is making me second-guess my doubts.

Kalleli shifts again in my lap, resting her head against my chest, and I wrap an arm around her, feeling the steady rise and fall of her breathing. I feel protective, but the fortune teller's gaze never wavers from me, as if she's waiting for me to settle, to accept that whatever's about to happen is already set in motion.

She reaches across the table, her hands hovering just above mine. "You have many challenges ahead of you," she begins, her voice low, almost a whisper, but it feels like it fills the room. "The war is coming, and you will face it head-on, but the path before you will be filled with trials. Some you've expected. Others, you cannot yet see."

My heart skips a beat, and I can't help but grip Ryat's hand a little tighter. I've known this. The war, the prophecy, it's all been looming over us, over me, but hearing it aloud from a stranger's lips feels different.

It feels real.

She studies my face for a long moment before continuing. "But the Fates have blessed you."

That makes me stiffen. My breath catches in my throat, and I feel Ryat tense beside me, as if we're both thinking the same thing. The prophecy. I open my mouth to ask, but before I can say anything, the fortune teller leans closer, her eyes never leaving mine.

"It's not what you think," she says softly, almost gently. "The blessing I speak of is not the one you're worried about. Though I know of that as well, this is something new, something unexpected, even by the gods."

I frown, confusion swirling in my mind. "What do you mean?"

She lets the silence hang in the air for a moment, as if weighing her next words carefully. "You are with child."

The world seems to tilt, and for a moment, I'm not sure I've heard her correctly. I stare at her, my heart pounding in my chest, trying to process the words.

With child?

No, that can't be right.

I would know, wouldn't I?

We had only been together once, the night after our bonding.

It is difficult to conceive in these lands, taking most couples years, if it happens at all.

How can it be possible?

I glance at Ryat, his eyes wide, shock mirrored in his expression. Confusion flowing throughout the room. He looks at me, then back at the fortune teller, but before he can say anything, the woman smiles softly, almost kindly.

"The Fates have blessed you, Emory. This child is part of that blessing."

I sit here, frozen, the weight of her words settling over me. Kalleli shifts in my lap, her small body warm and solid, and I instinctively hold her tighter, my mind racing. I came in here thinking this woman would be a fake, that this would all be smoke and mirrors. But now...

Now, I don't know what to think.

What to feel.

The bell above the door jingles softly as Ryat and I step into the pet shop, a quaint little cabin filled with the scents of fresh hay and pet food. Sunlight filters through the front windows, casting warm patches of light on the wooden floor. My heart feels heavy, a weight that lingers since the fortune teller's words. I glance at Ryat, who is still processing the news, his expression thoughtful as he takes in the colorful displays around us.

I squeeze his hand, seeking comfort in his steady presence. He looks down at me, his brown eyes filled with warmth, and gives my hand a reassuring squeeze in return. We wander deeper into the shop, my gaze flickering over the rows of collars hanging on the wall, each one a burst of color and personality. There are leather ones, sparkly ones, even some with tiny bells that jingle softly with each movement.

As I sift through the various options, I try to push

aside the thoughts swirling in my mind about what it means to be carrying a child. Instead, I focus on Kalleli. She deserves something special, a symbol of our bond.

I find a vibrant blue collar adorned with little stars and a bright green one with playful patterns, but they don't feel right. I want something that reflects her unique spirit, something that feels like home. My fingers trail over a series of collars until one catches my eye—a soft pink collar, its fabric smooth and inviting to the touch. It has delicate stitching and a small charm shaped like a heart hanging from the clasp.

"This is perfect," I whisper, holding it up to Ryat, who looks over my shoulder. He nods, a smile tugging at his lips, and for a moment, the weight in my chest lightens. "Kalleli will look lovely in this."

As I head to the engraving station in the corner, my mind drifts back to the fortune teller's words. I catch myself thinking about what being a parent means, the responsibilities and joys intertwined. I shake my head slightly, trying to banish the thoughts.

"Just focus on Kalleli," I remind myself silently, glancing back at Ryat. He watches me with an intensity that makes my heart race, his expression a mixture of pride and concern.

I hand the collar to the shopkeeper, who smiles warmly as I request the engraving. "What name would you like?" she asks.

"Kalleli," I reply, my voice barely above a whisper. Hearing it out loud feels grounding, a reminder of the life we're creating together.

As the shopkeeper gets to work, I return to Ryat's side. He slips his arm around my waist, pulling me close. The warmth of his body against mine provides a welcome distraction from my swirling thoughts. I lean into him, closing my eyes for a brief moment, savoring the closeness and the scent of him mixed with the shop's aromas.

"Everything will be okay," he murmurs, his voice low and reassuring.

I nod, though uncertainty lingers in the air between us. I can't help but wonder what the future holds, how our lives will change. But for now, I focus on this small moment—picking out a collar for Kalleli, feeling Ryat's warmth beside me.

When the shopkeeper returns, the collar is now engraved, the name shining back at us. I take it into my hands, marveling at how perfect it looks. "Thank you," I say, my heart swelling with affection.

Ryat watches me, a soft smile on his face. "It suits her perfectly."

We pay and head out of the shop, the bell jingling behind us. I quickly slide the collar onto Kalleli. The soft pink contrasts beautifully with her soft blue fur, the charm glinting in the sunlight as she wiggles excitedly in my arms. "Look at you!" I exclaim, laughter bubbling up as she tries to shake the collar off playfully. "You're stunning!"

Kalleli yips happily, as if she knows she looks adorable. I stroke her fur, feeling a rush of love and contentment.

Ryat chuckles, his smile infectious. "She really does look like a little princess now."

With Kalleli secured in my arms, we turn to head back into the bustling market, ready to find the rest of our party. The vibrant stalls are alive with colors and sounds, the air filled with the mingling scents of fresh produce, spices, and baked goods. I feel a rush of energy as we navigate through the crowd, Kalleli's tiny weight a comforting presence against me.

"Where do you think they went?" I ask, scanning the cabins for familiar faces.

Ryat shrugs, still holding my hand. "Maybe they found the bakery again. I could smell pastries all the way from here."

I laugh, imagining Hellion and Nox already indulging in sweet treats. "Let's go check there first," I suggest, feeling a small surge of excitement at the thought of rejoining our friends.

Together, we weave through the market, the lively atmosphere buzzing around us. With Kalleli nestled close, I focus on the warmth of Ryat's hand and her soft fur instead of the weight this journey has already held.

CHAPTER

THIRTY-TWO

The steady rhythm of the horse beneath me should be soothing, but I can't seem to shake the weight pressing down on my chest. The sun is low in the sky, casting a warm, golden light over the trees as we ride through them, but my mind is stuck elsewhere. We've been riding for six hours, and despite feeling the ache in my body, my mind is consumed with what the fortune teller said back in the shop.

You are with child.

The words keep circling in my head, refusing to settle. I shift slightly, adjusting Kalleli in my lap as she dozes, her small body pressed close to mine. Her blue fur is soft beneath my fingers, and I absently stroke it, trying to ground myself in the sensation, to push away the endless cycle of thoughts.

But it's no use.

What if I don't survive long enough to have this child?

I glance at Ryat, his powerful form behind me, his eyes scanning the woods ahead with quiet focus. He's always been the steady one, the calm in every situation. But I know he feels the weight of this, too. He has said little since we left the fortune teller's shop, but I can feel the heaviness drifting from him, feel the way he holds himself a little too still.

I tried reading earlier—the book of the princess that I had gotten from Eira—but I couldn't focus. The words blurred together, my mind too restless to take them in. Instead, I've been watching the trees pass by, listening to the steady sound of hooves on the dirt path, the distant rustling of leaves in the breeze.

The trees around us are thick, the shadows long now as the sun sinks lower. It's peaceful, in a way, but there's an edge to it. The kind of quiet that feels like it's hiding something, waiting for the right moment to reveal itself. I've always felt a strange connection to the woods, but today, it feels like they're keeping secrets from me.

Or maybe I'm just seeing shadows where there are none.

I let out a slow breath, trying to calm the anxiety bubbling under my skin. Kalleli stirs slightly in my lap, and I run a hand through her soft fur again, the motion soothing. She's been such a comfort to me, especially now when everything feels so uncertain. Her presence is a reminder of the small joys, the reasons we're fighting this war in the first place.

The rest of the party rides a little ways behind us, their conversation soft, though I'm too lost in my own thoughts to make out the words. I know they're trying to keep things light, to lift the mood after a long day of travel. But there's a heaviness hanging over all of us. The

Village we're camping in tonight, Valk, is still an hour away, and by the time we make camp, we'll all be feeling the strain.

I glance up at the sky, now tinged with orange and pink, and wonder if the fortune teller saw more than she told me.

Did she see what's coming?

Did she see my future?

My death?

I shake my head, trying to clear the thought. It's dangerous to dwell on it. I need to stay focused, to be present for the others, for Ryat. But it's hard. The fear of what's coming, of what I might lose, keeps creeping in.

As the sun dips below the horizon, casting long shadows over the path, I can see the outline of the Village Valkin the distance. Relief washes over me. We'll be able to rest soon.

"Almost there," Ryat says, his voice low and reassuring. He glances down, his expression softening as his eyes land on Kalleli, still curled up in my lap. "How are you holding up?"

"I'm fine," I say, though I'm not sure it's entirely true. But I don't want to worry him. Not now. Not when we're so close.

He studies me for a moment, like he knows there's more going on beneath the surface, but he doesn't press. Instead, he brushes his hand over my own, where it rests on Kalleli's back.

I cling to that touch. As the Village grows closer, I can't stop my mind from wandering back to the fortuneteller's words again.

You are with child.

It's strange, really. I haven't even confirmed it, but in my heart, I know she was telling the truth. I feel it—the weight of something new and precious growing inside me. And despite the fear, despite the war that looms over us, I already love this child. I didn't expect to, not like this, not so soon. But the love is there, blossoming quietly, like a warmth in my chest.

What will they be like?

I wonder if it's a boy or a girl. A daughter who might inherit my silver hair, or a son with Ryat's brown eyes. My heart swells at the thought of either—no matter who they are, I know I'll love them beyond reason. Will they look more like me or like Ryat? Will they have his strong, quiet nature, his strength that's always made me feel safe? Or will they be wild and curious, always seeking something new, something beyond the world they know?

I smile softly to myself, imagining Ryat holding our child for the first time. It's certain that he will be the kind of father who loves fiercely and protects without question. I can already see the softness in his eyes when he looks at Kalleli. How much more will he feel when he holds our own child?

I glance over at him, his expression focused on the path ahead, but I can see the subtle tension in his shoulders. I know he's thinking about it as well, about what this means for us, for the future we're trying to save.

A daughter with his eyes, his quiet resolve. Or maybe a son with my stubborn streak, fierce and determined. I can't help but smile again, even as the anxiety twists in my gut.

What kind of world will we bring this child into?

Will I be there to watch them grow, to see their first steps, hear their first words?

I push the thought away. I can't let fear rob me of this moment. Whoever this child is, they'll be loved. By me, by Ryat, by anyone of this group who lives through this war.

Even now, as I stroke Kalleli's fur, I feel the tug of that love, like a thread winding its way through my heart.

The thought of holding them—of cradling this little piece of us in my arms—makes the world around me fade just a bit. For now, I have this moment, this ride, this peace. And the hope that somehow, some way, I'll make it through whatever's coming.

Dinner is quick tonight and words are few and far between. We nibble on my new spicy breads and Kalleli wears a soft pink collar we got her before departing. We haven't told anyone of our visit to the fortune teller yet, but it seems everyone's thoughts are on the days ahead of us. The sound of the fire and the occasional animal within the woods is the only noise to be heard. We are over halfway to Eldevand now and I can almost feel the war breathing down my neck.

Me and Ryat go to our tent, the fabric rustling softly as we step inside. We climb into our sleeping bag and before I drift off to sleep, I hear him say, his soft voice filled with determination, "I will not let this war take you or my child. I love you both," his words lingering in the air, "and I will protect you both with my very last breaths."

CHAPTER

THIRTY-THREE

When I go to feed the horses their morning oats, one of them is lying motionless on the ground. I feel anxiety stirring in my chest as I rush towards the brown mare and bend to check on her, hearing my footsteps echoing on the soft earth. But I know, even before I've touched her cold body, that she is dead. The rest of the horses have shifted their bodies as far as their taut reins allow, their ears twitching nervously, betraying their fear. I stand and look around, wondering what could be the cause of her death.

And then, with a sudden movement, I catch sight of it, slithering towards me faster than I thought possible. The Tencan is large, most likely full grown and has fangs the length of my pinky hanging out of its wide mouth. The rustling of leaves under its weight fills the air. The scent of the forest intensifies, a mix of damp earth and decaying leaves, mingling with the acrid smell of the snake's venomous breath as it quickly reaches me. As panic grips me, a wave of fear courses through my veins, causing my heart to pound in my chest. I feel the scream leaving my lips but I do not hear it. My body caught in its freeze and cut off from the world around me. The snake is at least twenty feet long and has dark black scales, as dark as the night sky. Its eyes, burning like fiery embers, fixate on me with an eerie intensity, momentarily transporting my thoughts to ancient tales of the underworld, where such flames are said to be seen.

In that split second, survival instincts kick in, flooding my body with adrenaline. My muscles tense, coiled like a spring ready to strike. Time slows down, each second stretching into eternity. I can hear the rapid thump of my own heartbeat, pounding in my ears, drowning out all other sounds. The world around me blurs into a chaotic whirlwind of motion and darkness. With lightning speed, the Tencan lunges at me, its jaws unhinged, ready to devour me whole. The air crackles with anticipation, a storm seeming to brew in the midst of this deadly encounter.

Instinctively, I dodge to the side, narrowly escaping the razor-sharp fangs that would have pierced my flesh. The ground trembles beneath the Tencan's weight as it crashes into the earth, leaving a deep divot in its wake.

My heart races, my breath coming in ragged gasps as I scramble to my feet, desperate to put distance between us. But the Tencan is relentless, its slithering form undulating like a dark river, relentlessly chasing after me.

I sprint through the woods, branches whipping against my face, leaves crunching under my feet. Fear fuels my every move, pushing me beyond my limits, driving me to survive. The Tencan hisses, its venomous breath a constant reminder of the danger lurking behind me. Its monstrous form looms closer, each moment closing the gap with terrifying speed. Adrenaline courses through my veins, heightening my senses. I can smell the earthy musk of the Tencan, taste the metallic tang of fear on my tongue. Every fiber of my being screams for escape, for freedom from this merciless predator.

With a surge of desperation, I feel my body begin to change forms. I can sense the scales growing across my skin, their rough texture sending a shiver down my spine. As my legs change in length, I feel a strange sensation of stretching and flexing in my bones. The sound of a low, menacing hiss escapes my mouth as my fangs grow into place, the sharp points grazing against my tongue. Simultaneously, my tail elongates, its whip like movements creating a faint swishing sound in the air.

I turn, my body now transformed into the massive shape of a 60-foot Cayman. My eyes widen as I take in the sight of the Tencan, its long body grinding to a halt. The pungent smell of its poison still fills the air as the creature wastes no time changing course, slithering away with the same intense speed. Relief washes over me, mingled with the acrid scent of fear. Thankfully, it is not heading towards our camp.

A wave of pain courses through me as my body abruptly shifts back to its human form. Gasping for air, I collapse to the ground, the weight of exhaustion pressing down on me. My limbs tremble uncontrollably, like leaves in a fierce wind. As the adrenaline subsides, I am overwhelmed by a mixture of relief and disbelief.

I feel myself drift unconscious as I think about the memory of those burning eyes, their intense glow piercing through me.

CHAPTER

THIRTY-FOUR

I wake up to a gentle rocking motion and the soothing touch of a hand caressing my hair. Fatigue is weighing heavily on my body, making it feel heavy, and my throat is dry. I try to pry my eyes open, but they resist, sealed shut by the remnants of a long slumber, gritty and sticky on my eyelids. As my body shifts, I become aware that I am on a horse, though I do not remember getting onto one, and falling asleep after giving the horses breakfast eludes me.

A groan escapes my lips as the memory of the Tencan encounter floods my mind. Another shift, and I realize

Ryat is holding me, his presence offering solace, his warmth seeping into my skin where our bodies are touching.

I feel his hand gliding across my face as he softly asks, "Emory. Are you awake?"

I manage to nod, my voice hoarse and strained when I reply, "I am." A cough and another groan escape me, and I lean my head further into his chest. "What happened after the Tencan?"

I feel his body tense beneath me. "We didn't know there had been a Tencan. I woke up to your screams, and when I found you, you were unconscious in the woods. We didn't know why you had run or screamed, just that it had happened."

I nod again, clearing my throat before speaking. "The Tencan that killed Eira's mare was chasing me. I shifted into my Cayman form to escape, and it fled. But I had shifted into a much larger form than I'm used to and when I shifted back, it drained me more than I expected."

Ryat pulls me closer, his grip firm yet gentle. "You've been asleep for almost eight hours. We'll reach the next camp soon. We're staying with Fenor's parents in their village, Alepoy, for the night. Raya will stay with them when we leave. I was so worried about you and our child, I could hardly keep my eyes on the path. Fenor is leading us now." I can sense his worry dissipating, replaced by an overwhelming love.

"We're both fine, though it was too close for comfort. I'll have to be more cautious now that I'm carrying our child," I say, feeling a surge of guilt in my gut, aware of the risks our unborn child already faces from inside of me.

Ryat holds me until we get to Fenors family cabin, even though I have been able to open my eyes and talk for some time now. His family's cabin is moderately sized and looks to be well taken care of. The sight of hydrangeas adorning the window sills adds a splash of color, while the walkway, lined with lovely stones of coppers and golds, guides our path. As we secure our horses to a tree nearby, I hear the sound of soft gasps escape Fenor's parents. Curiosity compels me to turn, and I witness their tear-filled eyes fixated on the copper Silky resting in Fenor's arms. Their soft cries fill the air around us as they rush towards Fenor, enveloping their children in a hug.

Fenor's mother, Tanli, a striking woman with graying red hair and delicate features, exudes elegance. It becomes clear that their children inherited the enchanting green eyes from her, while their father contributed the warm brown hues.

They release Fenor and Raya from their grip and turn towards the rest of us with soft smiles. Fenor's mother steps forward and her smile grows as she speaks. "Hello! When Fenor had written to tell us he would visit with friends, we never expected he would carry our daughter back as well, so you'll have to excuse the tears. We have prepared a couple rooms with cots and started dinner. It should be ready any moment and we would love to hear how the journey has been so far. Please go inside and freshen up while Havel cares for your horses."

She leaves us no room for arguing that we can do

so ourselves, quickly pushing us forward and into their home. I look around the entryway and notice that the inside is even nicer than the outside. The space, though minimally decorated, bursts with the vibrant colors and sweet fragrance of fresh flowers that fill the air. As I look along the walls, I notice the photos hanging. I step closer to a photo of Fenor and Raya as children when we pass it and smile, thinking of a similar one in my own family's cavern. Me and Arden had lined the walls just like this and it brings a familiar sense of peace to see Fenor's family home the same way.

Tanli leads us through the rooms, their wooden floors creaking softly under our weight. Each room holds five cots neatly arranged along the walls. We choose a cot by the wall, feeling the coolness of the surface against our skin. Arden settles next to us, his presence comforting and familiar. Hellion takes his place beside Arden, the sound of his breathing creating a soothing rhythm in the room. Meanwhile, Haven's boisterous declaration about claiming one of the bathrooms echoes through the house, her excitement palpable. Azrael dutifully follows her, his footsteps fading into the distance. Ryat's grip tightens around my hand as he eagerly leads me towards the other bathing chamber, his anticipation clear in his hurried pace.

As we enter the bathing chamber, the sight of warm, glistening steam envelops me. Intricate tiles line the room. The soft glow of candlelight dances on the walls, creating an almost stone like shadow. The sound of trickling water fills the air as a gentle stream cascades from a fountain into their marble tub.

I smell the scent of bath oils and fragrant flowers wafting through the chamber, mixing with the warm, earthy aroma of their heated flooring. The scent of a calming blend of lavender and eucalyptus fills the air, bringing a smile to my face.

As I dip my hand into the tub, a gentle warmth envelops my skin, easing away some of my tension from the day. The smooth, polished stone beneath my feet provides a comforting sensation, grounding me in the present moment.

I sense Ryat gently tugging the straps of my dress,

causing them to slip off my shoulders, exposing my bare skin to the cool air. As he lifts my arms, I feel the fabric of the dress sliding off my body, hear it graze against the rough stone floor with a soft rustling sound. Moving forward, I step into the warmth of the tub, the scent of fragrant bathing oils filling the steamy air, filling my nostrils. Ryat joins me in the tub, his presence tangible as I feel the remnants of his touch lingering on my skin while he washes my body. I feel him pause as his hands gently caress my stomach, cradling our child.

Our bath is quick. We hastily cleanse ourselves, and then we dress in the plain clothing that was left in the bathing chambers before making our way back towards the room that holds our cot. But once we get there, we notice the room is empty. Ryat pulls me farther down the hallway, towards where the dining area is.

The table is full of our friends, sitting with Fenor's parents and laughing. We take two open seats next to Arden, and someone places a bowl of what looks to be blackened chicken and rice in front of us. The vibrant colors and enticing smells make my mouth water.

I raise my eyes to Fenor's father and smile. The room filled with the sound of clinking glasses and joyful conversation. "Thank you," I say softly.

He nods, his smile mirroring my own. "If your child craves anything else, please don't hesitate to let us know. We remember the early cravings all too well from when we had our own two."

Suddenly, the atmosphere turns tense; the silence punctuated by the sound of a dropped spoon hitting the table. A wave of confusion and shock fills the air, enveloping me and mirroring the shock coming from Ryat.

He glances at Havel, his voice barely a whisper, "How did you know she's with child? We just found out ourselves."

I feel Arden shift beside me, and look over to see his eyes widening. "You're with child?" he exclaims, his voice tinged with a mixture of excitement and awe. The sound of his words fill the otherwise silent air. As he leans in to hug me, his touch is gentle, as though he's holding something fragile. I can sense the nervous energy flowing from him, a palpable tension in the air.

Tanli's speaks, her words carrying a warm smile. "We can smell it on you, dear," she says, her voice laced with a hint of laughter. "The scent hangs in the air, a sweet and earthy one that only those who have witnessed the miracle of new life as often as we have can recognize." She glances at her husband, a knowing look passing between them. "Our Foxe senses have also gotten better with age."

The rest of our party erupts in a chorus of excited voices, their congratulations filling the air like a symphony of joy. They all speak at once, their words intertwining in a cacophony of excitement as they all ask when we discovered the news. The scent of the dinner lingers, blending with the anticipation that hangs in the air. We share our tale of the fortuneteller, the flickering candlelight casting dancing shadows across our faces as we speak. The conversation continues throughout the meal, filled with animated discussions about the future of our child, the sound of laughter and clinking glasses adding a joyful melody to the atmosphere. Yet, amidst the joy, a hint of unease lingers, unspoken but palpable, all of us avoiding any mention of the prophecy that had hinted at my potential death in only a few days.

CHAPTER

THIRTY-FIVE

A s the first rays of sunlight creep through the cabin's window, I wake and go to the stables to give the horses their breakfast. But when I arrive, my eyes widen in horror as I discover our horses are gone. A chilling stench of death mars the scene, and I quickly notice the lifeless body of the family's stable boy, his blood staining the ground. Knowing that this is likely someone on Ymirs side of the war, we set out for Eldevand quickly, having only three days left until we are required to be present and no time to waste.

We are facing a long and hurried walk to Eldevand. The path stretches out before me as we wind through dense forests and vast open fields. In my ears, I hear the echo of our weary footsteps, their rhythmic thumping resonating with each step we make. Ryat carries all of my bags and sometimes carries me when it has been over twelve hours of walking straight. With no time for a full night's rest, our sleep breaks are short and restless, and our meals are nothing more than a hurried meal of roasted animal cooked over a blazing fire. Kalleli relishes in moments of independence, bounding ahead of us for a few hours before returning to be carried. Her trust in the rest of the party grows exponentially, and soon after we start the hike, she is willing to be in the arms of whoever offers to hold her.

As we hastily set up at the final campsite before the impending war, the weight of stress and fear hangs heavy in the air, seeping into every breath I take. The scent of anticipation fills my nose, mixing with the lingering musk of sweat-soaked clothes, a testament to the relentless two-day trek with little rest. Fatigue gnaws at my bones, causing my muscles to ache and my feet to feel as though they are treading on air. We are in Eldevand now, only an hour out from the Tower of the Gods, and I am terrified.

Terrified for my friends, my brother, my mate, for me.

For my child.

The quickly built tent is quiet, other than the soft rustle of fabric as the wind brushes against it. The world beyond feels heavy with the weight of the war that looms over us, and inside, my heart races with a mixture of fear and anticipation. Ryat sits beside me, his eyes searching mine, sensing the turmoil I can't quite hide.

I can't stop thinking about the final battle—about what might happen. About what I might lose.

"I'm terrified," I whisper, my voice barely audible. I reach for his hand, needing to feel the warmth of him, to remind myself that for now, at least, we're here together.

Ryat's hand tightens around mine, and he pulls me closer until I'm resting against his chest, his arms wrapping around me like a shield against the darkness outside. "I know," he murmurs, his lips brushing my forehead. "But you're not alone. You'll never be alone."

The feeling of his steady breath calms me, but the fear still lingers, a shadow I can't quite shake. I tilt my head up, meeting his gaze, and the unspoken understanding between us is enough to make my throat tighten.

I don't want to think about what's coming.

I don't want to dwell on the uncertainty of our future.

"Ryat..." I swallow, my voice trembling. "I need you to help me forget. Just for a little while."

His eyes soften, and without a word, he rises, pulling me up with him. He leads me out of the tent, the cool night air brushing against my skin as we step into the quiet woods surrounding the camp. The night is dark, but with Ryat beside me, I feel safe, even with the uncertainty that clings in the air.

"Be as quiet as you can," he whispers, his voice low and intimate, sending a shiver down my spine. I nod, trusting him completely.

We move deeper into the trees, away from the camp. When we reach a small clearing, bathed in moonlight, Ryat turns to me, his expression tender but filled with a quiet intensity.

"Emory," he breathes, brushing a strand of hair from my face, "no matter what happens tomorrow, tonight is ours. Just us."

I nod, my heart swelling with love for him, with the need to hold on to this moment. He leans in, his lips capturing mine in a slow, deep kiss, and I melt into him, letting the world beyond the forest fade away.

His hands move to the ties of my dress, slowly, reverently, as if savoring each moment. As the fabric falls away, I feel the cool air against my skin, but it's Ryat's touch that keeps me warm. He guides me gently, pressing me closer to the rough bark of a tree, his hands steady on my waist.

"Trust me," he whispers, and I do, completely.

I place my hands against the tree, the texture grounding me, and I feel Ryat's presence behind me. His touch is careful, deliberate, and filled with love, every movement a reminder of the connection we share.

"Emory," he whispers, his voice low and filled with something more than desire—reverence, love. "Look at me."

I turn my head slightly, meeting his gaze. His dark eyes are intense, but there's a softness in them, a tenderness that makes my breath hitch. He leans in, pressing a kiss to my shoulder before his hands move up, tracing the line of my back.

"You're so beautiful," he murmurs, his voice thick with emotion. "Do you know that? So gods damn beautiful."

I shiver at the words, feeling them sink deep into

my chest. His hands come around to rest on my hips, steadying me as I brace my hands against the tree. There's a brief moment where everything feels suspended—the quiet of the woods, the tension in the air—and then I feel him press into me, his breath hot against my neck.

The world seems to fall away at that moment, leaving only the two of us bound by something deeper than words. His movements are slow at first, controlled, like he's savoring every second, every breath. I press my hands firmly against the coarse bark of the tree, feeling its rugged texture against my skin, anchoring myself in the earthy sensation. But it's Ryat's whispered words, his tender guidance, that make me feel safe, cherished.

"You're perfect," he whispers, his lips brushing the shell of my ear, his breath warm and steady. "You feel perfect."

I let out a quiet gasp, my body responding to him instinctively, and he thrusts deeper than I thought possible. My skin tingles as I feel his chest pressed against my back, his mouth trailing soft kisses along

KAY HUGHES

my neck. There's a rhythm between us, a shared pulse that quickens as he thrusts behind me. Each touch, each breath a reminder of the love we've built, the trust we share.

Ryat's hand slides up to my waist, steadying me as he leans in close, his lips brushing against my temple. "Emory, I need you to cum with me," he whispers, his voice soft but commanding, filled with the tenderness that only he can offer.

I nod, breathless, my heart pounding in time with the rhythm of our bodies. "I'm with you," I moan, my words barely audible. "Always."

As we move together, I feel the tension inside me build, coiling tight until it snaps, and I bite my lip to keep from crying out. I feel Ryat's hand tighten on my hip, his own breaths coming in short, ragged bursts as he follows me over the edge.

For a moment, we stay like this, our bodies pressed close, our breaths mingling in the cool night air, and then slowly, gently, he pulls me back toward him, turning me around so I'm facing him. His eyes meet mine again, and I see the love there.

He presses his forehead to mine, his breathing still uneven as he cups my face in his hands. "I love you," he whispers, his voice rough but sincere.

"I love you too," I reply, my own voice shaky with emotion, my hands reaching up to rest on his chest, feeling the steady beat of his heart beneath my palms.

After a moment, Ryat pulls back slightly, his lips brushing mine in a soft kiss before he helps me gather my discarded dress, his movements gentle, as if we have all the time in the world. We slip back through the trees, the quiet of the woods surrounding us once again, but this time, the weight that had pressed on my chest earlier feels a little lighter.

We make our way back to the tent, slipping inside as the night deepens. Ryat holds me close, our bodies wrapped together in the warmth of our shared sleeping bag, and for the first time in hours, I feel a sense of peace wash over me.

"Together," I whisper into the darkness, my voice soft but sure.

Ryat's arms tighten around me, his breath warm against my hair. "Together. Always."

And with that, I let myself fall into sleep, comforted by the steady beat of his heart beside mine, knowing that no matter what tomorrow brings, we'll face it.

CHAPTER

THIRTY-SIX

I wake slowly, the cool morning air brushing against my skin, but it's Ryat's touch that stirs me fully awake. His lips trail down my spine in soft, lazy kisses, his warm breath a gentle contrast to the chill of the early hour. My eyes flutter open, and I smile into the pillow, a quiet hum of contentment escaping me as I stretch beneath his touch. Beside me, Kalleli is curled up, purring softly in her sleep, her small, warm body pressed against my side. I can feel her gentle rise and fall with each breath, the peacefulness of it a balm against the tension I've been carrying for days.

"Ryat," I murmur, my voice thick with sleep, "we should probably get up. We need to get breakfast started for everyone."

His response is a low chuckle, and his lips pause at the small of my back before he leans up, his breath warm against my ear. "Not yet," he whispers. "You don't need to rush. Rest a little longer, Emory. Think about our child."

His words send a warmth blooming through me, and I close my eyes again, letting myself sink back into the quiet of the morning. Our child. The thought of it still fills me with an overwhelming mix of emotions—love, joy, and a lingering thread of uncertainty. But with Ryat here, the world feels just a little bit lighter, the weight of everything else easing, if only for a moment. He kisses the back of my neck, his hands sliding along my sides in slow, soothing strokes. "It's not every day you get a few more minutes of peace," he says softly, and I can hear the smile in his voice. "Take it. For us. For them."

I nod, biting my lip as I try to relax into his touch.

But even as I do, my mind wanders back to the fortune teller, to the war, to the battle that we know is coming but can't predict. I place a hand on my stomach, still flat but holding so much potential. Who will this little one be? I wonder. Will they take after Ryat's calm strength, or will they have my stubborn streak?

I turn slightly, shifting to look at him, my heart swelling as I take in the sight of him, already watching me with that quiet intensity that always makes me feel seen, loved. "What do you think?" I ask softly, my fingers tracing the outline of his hand as it rests on my hip. "Will they have your eyes?"

Ryat chuckles, his thumb brushing a light circle against my skin. "Maybe," he says, a glint of amusement in his eyes. "But if they're anything like you, they'll be beautiful."

I laugh softly at that, feeling a warmth spread through me, but before I can say more, the atmosphere in the tent shifts. There's a subtle shift in the air, a tinge of something otherworldly that raises the hairs on the back of my neck. I sit up slightly, my eyes narrowing as the tent's soft fabric ripples, though there's no wind. Ryat notices it too, his body going still beside me as he instinctively moves closer, his arm wrapping protectively around me and Kalleli.

And then, suddenly, he's there.

A figure, tall and imposing, stands at the entrance to the tent, his presence unmistakably divine.

A god.

Which one I do not know but his pale eyes are glowing with the kind of power that makes my skin prickle with awareness. His dark, otherworldly robe seems to shimmer in the dim light of the tent, and though his expression is calm, I can feel the weight of his presence pressing down on us.

"Apologies for the interruption," He says, his voice smooth and unhurried, as if appearing in people's tents uninvited is perfectly normal. "But I've come with a message."

I glance at Ryat, who's already sitting up beside

me, his hand still resting protectively on my back. "A message?" Ryat asks, his voice steady, though I can sense the tension building in him.

The god smiles faintly, his gaze flicking between us. "There is a ball being held at the Tower of the Gods this afternoon," he says, folding his hands in front of him. "And you, along with your entire party, have been added to the guest list."

I blink, trying to process his words. "A... ball?" I repeat, incredulous. With everything that's been happening—the impending war, the looming final battle—it seems almost absurd to think about attending a ball.

"Yes," He replies calmly, as though he's discussing the weather. "The fates have dictated that you must attend. The final battle will not happen there, but your presence is required nonetheless."

My heart skips a beat at the mention of the final battle. We've been waiting, preparing, knowing it could come at any moment. But somehow, knowing that it's still out there, waiting, makes the idea of dressing up for a ball feel... surreal.

Ryat sits up fully now, his expression unreadable. "Why us?" he asks, his voice low. "Why the ball?"

The god's eyes gleam slightly, and he tilts his head, as if considering his answer carefully. "Because the fates have woven this path for you," he says. "And because certain threads must be tied before the next chapter begins."

I feel a shiver run through me at his words. There's something in his tone, in the way he speaks of the fates, that makes my stomach twist. There's no escaping the destiny that's been laid out before us, and though I've known this for a while, hearing it from a god makes it feel more real than ever.

"We'll be there," Ryat says after a moment, his voice steady, though I can hear the edge of determination in it.

The god gives a slight nod, his pale eyes flicking to me for a brief second before he steps back toward the entrance. "Good. I'll see you there, then."

And just like that, he's gone, his form dissipating into the morning air as if he was never here at all.

I release a breath I didn't realize I was holding, my mind spinning with the weight of what just happened. A ball. The Tower of the Gods. The fates weaving our path.

Ryat pulls me close again, pressing a kiss to my temple. "Don't think too much about it," he murmurs. "For now, we take it one step at a time."

I nod, leaning into his touch, though the tension in my chest remains. One step at a time. I just hope the next step doesn't lead us too close to the edge.

I pull myself out of bed, the lingering warmth of Ryat's touch still tingling on my skin. The air in the tent feels cooler now that the god is gone, though it's more from the weight of his words than the actual temperature. I move slowly, careful not to wake Kalleli, who's still curled up at my side, her small body rising and falling softly with each breath.

I glance at Ryat, who's already tugging his shirt over his head. He meets my eyes, his brow furrowing slightly as he steps closer. "Are you okay?" he asks, his voice low.

"I'm fine," I whisper, though my heart is still racing from the encounter. I try to smile, but it comes out half-formed. "Just... processing."

He brushes a strand of my still slightly pink tinted silver hair away from my face and leans in, pressing a kiss to my forehead. "We'll figure it out," he says, and somehow, his steady presence helps ease some of the tension twisting inside me. "One thing at a time."

I nod, reaching for my dress and pulling it over my head, feeling the fabric settle against my skin. There's an odd contrast between the normalcy of getting dressed and the enormity of what just happened. But I focus on the simple task, trying to ground myself.

As we step outside the tent, the sun has just begun to rise, casting a soft glow over the camp. The fire in the center crackles quietly, and I can see the rest of our party starting to stir. Vulcan is already up, poking at the fire with a stick, while Fenor and Eira stretch lazily near their tent.

We walk over to the fire, Ryat's hand resting gently on the small of my back as we approach. The familiar warmth of the flames greets us, and I feel a little more like myself.

Vulcan looks up, raising an eyebrow as we near. He nods as Eira looks over at us and speaks. "Morning," she says, her voice rough from sleep. "You two look like you've seen a ghost."

"Not a ghost," I say with a small sigh, sitting down on one of the logs beside the fire. "But close."

Fenor frowns, his eyes narrowing. "Who, then?"

I glance at Ryat before answering. "A god came to see us."

That catches the attention of everyone nearby. Haven, who's been brushing the knots out of her copper hair, pauses and turns toward us, her eyes wide. "A god? Here? In our camp?"

Ryat nods, sitting beside me. "He said we've been added to the guest list for a ball at the Tower of the Gods this afternoon."

"A ball?" Haven repeats, blinking in surprise. "As in, we need to be there, dressed to impress?"

"Apparently," I reply, rubbing a hand over my face. "The final battle won't happen there, but we have to go. It's some... fate thing."

Fenor sits back, scratching his chin. "So, a god shows up and invites you to a ball, and we're supposed to just drop everything and attend?"

I laugh softly, the absurdity of it not lost on me. "Pretty much."

"And who was this god?" Vor asks, his voice skeptical.

"I... don't know." I admit, glancing at Ryat for confirmation. He shakes his head slightly, confirming my uncertainty. "He's not one we've dealt with before and he did not introduce himself."

Haven stands, brushing off her trousers. "Well, we can figure out who he is later. Right now, the important question is—what are we going to wear?"

Her comment earns a laugh from Hellion, who's stretching his arms above his head. "I'm sure we'll all look stunning in our camping gear," he jokes, his grin wide as he moves closer to the fire. "Or maybe we should just show up in our battle armor—make a statement."

"We can't go in this," Haven says, her tone serious. "If we're going to a ball, we need proper attire. Ryat, Azrael, and I will go to the nearest village and find something for us to wear."

Ryat nods beside me, already thinking ahead. "We should leave soon then. The nearest village is a couple of hours away."

Azrael, who's been quiet until now, gives a nod of agreement. "I'll get our bags and canteens ready."

As they start discussing logistics, I feel a small tug of worry. Not about the ball, but about Ryat leaving for even a short time. I know it's irrational—he's just going to the village—but after everything that's been happening, the idea of him being away, even for a few hours, makes my chest tighten.

Fenor stands, stretching his arms before turning to me with a grin. "I'll get breakfast started while you guys figure it out. Something hearty to keep everyone going." He winks, already moving toward the supplies.

I smile at him in thanks, but my focus is on Ryat. As he stands to get ready for the trip, I rise too, following him a few steps away from the fire. The rest of the camp fades into the background as I look up at him, biting my lip.

"You'll be careful, right?" I ask, my voice quieter than I intended.

He smiles softly, reaching out to cup my cheek. "It's a quick trip, Emory. I'll be back before you even miss me."

"I always miss you," I say, leaning into his touch. The weight of everything feels heavy on my shoulders—the ball, the war, the child growing inside me—but right now, I just want him close.

Ryat leans in, pressing a kiss to my forehead. "I'll be fine. You rest, take care of Kalleli, and by the time I'm back, we'll have something proper to wear to this ridiculous ball."

I laugh softly despite myself, nodding as I reach up to kiss him. "I'll hold you to that."

With one last look, he pulls away, heading toward Azrael and Haven as they prepare to leave. I stand there for a moment, watching him, before turning back to the fire where Fenor is already cooking.

As the smell of breakfast fills the air, I sit down, Kalleli stirring at my side and curling closer to me. The morning is calm, but my thoughts keep drifting back to the gods visit, to the ball, and to the uncertainty of what comes next.

CHAPTER

THIRTY-SEVEN

As the sun sinks lower as I sit by the flickering fire, its flames dancing and crackling. The warmth seeps into my skin, creating a cozy cocoon around me. Kalleli is curled up at my feet, her small body breathing softly, while Eira and Teirney sit across from me, their faces illuminated by the firelight.

"So, what do you think of the book so far?" Eira asks, leaning forward, her curiosity evident.

I hold the worn pages of the book in my hands, glancing between them. "I can't believe the princess just left her home like that. How can she be so in love with someone who shares so little about himself? It's reckless!"

Teirney giggles, her eyes sparkling and mischief pouring from her. "But that's what makes him so mysterious and dreamy! She's drawn to that allure, Emory."

"Sure, but she's risking everything. Her kingdom, her family... for a stranger?" I shake my head, still in disbelief.

Eira chuckles, leaning back with a knowing smile. "Sometimes it's that thrill that makes it exciting. Besides, he's a good kisser."

Teirney nods vigorously, her hair catching the firelight. "And you haven't even gotten to chapter thirty yet! Wait until you read about their first time! You're going to be blushing like crazy."

I roll my eyes but can't help the smile creeping onto my face. "Oh, great. Just what I need—more scandalous details to mull over. I'm still trying to process the fact that she's risking her life for someone who seems to be hiding everything and that she kissed him the first day they met!"

"Maybe he has his reasons," Teirney suggests, her tone thoughtful. "Sometimes people keep things to themselves to protect those they care about."

"Or maybe he's just not as interesting as she thinks," I counter, but even I can hear the doubt in my voice. The chemistry between the characters is palpable, and a part of me can't help but get swept away in the fantasy of it all.

Then, the sound of footsteps pulls us from our conversation. The crunch of leaves underfoot and the distant hoot of an owl remind me of the world beyond our camp. I turn my head and see Ryat, Haven, and Azrael approaching, their footsteps creating a rhythmic cadence that echoes in my ears. Each of them carries large garment bags slung over their shoulders, the soft swishing of fabric filling the air. They approach the fire, and I rise to meet them, brushing off my dress as Ryat sets the garment bag down carefully on a nearby log.

There's a glint in Ryat's eye when he looks at me, and despite everything—the looming war, the uncertainty of what lies ahead—my heart skips a beat just at the sight of him.

"Got something for you," he says, his voice low, full of that quiet affection I love so much.

I raise an eyebrow, glancing at the bag. "You're not going to make me guess what it is?"

Haven laughs as she tosses a bag toward Teirney, who catches it with a raised eyebrow. "No surprises, Emory. But trust me, you're going to like it."

Azrael hands a bag to Eira, who thanks him with a soft smile. The camp hums with excitement now as everyone heads toward their tents to change. Ryat takes my hand, and together, we walk toward our tent, his other hand carrying two garment bags.

Once inside, he sets them down on the sleeping bag and begins to unzip one of them. The sound of the zipper cuts through the quiet, and when he pulls the bag open, I feel my breath catch.

The gown he picked for me is beautiful—stunning, really. A soft silver fabric that twinkles in the light, almost like moonlight woven into cloth. Smooth and cool under my fingertips, the bodice is fitted and adorned with delicate embroidery that dances across it in swirling patterns. Delicate lace adorns the wrists of the long, sheer, and flowing sleeves. The skirt is full and sweeping, with a slit along the side that I hadn't expected but instantly love. The dress is elegant and regal, yet it has a softness that makes it feel personal, intimate—as if it was tailored specifically for me.

I turn to Ryat, my voice caught in my throat for a moment. "It's… it's perfect," I whisper, feeling the emotion swell in my chest.

He smiles, his eyes soft as he steps closer. "I'm glad you like it," he says quietly, taking the gown from my hands and gently holding it up. "Let's get you dressed."

I slip out of my current dress, feeling the cool air against my skin for just a moment before Ryat helps me into the gown. The fabric glides over my body like water, cool and smooth, settling perfectly into place. I feel him behind me as he begins to fasten the buttons along the back, his fingers working deftly but with care.

His touch lingers as he moves from one button to the next, and each time his fingers brush against my skin, a soft warmth blooms beneath them. I close my eyes for a moment, letting myself get lost in the feeling of him, in the quiet intimacy of the moment.

When he finishes the last button, he leans in, pressing a soft kiss to the back of my shoulder. "You look beautiful, Emory," he whispers, his voice deep and warm.

I turn to face him, my breath catching again—not because of the dress this time, but because of him. He's changed into a suit, dark and perfectly tailored to his form, with a crisp white shirt and a tie that matches the silver of my gown. He looks... gods, he looks beautiful.

The sight of him takes me by surprise, even though I've seen him countless times before. But here, now, dressed like this... he looks every bit the warrior, the leader, but there's also a softness in his eyes that's just for me.

"How did I get so lucky?" I murmur, reaching out to run my hand along the front of his suit. He catches my hand, bringing it to his lips and pressing a kiss to my knuckles.

"I'm the lucky one," he says softly, his eyes meeting mine with that intensity that always makes me feel like the most important person in the world.

For a moment, we just stand there, the world outside the tent falling away as it so often does when it's just the two of us. But then, the sound of movement outside reminds me we're not alone, that there's a ball to attend.

I smile up at him, letting out a small sigh. "We should go."

He nods, but there's a warmth in his eyes as he leans in and kisses me softly. "Let's go show everyone how stunning you look."

When we step out of the tent, the camp is alive with

movement. Everyone is finishing getting dressed, and as I look around, I take in the sight of our party.

Haven is in a similar dress to my own. The fabric, a vibrant shade of red, catches the eye with its richness and boldness. Intricate detailing embellishes the gown, adding an air of regality to her presence. As the sunlight bathes her, her copper hair glows with an otherworldly radiance, perfectly complementing her golden eyes. It makes her look ethereal in the sunlight.

Eira is wearing a light blue, flowy dress that seems to float around her, soft and ethereal, like something out of a dream. The dress rustles gently in the breeze, creating a delicate sound that harmonizes with the distant chirping of birds. The scent of fresh flowers wafts through the air, mingling with the faint fragrance of her perfume. As I admire her, the dress's smooth fabric brushes against my fingertips, evoking a sensation of coolness and softness. The combination with her captivating blue eyes is stunning, creating a mesmerizing sight that feels like a perfect match.

And Teirney... Teirney looks absolutely radiant in a

black gown that glitters with gold details, the fabric shimmering in the sunlight. When I see her, it feels like I'm in a magical dream where characters come to life. The gown hugs her figure in all the right places, accentuating her natural beauty. The sunlight dances off the golden embellishments, creating a dazzling display of glittering light.

They all turned when we approached, and Haven's eyes widen as she takes in my dress. "Emory... you look incredible. Ryat picked the dress, but I knew it would be perfect for you when he showed me."

I smile, feeling my cheeks heat. "So do you," I reply, glancing at the rest of the group. "All of you."

Hellion grins, looking around at the group. "Looks like we're ready for the ball, then."

I glance at Ryat beside me, his hand resting gently at the small of my back. The tension from this morning still lingers in the back of my mind, but right now, standing here with him, with our friends, I feel... hopeful. Maybe, for just tonight, we can forget about the war, about what's coming. Maybe, for just one night, we can dance.

The air is crisp as we begin our walk toward the Tower of the Gods, the soft click of heels against the rock path filling the silence between our party. The glow of the afternoon sun bathes the landscape in a soft golden hue, but I'm more focused on not tripping in these shoes. I'm grateful for the steady arm of Ryat beside me, his warmth grounding me as we make our way.

It's an hour and a half hike, longer than it would normally take because Haven, Eira, Teirney, and I are all in heels. My silver gown sways as I walk, the hem brushing against the grass beneath me. The men stroll along at a leisurely pace, their formalwear perfectly suited for the walk, yet I can sense the exertion with each step. I glance at Ryat, who catches my eye and gives me a reassuring smile.

"You're doing fine," he says softly, his hand steady at the small of my back.

I nod, giving him a grateful smile, though my nerves flutter in my stomach. This isn't just a ball, it's the ball, held in the Tower of the Gods—a place I've only ever heard of in stories. The grandeur of it, the sheer weight of the event, has me feeling excited and anxious all at once. I've never been to anything like this before, and I can't shake the feeling that I'm about to step into a world that I don't quite belong to.

As we near the tower, it becomes increasingly imposing and larger than I had envisioned. Reaching high into the sky, the walls of white marble, along with the golden accents reflecting the sunlight, give the entire structure a subtle radiance. The entrance is a spectacle, with horses and carriages neatly arranged, and as guests dressed in exquisite attire and the air is full of the delightful sound of their laughter and animated conversations. The scene resembles a whimsical daydream, with vibrant hues and a contagious energy that fills the air.

I take a deep breath as we reach the entrance. A guard in gleaming armor steps forward, clipboard in hand.

"Names?" he asks, his tone formal.

Ryat steps forward, giving the names of each member of our party, and the guard nods before stepping aside to let us pass. We enter through the massive arched doors, and as soon as we step inside, my breath catches in my throat.

The inside of the tower is stunning. Polished white marble floors gleam under the light of the grand chandeliers hanging from the high ceilings. Casting a soft glow over the ballroom below, the chandeliers themselves are breathtaking—each one a massive, intricate creation of glass and gold. People, all dressed in the most elaborate and elegant attire I've ever seen, fill the room. Silks and satins in every color imaginable, embroidered gowns glittering with jewels, and hair styled in intricate updos that make me feel plain in comparison.

I glance down at my shimmering silver gown, the soft fabric cool against my fingertips, suddenly feeling self-conscious in the elegant crowd. But as Ryat's hand tightens around mine, I feel a comforting warmth spreading through my palm. I look up at him, the soft glow of the chandeliers reflecting in his eyes, and the gentle hum of conversation fades into the background. The sweet scent of flowers and perfume lingers in the air, mingling with the sounds of faint laughter and the soft melodies of the live orchestra. In that moment, as I catch a whiff of anticipation and excitement, the way he looks at me—like I'm the only person in the room— fills me with a sense of belonging, even in this grand ballroom.

The music is soft, slow, flowing through the room like a river. It's beautiful, and I can feel it weaving its way through me, building my excitement even as my nerves continue to tingle in the back of my mind. There are so many people, more than I've ever been around before, and I'm not sure if I should be excited or terrified.

"Are you all right?" Ryat's voice is gentle, pulling me from my thoughts. He's watching me carefully, as if he can sense the swirl of emotions running through me.

"I've never been to a ball before," I say, my voice quieter than I intended. "And I've definitely never been around this many people."

He smiles, his eyes softening. "I know, but you'll be fine. Just follow my lead."

I nod, trying to steady my breathing, but then he steps closer and holds out his hand. "Would you like to dance?"

I blink, feeling my heart skip a beat. "I... I don't know how."

His smile widens, and there's a softness in his eyes that eases some of my nerves. "I'll teach you," he says, his voice low and reassuring. "Just follow my steps."

I hesitate for only a moment, my heart pounding in my chest, before mustering the courage to take his hand. The dimly lit dance floor beckons us, the soft glow of colored lights reflecting off the polished marble. The rhythmic melody of the music envelops me, filling the air with a vibrant energy that resonates in my ears.

As we step into the middle of the room, the sound of laughter and conversation fades into the background, replaced by the melodic beats and harmonious lyrics. The mingling scent of perfume and sweat mingles, creating a heady fragrance that lingers in the air. I can feel the weight of other gifted looking at us, their eyes like spotlights casting a glow on our every move. But even in this crowd, all I can feel is Ryat's presence beside me, radiating a comforting warmth that seeps through my fingers, intertwining with mine.

He positions me gently, his touch sending a gentle shiver down my spine. I become acutely aware of the smooth texture of his hand, the calluses that tell tales of his experiences. His hand rests securely on my waist, a firm yet gentle anchor that grounds me in the moment. As the music swells, he leads, his movements fluid and effortless. I try my best to mimic the other dancers, my steps becoming a mix between uncertainty and determination.

Each step I take, I can feel the friction of my heels against the polished marble, the slight give and resistance beneath my feet. With every sway and twirl, the music envelops us, embracing our bodies and souls. I can feel the rhythm pulsating through my veins, synchronizing my heartbeat with the melody. Though my steps falter slightly, I surrender to the music's guidance, allowing it to carry me through the dance.

"Just watch my feet," Ryat murmurs, his voice soft. "And listen to the music. Let it carry you."

I nod, focusing on the rhythm of the song, on the way his feet move in time with it. I step where he steps, follow where he leads, and slowly, the nervousness fades. His touch is gentle, steady, and soon I find myself moving with him more naturally. The music flows through me, and with Ryat's hand guiding me, it starts to feel almost effortless.

"You're doing great," he whispers, his lips close to my ear, and I smile, feeling a warmth spread through my chest.

As we move across the floor, I can't help but feel a quiet sense of awe. The beauty of the room, the elegance of the people around us, and the way Ryat looks at me —it all feels like something out of a dream, something I never thought I'd experience. And yet, here I am, in the arms of the man I love, discovering the wonders of a room that feels like it has been pulled from a fairytale, and I am learning to dance.

"How did I get so lucky?" I whisper, the thought slipping out before I can stop it.

Ryat's gaze softens, and he pulls me a little closer. "I think the same thing every day," he murmurs, his voice so full of love that it makes my heart ache in the best way.

We continue to dance, the music carrying us, the world around us falling away as we move together. Everything feels surreal, like I am living in someone else's dream, but the solid warmth of Ryat's hand at the small of my back keeps me grounded. He gently guides me across the dance floor while clasping his other hand with mine, and for a moment, I surrendered myself to the rhythm of the waltz, to him.

The silver gown he bought for me moves like water with every step, catching the light as we spin. My hair, back to its natural silver, falls in soft waves around my shoulders, the pink dye gone now from my last bath.

"You're beautiful tonight," Ryat murmurs, his voice low, just for me.

I smile up at him, my heart fluttering at the sound of his voice. "You bought the dress," I tease lightly, though I know he isn't just talking about the gown.

He chuckles, his grip tightening on my hand as we continue to move. "The dress is just fabric. You are the one who makes it shine."

His words make my heart swell, even though a part of me resists the comfort. I know this isn't forever. The final battle looms on the horizon, closer with every passing day, and yet here we are, pretending that for tonight, everything will be okay. That we can just be two people, dancing.

From the corner of my eye, I catch a glimpse of

Haven, laughing as she dances with Azrael, her energy as infectious as ever. She spins in his arms, carefree, and it makes me smile. At the banquet table, Nox is piling food onto his plate, his appetite never-ending. He is sitting beside Vulcan, Hellion, and Eira, who are deep in conversation, sharing smiles and laughter as they enjoy the evening.

It is a beautiful sight. It's enough to make me believe, for just a second, that we can hold on to this peace.

But then my gaze shifts, drawn to the far end of the room where the shadows linger just beyond the light of the chandeliers.

And that's when I see him.

A dark and terrifying god.

He stands there, half-hidden in the darkness, watching me with cold, calculating eyes. A chill runs down my spine, and the weight of what is coming crashes into me all over again. The God of Revenge is here, a silent reminder of the war still to come, the battle that will decide everything. I don't know how long he has been watching us, but the sight of him twists my stomach with dread.

Instinctively, my hand tightens around Ryat's. I know what Ymir's presence means. The final battle is close—closer than I want to admit. The dance, the ball, this moment... It is all temporary. Everything is temporary.

I look up, expecting Ryat to give me some kind of reassurance, but it isn't him I see.

It is Dyra, standing just beyond the edge of the dance floor. Her gaze locked on mine. She shakes her head slowly, her eyes calm but firm. Not yet. Her message is clear.

I exhale slowly, forcing myself to nod, to trust her. Dyra has always known when the time would come, and if she says it isn't now, I would believe her. The battle could wait. Tonight wasn't for that. We had already been told that.

I let my grip on Ryat loosen, let my body relax back into the rhythm of the dance. Ymir can wait. The battle can wait. Tonight is for this—just for a little while longer. I lean into Ryat, resting my head against his chest, and let the music carry me across the floor. I focus on the steady beat of his heart beneath my cheek, the warmth of his body against mine, and the way my silver gown shimmers around us as we move.

For now, the world outside doesn't matter. Not Ymir, not the looming battle, not the weight of the future pressing down on my chest.

Tonight, I am here. Here with Ryat. Here in the ballroom's warmth, in the shimmering light and the music, with our friends around us. I can feel the gentle fluttering of my baby inside me, reminding me why I have to hold on to this moment. Why it matters.

For tonight, I am just here to dance.

CHAPTER

THIRTY-EIGHT

T he music swirls around us, and for a moment, I'm lost in the rhythm of it, moving in perfect sync with Ryat as if we've been dancing together our whole lives. His hand is warm on my waist, his touch steady, grounding me in this sea of elegance and jewels. The nerves I felt earlier are gone now, replaced by a warmth that's only grown since we stepped into the Tower.

But then Ryat leans down, his breath soft against my ear. "Come on," he murmurs, giving me a mischievous smile. "Let's take a break. Before Nox and Hellion eat all of the food they have prepared for the dinner."

I glance over toward the dining tables and spot Eira, Hellion, Nox, and Fenris seated together, plates in front of them, the table already scattered with fancy dishes. My stomach rumbles softly, reminding me that I haven't eaten since we left camp, and I laugh, nodding in agreement.

He leads me off the dance floor, our fingers still intertwined, and we make our way over to the table. Eira looks up as we approach, her pale blue gown flowing like water as she shifts in her seat to greet us.

"Finally decided to join us, did you?" Hellion teases, his fiery hair glinting in the soft light of the chandeliers above.

"We had to warm up first," Ryat replies, pulling out a chair for me. I smile at him as I sit, feeling the warmth of the room sink into my skin.

The food laid out in front of us is almost too beautiful to eat—delicate fishes seasoned with herbs, slices of tender meats, and plates of vibrant vegetables arranged like art. The aroma is mouthwatering, and I waste no time in filling my plate, eager to try everything.

As I take my first bite, the flavors explode in my mouth—rich and savory, with just the right amount of seasoning. It's unlike anything I've tasted before, and I catch Ryat's eye across the table, raising an eyebrow in appreciation. He grins at me, clearly enjoying my reaction more than the food itself.

I find that the slow-smoked brisket is my favorite of the meats, tender and infused with deep, rich flavors. I pair it with a generous serving of olive salad, vibrant with both green and black olives. The briny richness of the olives complements the crumbled feta sprinkled on top, while the chili flakes add a subtle kick that dances on my tongue. The cornbread arrives still warm from their ovens, its golden crust giving way to a sweet, soft interior. I can taste the honey they mixed into the batter, enhancing the natural sweetness. As I take a bite, I spread a dollop of cinnamon butter on top, watching it melt and seep into the bread, creating a heavenly combination of flavors. Each bite is a perfect balance of savory and sweet, making it hard to resist going back for more.

For dessert, a server brings out a tray of baked goods—tiny cakes, pastries, and muffins. My eyes immediately lock onto the muffins, small and golden brown, and I grab one without hesitation. I bite into it, the soft texture melting on my tongue, and I hum in satisfaction.

"I never forget how much I love muffins," I say, more to myself than anyone else, but Fenor, now seated beside me, hears and chuckles.

"You know," he says, leaning in a little, "we still haven't found that muffin pan we were talking about. I think it's time we make some ourselves once this is all over."

I laugh, nodding. "You're right. When we're back at camp, we'll hunt down a proper muffin pan, and I'll show you my mother's recipe."

"I'll hold you to that," Fenor replies with a grin, and I can already picture the two of us and Vulcan kneading dough, a sense of normalcy returning to our lives after everything that's happened.

As we're finishing up, Arden joins us, slipping into the seat next to me. His face is lit with a mischievous grin, and I know instantly he's about to launch into one of his stories.

"You should've seen Emory as a kid," he begins, his voice loud enough for the whole table to hear. "She never went easy on me when we played games, even though I was three years younger and much smaller at the time."

I roll my eyes but can't help but smile. "That's because you were always trying to outdo me, and I couldn't let you win."

Arden laughs, shaking his head. "Remember that time we played hide and seek in the woods? I was looking everywhere for you, and after hours of searching, I found you asleep in a tree!"

Everyone at the table bursts into laughter, and I can't help but join in, even though I feel a little sheepish. "I didn't mean to fall asleep! That tree was comfortable."

Arden grins wider, leaning back in his chair. "I was convinced something terrible had happened. I nearly had a heart attack. And then there you were, snoring away like nothing in the world could bother you."

I laugh again, my cheeks warming at the memory. "I guess that's the reason I always won. You weren't prepared for me to nap mid-game."

The laughter at the table is infectious, and soon we're all reminiscing, trading stories of childhood antics and adventures. Even Azrael, who doesn't often join in stories, joins in, sharing a tale about chasing rabbits through the fields as a pup, much to Haven's delight. The meal stretches on, the conversation light and filled with joy, and for a moment, the world outside the Tower —the war, the uncertainty—fades away.

As the plates are cleared and the final sips of wine are taken, Ryat stands, extending his hand toward me again. "One more dance?" he asks, his eyes soft as they meet mine.

I feel the familiar flutter in my chest, and I nod, placing my hand in his. He leads me back to the dance floor, the music swelling once more as we step into the rhythm. This time, I don't feel nervous at all. I move easily with him, the steps coming naturally, and for a moment, it's just us—floating through the room, lost in the music and each other.

By the time the song ends, the night has deepened, and the sky outside the tall windows is filled with stars. It's time to head back to camp, and though part of me wishes the night could last a little longer, I know the real world waits for us beyond these walls.

Ryat keeps his arm wrapped around me as we gather with the others, and together, our party begins the walk back to our camp. The stars shine overhead, and I can still feel the warmth of the evening in my chest as we make our way through the quiet night. I glance up at Ryat, and he looks down at me, his eyes soft and filled with a quiet kind of love.

Tonight, we danced. And for now, that's enough.

KAY HUGHES

CHAPTER

THIRTY-NINE

I wake suddenly, a jolt pulling me from the depths of sleep, the reason elusive in the fog of my mind. Ryat lies beside me, his soft snores a gentle rhythm in the quiet of the tent, while Kalleli is curled up in his arms, her tiny body rising and falling in sync with his breaths. I blink my heavy eyes, trying to shake off the grogginess as I scan my dim surroundings. The canvas walls of the tent are shadowy and still, the only sound my own heartbeat echoing in the silence. Yawning deeply, I sit up in our sleeping bag, the fabric cool against my skin as I cross my arms over my chest to ward off the chill that seeps into the air. The tent feels slightly damp from the cool night, and I shiver involuntarily. Confused and a little disoriented, I wonder why I woke up to begin with. The scent of earth and moss lingers, mingling with the faint, warm smell of the campfire still lingering in the air, but nothing feels off.

Sleep has left me and I know I will not be able to go back to my dreams, so I decide to step outside and start on breakfast. The final battle will be today, though we have not been told when or where, so I figure a good breakfast will be a pleasant start and it's only a bit before when I would normally wake gauging by the night sky peeking through the small opening in the tent's roof.

Carefully, I pull myself from the sleeping bag, trying not to disturb either Ryat or Kalleli as I rise and step outside. The moment I do, the air hits me with the invigorating scent of fresh rain, a clean, earthy fragrance that fills my senses. Even though the ground is dry beneath my feet, I can almost taste the dampness lingering in the air.

Tilting my head back, I'm captivated by the sight above—a sky adorned with countless shimmering stars. Each one twinkles like a tiny beacon, creating a symphony of lights that dance against the darkness. A full silver moon hangs proudly, its ethereal glow bathing everything in a soft, silvery sheen. Tranquility washes over me, a wave of calm that soothes my racing thoughts. A contented smile graces my lips as I make my way toward my cooking supplies, my heart lightened by the beauty surrounding me.

Suddenly, the world feels distant as I now move through the forest, my feet carrying me forward with a will of their own.

The silver bark of the Wishing Tree gleams ahead, its massive branches stretching high into the twilight sky, shimmering with a light that pulses faintly in the early morning sun. My heart thuds in my chest, a dull, steady rhythm that seems to echo in the quiet air. I don't know how I got here—how the path I was walking towards my cooking supplies had instead led me to this far away place—but I can feel a tinge of magic in the air and my skin hums with the familiar, unsettling energy.

My steps slow as I near the tree, and the sharp awareness of something wrong creeps into my bones. The ancient magic of the Wishing Tree swirls around me, its presence is usually a piece of comfort, but there's something else—something darker—that sends a chill down my spine.

Then I see him.

Standing beside my beautiful silver tree, his back to me, is a figure I recognize instantly.

Ymir, the God of Revenge.

His presence is impossible to mistake—the dark, heavy cloak that billows slightly in the still air, the cold energy that radiates from him, sharper than ice. His casual, relaxed posture and the way his hands are clasped behind him make me feel as if he has been waiting on me for a while.

My breath catches in my throat, and I stop, my body freezing in place as the weight of realization settles over me like a suffocating fog. This is it. The final battle. The one I had been hoping to avoid, the one I had hoped wouldn't come when we were told to expect it—not yet, not while so much was still unknown and i am still so unprepared.

But fate didn't care about my plans. It had brought me here, to this moment, whether or not I was ready.

I press a hand to my stomach and feel the soft flutter of life stirring within me—my baby. My heart clenches painfully, and I close my eyes for a moment, grounding myself in that small, gentle movement. A reminder of why I can't give up. Why I have to keep fighting, even now, when the odds feel impossibly stacked against me.

When I open my eyes, Ymir has turned to face me.

"Hello, Emory," he says, his voice low and smooth, like a whisper of wind through dead leaves. There is something eerily calm about him, as if the gravity of this moment means nothing to him. As if the world could end, and he would simply watch it burn.

My throat feels tight, but I lift my chin and meet his

gaze. "Ymir."

The god's eyes, dark as storm clouds, flicker over me, lingering for a moment on my stomach before rising back to my face. His lips curl into a faint, almost imperceptible smile.

"I see you've brought company."

My hand tightens protectively over my belly, the weight of my unborn child suddenly feeling like the only real thing in this moment. I can feel the quiet strength of life growing within me, a spark of hope that flickers even in the presence of such overwhelming darkness. But as I stand here, facing the god of revenge himself, that hope feels fragile, like a flame flickering in a storm.

"I didn't bring anyone," I reply, my voice steadier than I expected. "I am alone."

Ymir tilts his head slightly, his smile fading as his eyes bore into my own. "Yes," he murmurs, stepping closer, his movements fluid, predatory. "You are alone."

The words hit me like a blow, a reminder of the grim truth I had tried to push away. This battle is mine alone to fight. Ryat isn't here. Haven, Hellion, Arden—they are all somewhere far from this place. And my child... my child is inside me, defenseless.

But I am not defenseless. Not yet.

The air around me thrums with the magic of the Wishing Tree, vibrating against my skin like an old song that generations have sung. I can feel it, the power that has been locked away for so long, the power that has shaped destinies and ended wars. But it isn't the tree's gifts that will decide this battle.

It's mine.

I let out a slow breath, my eyes never leaving Ymir's. I can feel the fear creeping at the edges of my mind, the weight of the impossible choice before me. I had always known that this moment would come, that I would have to face Ymir alone. But now that it was here, standing on the edge of this final battle, the enormity of it threatens to crush me.

Ymir steps even closer, his voice soft, almost tender. "You know how this ends, don't you, Emory? You've always known."

My hand tightens over my stomach, the fluttering of my baby a gentle reminder of why I can't—won't—let him win.

"I know how it begins," I say, my voice stronger now, defiant. "And it doesn't end with you winning this war."

For a moment, silence stretches between us, the air thick with tension, as though the world itself is holding its breath, waiting.

Ymir's smile returns, cold and knowing. He nods slowly, as if in acknowledgment of my resolve. "Very well," he says softly. "Then let it begin."

The moment he finishes his sentence I feel the sun's warmth on my skin, a cruel contrast to the dark magic roiling within me—untamed and feral, like a storm ready to unleash its wrath. It thrums in my veins, a chaotic energy clawing for release, a primal urge that threatens to consume me from the inside out. The warmth clashes violently with a bone-deep chill of dread, a volatile concoction that ignites every nerve ending, leaving me teetering on the edge of something unnameable.

As the shadows begin to coil and twist around us, I grasp the suffocating weight of the moment. My mind races, thoughts spiraling into a chaotic whirlwind of the horrors that lie ahead. The darkness feels sentient, a ravenous entity, eager to devour everything it encounters—my hopes, my will, my very essence.

But just as panic surges within me like a tidal wave, two final thoughts flicker through my mind, desperate and fleeting, like the last gasps of a fading memory.

The final battle is here.

And I will face it alone.

ACKNOWLEDGEMENT

I'd like to start by acknowledging the amazing journey this book has been. I am thankful to each person who strapped on their seatbelt and joined me on this adventure.

I couldn't have written a single word without the love and support of my mother, Yvonne, who read every word at least a dozen times. She stood by me through the drafting of maps, the naming process and all of the book events. You're my rock mama, my best friend. When I wrote about the love Emory felt from her mother, I could only write that from the experience of feeling yours.

Speaking of the naming process, I would be nowhere at all without my brother, Brendan. When I told him that I was going to write a book, he had nothing but support for the crazy world I would have to create myself. He worked with me on naming both the gifts and the creatures they encountered, fireballing ideas off of me for days on end. Thank you B, without you I would be half the woman I've grown to be today, and my world would be a flat nameless place.

Writing this character, with so much confusion in her heart, reminded me of myself so long ago. My uncle, Steven, was one of the best people who has ever been a part of my life, and he was with me in my time of confusion. Uncle Steve once told me that every person we meet is either a blessing or a lesson. For me, he was both. Steve was a good man, a kind man, a man strong in his faith. As I wrote about Emory's travels and the struggles she faced, I knew that she needed to possess the same qualities. So, thank you Uncle Steve. I hope you're proud from your home up in heaven. We miss you down here.

Lastly, I want to express my gratitude to Anthony, my best friend and the love of my life. Writing a book, constructing an entire world, and designing maps is a lengthy and challenging process. Yet, you never once hesitated in offering your unwavering support. Thank you for your constant love and giving extra love to our pups when I was engrossed in my writing. The world I've created is filled with strong, kind, and amusing men (even if they can be a bit eccentric at times), and I owe it all to you. Your humor in our everyday lives allows me to give my heroines true love as well.

ABOUT THE AUTHOR

Born in the small town of Keosauqua, Iowa, Kay
Hughes spent the first twelve years of her life traveling
the United States with her parents and younger
brother, an experience that inspired her boundless
imagination. Specializing in Fantasy Romance,
Kay crafts vivid worlds filled with epic battles,
enchanting magic and unforgettable love stories.
When not writing, Kay enjoys crocheting, reading,
and swimming with her three beloved dogs.